# CRAZY OVER YOU

A small-town enemies to lovers romance novel

LILY MILLER

# About the book

**Crazy Over You is the exciting fourth novel in the steamy and addictive Bennett Family Series.**

The first rule of business: *never* mix it with pleasure.

…and never fall in bed with your biggest competitor.

I've been in the boardroom long enough to know that some men are just off-limits. As head of marketing for my family's successful boutique hotel business, I'd never jeopardize our brand's success for someone like Beckett Taylor. He's arrogant and cocky. And completely ruthless when it comes to getting his way in business.

But when we're forced to spend the weekend together at a conference, I find myself unable to resist the fire that has been burning between us. He is, after all, ridiculously sexy. *One night*, I tell myself. *One hot, steamy, forbidden night with a man I find too tempting to resist.* What possibly could go wrong?

The problem is, it turns out he may not be the alpha-hole I thought he was- he's sweet and charming and has a dirty mouth that I can't seem to get enough of.

I know this isn't going to end well. Falling for my rival wasn't part of my plan.

I know that I should walk away before he breaks me into a million tiny pieces. But I've never been any good at resisting what I want, and my heart wants him.

**A steamy, enemies-to-lovers, forbidden romance, Crazy Over You is the final book in The Bennett Family series.**

Crazy Over You

Cover design/Illustrations: Jayde Ubels

Editing: Carolyn De Melo

Publicity: Katie and Brey PA

*For my Family*

*The best things in life are better with you.*
*P.S. I love you.*

## Chapter One

Jules

The lobby of The Peninsula Hotel is buzzing as I roll through the lobby doors dragging a suitcase with only two working wheels. Just my luck. Of course it's *my* suitcase that was manhandled on the three-hour flight from JFK to Miami—a flight that was delayed on the runway for what felt like an eternity. Doing my best to maneuver the broken bag through the crowded lobby, I join the check-in line and drop my duffle on the floor with a wince.

I'm in Miami for work, attending the annual Boutique Hotel Association Conference at the bougie Peninsula. No complaints here. Between presentations and the usual networking, I plan on lying poolside with a good book, sipping mojitos under the Florida sun. Oh, and I will definitely be taking advantage of the Peninsula's gorgeous spa. I'm travelling solo this time—my older brother, Parker, normally joins me on business trips, but he's on what he calls a "babymoon" with his wife Olivia. They're expecting their first child later this year and want to enjoy some peace and quiet while they still can.

Parker and I both work for our father at The Seaside, a chain of luxury boutique hotels he took over from his father when we were just kids. Parker is the COO, and I head the marketing team—a job I've loved since joining the family business straight out of university four years ago.

I let my eyes drift over the lobby, taking in the gleaming black-and-white marble floors and sweeping staircase. The chandelier overhead glitters in the glow of the early afternoon sun that streams through the large, arched windows. I exhale, trying to let go of the stress of the travel day, and watch the steady stream of men and women clad in business suits move past me. I recognize a few familiar faces from past conferences before my eyes fixate on one in particular. I feel the tension immediately return to my shoulders. And here I thought this day couldn't get any worse.

*Of course* he's here.

Beckett flipping Taylor, the pain in my side and Mr. Man Wonder of the Liberty Hotel empire. Our rivals. Our arch nemeses. Okay, maybe that's a tad dramatic, but we have a past. The Liberty team take no prisoners when it comes to doing business, and Beckett leads the way. We went head-to-head in a business deal a couple of years ago where Beckett came out the victor, and I still feel the sting of the pain on that one. I have a fierce competitive streak in general, but some losses are tougher than others.

The thing is, Beckett is like a shark. As soon as he sniffs out the weakness in his competitors, he moves in for the kill —and he enjoys himself while he's at it. He's been the bane of my company's existence for the last four years and I would love to be the one to knock him down a notch.

I watch him tip the bellman, slipping a bill into the palm of the man's hand. Beckett is wearing a button-down white dress shirt tucked neatly into the waist of his tailored pale gray dress pants. A tan belt and matching tan shoes complete his king-of-the-hotel-business look. If I didn't loathe him as much as I do, I would maybe appreciate the view. But I don't.

I'm positive I can smell his pompous attitude from here.

God. Beckett is such a dick. He exudes arrogance. He thinks he's better than everyone else in the room, and he always wants the last word.

Our eyes meet and I don't back down, holding his gaze. His dark blue eyes laser on mine. Okay, fine, I admit it. Beckett is blessed with unbelievable DNA: a six-foot athletic frame, sex-tousled light-brown hair, full lips. I could go on.

He's the kind of man that should grace magazine covers. The kind that makes you stop and stare. Which, I realize, is exactly what I'm doing when he suddenly smirks an infuriating smile at me and winks.

*Ass.*

I straighten my shoulders and flash a don't-start-with-me grin. He knows exactly what my expression means. His steel blue eyes narrow in on me and a jolt of heat ripples down my spine at the intensity of his stare. He is so annoyingly cocky.

"Miss," comes a gentle male voice from behind me. I startle, my attention suddenly pulled away from Beckett. The man signals to me to move ahead, and I realize I've been standing still while the line has kept moving. I shuffle a few steps forward with my bags and then glance at my phone and try to pretend that Beckett isn't here. I make a mental note to avoid him this weekend at all costs. I briefly consider moving to the hotel next door, or maybe into one on a different planet.

Once I've checked in, I sling my bag onto my shoulder and turn to find Beckett watching me. I realize I'm going to need to drag my broken suitcase past him to get to the elevators. *Fantastic.* I could ask a bellman to do it, but they're all busy dealing with the crowd of convention goers who seem to be checking in all at once. Screw it. I straighten my shoulders and meet Beckett's amused stare. I won't let him get to me. He enjoys thinking my position in my father's hotel chain was handed to me on a silver tray. He thinks I'm a spoiled brat. He thinks he's better than me in the boardroom.

He's wrong.

The truth is, when I lost that major event to Beckett a few years back—a high profile celebrity wedding we were both vying for—things got ugly. I may have told him that the only way the couple would love his hotel was if they enjoyed sleeping with bed bugs. I know, not my finest moment. In my defense, Beckett had been pretty ruthless in his attempts to secure that deal. In any case, once the dust cleared and the wedding was over, I sent him an olive branch in the form of a bottle of Macallan… but it was too little, too late. The damage was done.

I grip the handle of the suitcase and drag the stupid thing in Beckett's direction. It knocks and bounces and hits me in the ankle, but I keep going, refusing to look in his direction. I'm halfway to the elevators—*must keep going*—when I hear him say my name.

"Yes?" I stop and our eyes briefly meet before his do a full sweep of me, from my hair down to my busted suitcase.

Beckett's lip curls up. "Need a hand?"

I can't stand him. I'd like to tell him to go for a long

walk off a short pier, but I don't. This could be a very long three days if I poke the bear. Instead, I force a smile to my lips.

"Nope." I say it as sweetly as I can, but I'm sure "you're such a douche" is written all over my face.

The guy standing next to him stifles a laugh. I'm sure it's not every day that the Golden Boy, Beckett Taylor, is turned down. Well, the rest of the world can spin around his axis, but I'm not interested.

I yank on my suitcase, not wanting to spend a second longer than I have to in his company.

"Wait. Why such a rush, Jules?" Beckett asks with a grin. "You weren't going to say hi to me? Ask me how my flight was?"

"Hi. How was your flight?" I ask sarcastically, noticing his friend's eyes flick from me to Beckett. He looks amused. I am anything but.

"My flight was smooth. The peanuts were superb. Thanks for asking," he says.

"I may have asked," I tell him. "But between me and you, I really couldn't care less."

He smirks, then presses his lips together in a pout. "Maybe just a little?"

"Definitely not," I say, my hand gripping the handle of my suitcase so tightly that I may need pliers to pry it off later.

He laughs. "Maybe we should take this to the bar. Grab a drink and catch up like old friends."

"That would be lovely if we *were* friends, but we're not, so I'll see you around."

My feet remain firmly rooted to the floor. Normally, I wouldn't bother engaging in such a petty conversation, but it's been a long and frustrating day and taking it out on Mr. Man Wonder is proving to be a pretty good stress reliever.

For a moment Beckett and I just stare at each other in silence as the sounds of a Michael Bublé song float through the lobby speakers. The spell is broken by the guy who's still standing next to us, having watched our heated exchange with his eyes wide. "Okay, you guys are acting weird," he interrupts with an awkward laugh. "Do you two actually know each other?"

Beckett maintains his infuriating eyebrow arch. "We do," we both say in unison. I roll my eyes. Beckett continues. "Grayson Scott, meet Jules Bennett. Jules is with The Seaside."

Grayson resembles Austin Butler with his bleached blond hair, slim build and boy-next-door vibe. He seems nice too, like the kind of guy I should be interested in.

"Pleasure," Grayson says, holding out his hand. "I work with Beck." I smile and shake his hand, my eyes meeting his. No zing. No spark. Nothing.

"Pleased to meet you, Grayson. Working with Beckett…" I add, lowering my voice, but just enough so that Beckett can still hear me. "I don't know how you can stand it."

Grayson stifles a laugh the best he can while Beckett rolls his eyes.

"Now that I know you enjoy nuts, I best toot aloo to my room." I say, hitching my duffle on my shoulder.

"Wonderful to catch up with you again, Miss Bennett," Beckett says. "I'm happy we were able to exchange pleasantries."

"Right," I reply with a smirk. "And on that note…" I grab the handle of my busted-up bag and silently beg it to cooperate. Beckett watches me, his expression full of amusement, and I scowl, knowing what a mess I must look like. I do my best turn-on-my-heels pivot and head in the direction of the elevators. My suitcase flops to the left and then to the right as I walk past them, breathing a sigh of relief when the door to the elevator opens and I step in. Flashing a brief smile to the couple already inside, I avert my eyes from the lobby and will the doors to close.

As soon as they do, I slump against the elevator wall and close my eyes. It bothers me how easily Beckett can get to me. I've never been very good at being able to control my temper around him. But can you blame me? He's such a know-it-all, a giant pain in my ass.

As the car ascends past the 14th floor, I realize that I forgot to push the button. Damn Beckett. I jab the number 14 and it lights up. The couple sharing the elevator with me apparently have the penthouse suite—obviously, because it's been that kind of day—and the ride up to the top floor and back again feels like an eternity. When the doors finally open to my floor I can't get to my room fast enough. My nerves are fried.

Minutes later, I'm standing outside of my room digging out my hotel key card when a familiar voice resonates beside me. "Hey, neighbor. Everything okay? You look a little agitated."

*You've got to be kidding me.* I turn to see Beckett stop at the door next to mine.

"Did you plan this?"

"No, but I'm actually kind of upset with myself that I didn't."

"Stalk much?" I frown. "I didn't realize your obsession with me had reached this level."

He shrugs, unfazed at my dig. His chiseled jaw is covered in a fine layer of scruff and the column of his neck is tan and smooth. Dammit, why does he have to be so handsome?

"Fat chance. Stalker is not my color, but you on the

other hand… I bet you have a poster of me on your bedroom wall."

*And here we go.*

"If I did, it would only be to throw darts at it."

"Ouch. You wound me." He mockingly sulks, clutching his hand to his chest and pushing his bottom lip forward. His blue eyes are wide. My knees tremble and something warm fills up my chest. *Stop it.* I am not looking at his eyes. Or his mouth.

Distracted (more like freaking the fuck out) by these strange thoughts suddenly popping up in my mind, I drop my key card to the floor.

"I got it," he says, bending down to pick it up. He passes it to me and our fingers brush, lighting a spark through my body and a wave of goosebumps over my skin. The feather-soft contact is brief and unintentional but my entire body hums. His usual resting smirk face is gone, and a peculiar expression takes its place. He pauses for a second, looking at me like I'm a mountain he can't figure out how to climb, then blinks. Did he feel it too?

He clears his throat and takes a step back. "Should I pick you up on my way to dinner tonight?"

"Why would I want you to do that?"

There is a welcome dinner this evening in the lobby, a chance for everyone to mingle before the conference starts tomorrow morning. I've already made plans to meet my co-worker Sierra there. Spending extra time with Beckett is not on my itinerary for the weekend.

"It's not a date, Jules. Relax. I just figured since we're both going in the same direction you might enjoy my company. I'm told I'm the life of the party."

He smiles, clearly very happy with himself, and I find myself actually considering his offer. The man can be charming when he's not being an egotistical ass. And he *is* incredibly good looking. How bad could it be to let my guard down for a night? We could call it a temporary truce.

*A truce with Beckett Taylor?* I hear the words running through my head and have to remind myself that Beckett isn't just any guy. He's the competition. I gather my will and try to forget how attractive he is.

"Life of the party? Says who? Your mom?"

"Well, yes, she's one of them," he says with a cheeky grin. "So, I'll pick you up?"

"This side of you is making me feel weird, Beckett."

"Because you can't resist me?"

"Do you ever stop?"

He smirks. "No."

He leans his tall, athletic body against the door and winks. He fucking *winks* at me and all at once, I feel butterflies flutter throughout my entire body. It's probably because it has been a long while since I've been with a man and being this close to all of his maleness is frying my senses. That's got to be it. It has nothing to do with his forearms, tan with a soft dusting of dark hair, or the fact that he smells like sex and a good time. Wild, inhibited sex that makes you scream for more.

*Enough, Jules.*

*Stop ogling Mr. Man Wonder.*

"So? 7 o'clock? You may even want to invite me in for a pre-dinner cocktail."

"When pigs fly." The words are out of my mouth before I have the chance to consider them. I almost feel bad because it seems like Beckett is trying. He may even be flirting with me. But our long and unpleasant history brings me back to reality, forcing me to remember that awful day in his office. I blink, flustered. *Don't get distracted by his charm.*

"Suit yourself."

Pressing the key card to the reader, the door to my room unlocks. I can feel Beckett watching me and sure enough, when I glance over at him, his gaze is sharp, avidly taking me in.

*What is his deal?*

Forget it, I tell myself. He wants me on edge. He's just trying to throw me off my game. Whatever game he's playing at, I don't like it. It would be much easier if we both just pretended the other didn't exist.

I'm annoyed that I'm letting him get to me. It's infuriating the way he can get under my skin. Whatever.

I enter my hotel room and let the door close behind me, leaving Beckett standing in the hallway.

Once inside, I drop my bags, toe off my heels and walk towards the patio doors. My view is of the pool, the beach and the ocean in the distance. There's a swim-up bar and the row of sunbeds built into the shallow end of the pool look very enticing.

Taking in the gorgeous scenery, I feel some of the tension that has built up in my body start to melt away.

This trip will be good for me—as long as it remains Beckett-free.

## Chapter Two

**B**eckett

"I wonder what they're doing back at the office?" Grayson says from the pool chair next to mine, one arm bent behind his head and the other holding a cold glass of Miller Lite. "Because it sure as shit isn't this."

"Cheers." We clink our glasses. It's 87 degrees, the patio speakers are pumping out Bruno Mars and we're both splayed out on poolside loungers under an umbrella. Seminars won't start until tomorrow—the only event in our calendars today is a welcome dinner scheduled for later tonight.

"The office is the last thing on my mind right now," I tell him. "My only priorities are getting another cold one and taking a dip in that pool. I'm just trying to decide which one I want more."

If only that were true. I've got a lot on my mind where work is concerned. I've been refreshing my emails constantly, hoping for the one I'm waiting on. The email that could change everything.

"Why choose?" Grayson grins. "Go on a spree."

"Go on a spree, hey?" I say, my attention distracted by a dad playing catch in the pool with his son. The boy must not be any older than 10. My chest tightens and that old, familiar lonely feeling sinks in. Disappointment. Inadequacy. Heartbreak. Twenty-seven years later and I'm still dealing with this crap.

"Yeah, man. Go on a motherfucking spree," Grayson laughs, interrupting my thoughts. "Drink the drink, swim the pool, do all the things."

"Is that all, Confucius?"

"Not even close. I sprinkle my wisdom whenever I see fit."

"You should be a life coach. Get your own podcast. Preach to the masses."

A wry grin pulls at his lips. "Now you're talking. I can call it 'Get that Spree with Coach Grayson.' Brilliant. I'll be hosting my own damn seminars in no time."

I laugh, laying my head back against the lounger. I'll miss Grayson if it all pans out like I'm hoping. We've known one another for three years, ever since he joined my team at The Liberty. We hit it off right away. Fresh out of university, Grayson was hired as an intern but quickly got promoted to an analyst. His department is responsible for making sure the hotel is maximizing profits in every aspect. He has a mind for numbers. I knew after that first week working with him that the guy was smart. He's one of the good ones too, a straight shooter and as loyal as a Golden Retriever.

"Ah, here we go. The afternoon is about to get interesting," he says, slapping my thigh with the back of his hand. "Two o'clock. Jules incoming."

I shift my attention to where Grayson is looking. Jules hasn't spotted me yet and my eyes are hidden behind my

Ray Bans, so I narrow my gaze and take her in. She's wearing a white, flouncy sundress that ends just above her knees. Her light brown hair is pulled back into a high ponytail at the crown of her head, the sun's rays illuminating the strands of gold. Tanned, toned legs stride towards us as she looks around for a vacant lounger. There aren't many around. There *is* one beside Grayson.

I stare, practically memorizing her. There's something about the way Jules moves that gets to me. I drink in the way the muscles in her legs flex when she walks, the slight sway of her hips and the wild strands of hair that have come loose from her ponytail.

She's wearing a pair of tortoiseshell-rimmed sunglasses so I can't see her eyes, but her cheekbones are high and her lips full and pouty and as she gets closer, I can see her toes are painted an almost fluorescent pink. She's polished, a beauty pageant-type. I'd put money on her having been class queen and the quarterback's girlfriend. Jules Bennett is Reed Point royalty—which is the furthest thing from me. I bet you she gets anything she wants.

*Not into her,* I say to myself, eyes still glued to her as she drops her bag on the edge of the chair next to Grayson's. *Not your type.*

I'm not her type either. That much was made very clear when she went up one side of me and down the other in my office a few years back. I can still see her standing there with her hands on her hips while she snapped at me over a business deal that went my way instead of hers. She was pissed.

I watch her take her towel from under her arm, spreading it out over the chair while I wait for the bomb to drop—the moment she realizes who she's sitting beside. I can't hold back the smirk that's already forming on my face. I like to rile her up, sue me.

Jules is pulling a book out of her bag when she suddenly stops, as though she feels our eyes on her. She turns her head and I watch her glance at Grayson before shifting her gaze to me. I can see the wheels turning in her head. I'm betting she's planning her exit, kicking herself for not noticing us sooner. The book drops to her chair as I flash her a wide smile.

"Best seat in the house," I say, and she furrows her brows, her lips pressed together in a straight line as she slips her sunglasses to the top of her head.

"Next to you two?" she grumbles.

"You got it."

She huffs under her breath, just loud enough for us to hear. "If there was a pool floaty handy I would choose that, but there's not."

*You're stuck with us, Jules.*

"You know, it's actually your lucky day," I say. "My associate Grayson over here," I point to him with my thumb, "and I are full of good times."

She rolls her eyes so hard I think she sees her brain. "Full of yourself is what you are. Now, why don't we play that game where we can see how quiet we can be? Whoever talks first loses. Starting… now."

Jules flops down onto the lounger, crosses her long, toned legs and opens her book. I'm curious what she's reading—I bet it's some romance novel or maybe a biography on Britney Spears. I resist the urge to ask her. She'd probably bite my head off.

Grayson does not possess the same self control. "Whatcha reading?"

I wince. He's obviously not picking up on her leave-me-alone vibe. *You're on your own, Grayson.* I'm bolting for the pool when shit goes south.

"It's a memoir," Jules replies. "*The Liars' Club*. Have you heard of it?"

"I haven't. Is it good?"

She dog ears her page. "I'm only four chapters, in but so far it's fascinating. Are you a big reader?"

"Big Harry Potter fan," he says, sitting up in his chair. "I've read every book twice."

My jaw gapes listening to the two of them. *Why is she being so nice to Grayson?* I guess it's just me that she hates.

Jules looks honest-to-God fascinated as Grayson does a deep dive into the various Hogwarts houses. I lean back on my lounge chair, determined not to care that they seem to be hitting it off so well. I give myself a mental beat down: *You don't care who she talks to. You can't stand her anyways. Grayson can have her.* But I can't seem to stop my growing annoyance. Why is seeing the two of them together making me crazy?

"Can I get you another?" a pool waitress asks, stopping at the foot of my chair. She's 20-something, cute with pink highlights tangled through her long blonde hair.

"Please. Thank you."

"And for yourself," she looks at Grayson. "Can I get you anything?"

"I'll have another too."

"I'll have a Pina Colada," Jules calls out. "And do you have potato chips? I'm feeling kinda snacky. Oh, and you can put it all on his tab," she says tossing her thumb in my direction. "Beckett Taylor. But he's probably already given you his name. He's flirty like that."

"Oh, I'm sorry, I didn't realize you two are together," the waitress says with an uncertain look, hesitating before writing down Jules' order.

"We are *very* together," she says drawing the *very* out into 13 syllables just to spite me. "He's my husband, but he cheated on me… four times. Can you believe it? He has that disorder… you know where he can't keep his dick in his pants? What do they call it? A sex fiend! That's the one. Anyways, he brought me on this trip to try to make things right with us. So sweet of him, really."

I stare at Jules, my jaw on the floor. Has she lost her fucking mind? Two can play this game, but our waitress leaves with a confused look on her face before I have the chance to say anything. Jules pulls a tube of sunscreen from her bag, crosses one leg over the other and in dramatic fashion begins to squirt the lotion into her hand.

Grayson busts a gut as soon as the waitress is out of earshot. "Slay, Jules. That was badass. You have to admit, Beck, that was good."

Jules laughs as Grayson high-fives her clean hand. Traitor.

Two can play this game.

"It's a shame our waitress left, sweetheart," I say to Jules, laying it on extra thick. "Before I had the chance to tell her about your porn addiction."

Jules shakes her head, returning her attention to her sunscreen.

I roll my eyes. She is exasperating. Why do I bother?

It doesn't take long for Jules and Grayson to return to their conversation. When they finally get the cheating husband jokes out of their systems their chat turns to work, their favorite TV shows, where they're from. I listen intently to every word, strangely interested to know that she loves sailing, hates mangoes and has watched every episode of *Bridgerton*. She's closest to her brother Liam, prefers tacos over enchiladas and identifies as a Swiftie. *Figures.* Frustration takes hold of me. She talks so easily with Grayson, meanwhile every word tossed in my direction is like a dagger.

Jules sips from her fruity drink, her lips forming this perfect O that gets my attention in more ways than one. My dick perks up behind my swim trunks wondering what her O face looks like. Then imagining her lips wrapped around my…

*Where the fuck did that come from?*

Since when have I ever had illicit thoughts about Jules Bennett?

She's definitely attractive. Any man with a heartbeat can see that. I allow my eyes to soak her in for a minute. With her hair up, I can see the elegant curve of her neck, the angle of her jaw and the multiple earrings in her ears. When my eyes drift lower, I notice the small tattoo on her wrist and another close to her ribs, both too small for me to see clearly.

My fingers itch to reach out and remove her sunglasses so I can see the look in her eyes. Is it the same as mine?

Fascination.

Curiosity.

She carries on reading her book, sipping from her drink, wanting nothing to do with me. I know she thinks I'm an arrogant ass, which is partly my fault. I haven't done much to convince her otherwise. I'm sure she's run into her share of hotshot losers in her work, and she assumes I'm just another one. That couldn't be further from the truth. Behind the walls I've built up, I'm a son who loves his mother, a brother who would do anything for his sister. I do whatever I can every day to make sure they have everything they need. I've lost my father, and because of that I know what betrayal feels like.

Jules takes another sip of her drink then sets her glass down and tugs her dress over her head. She's wearing a light-blue bikini, her skin golden, her stomach firm. I try to look away but it's impossible. I'm a hot-blooded man and

Jules has one of the hottest bodies I've ever seen. Lean with the perfect curves. She adjusts the strings around her neck. *Oh God*, make her stop. Swim trunks hide nothing. I try to think of my grandma, or three-legged cats. I shift in my seat. What I need to do is dunk myself in the cold pool. That's what I get for imagining Jules underneath me while I…

"You okay over there?" Grayson asks while I make a quick adjustment to my shorts. His eyes flip to my trunks and the situation happening down south.

"I'm fine."

"Bro, you were staring, and you have a hard-on for the girl."

"I was not," I say defensively.

He laughs. "Chill Beck. You look like you're coming unglued. Look at yourself, man. You're all wound up, your knee won't stop bouncing, and you have this weird, spaced out look in your eyes."

"I'm fine." I am not fine.

"Whatever you say."

"I'm going for a swim," I say, needing a change of scenery. My current view is making me hard. Standing, I slip off my sunglasses, walk to the edge of the pool and dive in, the cold water exactly what I need to clear my head and cool down my libido.

I swim laps until I'm out of breath then push out of the pool and sit on its edge facing the hot afternoon sun. I run my hand through my wet hair, feeling the cool droplets trickle down my chest. I tip my face towards the sunshine, my feet tracing lazy circles through the water.

When I open my eyes, I find Jules standing at the edge of the pool and immediately feel my lungs squeeze in my chest. She walks through the shallow end and my body buzzes. I can't take my eyes off her. She is so damn perfect.

As she makes her way deeper into the pool I sit back and take in the free show that is Jules Bennett dripping wet in a bikini.

I'm not the only one. I look around us and notice that plenty of other men and women around the pool are watching her too.

I inhale a deep breath and return my attention to Jules. Her swimsuit leaves little to the imagination. The triangle top ties at her nape and across her back, the bottoms held up by bows at her hips. Her chest isn't large, but perfectly proportioned. Hers is exactly the body type I fantasize over. *Fuck.* I try to remind myself that it's just a swimsuit. Not a big deal.

Jules ties her long caramel-honey hair up in a ponytail as she glides into the pool, her petite body disappearing under the water with every step. She stops when the water is at her belly button and looks in my direction, as if she senses my hungry eyes raking over her. I'm past the point of caring that they're no longer masked behind my sunglasses.

"You're not going to swim over here and give your husband a kiss?" I tease, just loud enough for her to hear it. "He *did* take you on this fabulous vacation."

She scoffs. "After he nailed a bevy of women." She wades a little closer. "Who said romance is dead?"

"Are you going to keep bringing up your husband's extracurricular activities forever, sweet pea?"

"Only until you stop talking in the third person," she says, dipping her body further under the water to her neck. "I don't think your indiscretions fazed our waitress though. She's been staring at you all afternoon like she wouldn't mind being your next extracurricular activity."

I laugh. "Someone sounds jealous."

"Keep dreaming."

Damn, her smart mouth is such a turn-on. "Just wait, you're going to love me like that waitress does."

"That waitress is 19. She has a brain that's not fully developed. You wanna know what I think?"

"I already know."

"Is that so?" She gives me that smirky grin, the one she flashes me when she's trying to act cheeky.

"That I'm incredible."

"Incorrigible, maybe. Immature, definitely." She smiles her perfect, pretty smile and I feel it all over. Why does she have to be sexy as hell?

"You're a ballbreaker!"

"I only call it like I see it." She shrugs but doesn't move further from where I'm perched on the edge of the pool. She's close enough that I could reach out and touch her. "Tell me why you're so incredible."

I sigh. "Is this a trap?"

"I'm not a sadist, Beckett. My mother could have named me Pollyanna." She moves her sunglasses to the top of her head, and I can see the green flecks around her irises. They glitter like diamonds lighting up her face.

"You *do* seem quite lovely to everybody else. So I guess it's just me that you don't like?"

"I think you like yourself enough for both of us," she replies with a smirk. "But if you're asking about our… history? Don't worry, I'm over it."

I squint at her. "Shoot me straight. Are you really over it?"

"You think I'm still holding a grudge. I'm not. I'm over our argument. I haven't thought about it in a long time."

I'm not sure whether to believe her. I'm silent, watching her nibble on her lip. Her head dips towards the water, as if she's hiding her expression, then she looks back at me and I'm awed. Her eyes are intense as they roam over my pecs to the grooves of my abs and down to my blue-and-white striped swim trunks.

I clear my throat and her eyes dart up to meet mine. She likes what she sees. I'm also enjoying my view. My lips tip up in a silky grin.

"What?" she huffs, a frown creasing her brow.

"I'm starving."

Jules frowns, then shakes her head. "You are such a man."

"I'm all man, trust me. I can show you if you don't believe me."

I grin. I can't help myself. If she's going to dish it, I can dish it right back.

"I'll take your word for it," she says, then begins to swim away.

"Hey! Where you off to?" I call after her. "I was just starting to enjoy this little chat."

"That makes one of us," she says over her shoulder. "Thanks for the drink."

Jules swims across the pool to the ladder and I watch as she climbs out, water dripping down her skin. She strides towards her chair without a look back in my direction.

"I'll see you tonight," I call out to her. "Offer still stands. Happy to escort my wife to dinner."

"I'd rather set myself on fire," she says with sass in her voice. I can't help but laugh at my own expense.

Jules packs up her things, throws her dress over her head and walks into the hotel.

As soon as she's gone, I slip back into the pool, needing to put out the fire she's left burning in me.

# Chapter Three

Jules

Two hours later, I'm walking into the Grand Ballroom of the hotel. Alone. The form-fitting red dress I'm wearing clings to my body, stopping just above my knees. I left my hair down in long, loose waves. I wondered if I might see Beckett in the hallway when I left my room but wasn't surprised when the corridor was empty. We didn't exactly leave one another on the best of terms. It doesn't matter anyway. I won't miss him.

I scan the room of seminar guests looking for Sierra, who texted me earlier to let me know she had arrived. She works for us at the Virginia Beach Seaside and took Parker's place on this weekend's trip. I'm glad she did. Sierra is close to my age, a bright spark who I always have a good time with.

I spot her at the bar and make my way towards her through the crowd of people dressed in suits and evening dresses, sipping from champagne glasses. There are round banquet tables scattered throughout the room, topped with linen tablecloths and flickering candles. The Peninsula has gone all out.

"Looks like you could use a partner in crime?" I say as I slide into the spot beside her at the bar.

"Me? Sorry, you must be mistaken. I am *all* business and zero pleasure this weekend."

She has an over-the-top expression of innocence on her face. I shake my head and smile. Sierra is pretty in a girl-next-door kind of way, with wavy blonde hair past her shoulders, wide brown eyes and a splatter of freckles across the bridge of her nose. She throws her arms around me and I laugh, happy she's here to keep me company. Just then I spot Beckett as he enters the room. Our eyes meet over Sierra's shoulder, and he nods, a small smile on his lips. He has no right to look that good in a suit. It's irritating, even more so when I suddenly find myself wondering what he smells like, what his chest feels like under his crisp white shirt. It's official: I've lost my mind.

I pull my eyes away from him when Sierra releases me from our hug. "It's so good to see you. I was just remembering the last time we were together. Do you remember, we crashed that wedding at the resort next to ours and jumped on stage with the band?" She hands me a glass of champagne. "Here, a drink for my accomplice."

"Do I remember?" I repeat. "Yes, clearly. Especially the part where you took over as the drummer and I sang a duet with the lead singer. We were like the worst imaginable scene in a drunk adaptation of *Bridget Jones' Diary.*"

"The best! So, what trouble can we get into this trip?"

"The world is our oyster, Sierra." We clink glasses and both drink to that. "What happens in Miami stays in Miami."

Our attention turns to the front of the room where the MC for the night welcomes us all to the 17th annual

Boutique Hotel Association Conference and asks us to take our seats. Sierra and I find our table and I try to listen as the woman talks about absorbing the art of the hospitality industry, but I've lost her. I'm a bit of a daydreamer, always have been. My mom tried to teach me mindful meditation and breathing techniques, but none of it did much to help. It's who I am.

"Can we move on already to the good part? Where's the food?" Sierra mutters beside me as the MC rambles on and on.

I sigh and take a sip of my champagne. "I'm going to need three more of these if this woman doesn't stop."

After dinner, Sierra and I are up and mingling. We know a lot of people here from attending these seminars over the years, so we chat with a few familiar faces and steer clear of those who only seem interested in grilling us for Seaside secrets. I look over at Beckett, who's standing with Grayson and two other men. He's watching me. He has a curious look on his face, and the next thing I know, he's walking over to me. Sierra must notice the shrewd look in Beckett's eyes because she murmurs, "Coming in hot," just loud enough for me to hear it before one of our colleagues from New York links an arm through Sierra's and pulls her towards the bar. She flashes an apologetic look my way, leaving me on my own in enemy territory.

"Hey," Beckett says when he reaches me. His eyes drift down my dress to my heels then back up to my face. The look in his eyes is hunter-meet-prey and I'm immediately flustered and on edge.

There's a tension between us that I wish wasn't there. I wish we could let bygones be bygones and be civil, but that's not my relationship with him and it probably never will be. I remind myself that Beckett is dangerous.

But I can't ignore this connection between us, as if

we're being pulled together. I'm curious about him. What does he do for fun? Does he even know the meaning of the word? Is he always in shrewd, cocky, business mode or would he crash a wedding too?

"You found your way to the ballroom," I say, noticing the stiffness in my tone. "I was worried you might get lost."

He ignores the dig, instead volleying one back at me. "It's not Dom Perignon," he says with a nod to my champagne glass. "Will you be okay, princess?"

*Dick.*

Here he goes again with the rich girl bullshit. I'm used to this, being a Bennett, but if you know me and my family, we don't fit the spoiled, wealthy stereotype. Yes, we have money. My father owns the largest luxury boutique hotel chain on the east coast and my brother Miles is one of Hollywood's highest paid actors, but I was raised to be humble, to give to others and to understand that money doesn't buy you happiness.

A tall, willowy blonde woman in her early 20s saddles up next to Beckett. She's beautiful, with a sultry smirk on her face and appreciation in her eyes. Her gaze runs the length of him, liking what she sees. I bet he gets this a lot. The man is attractive—okay more than attractive, Beckett is ridiculously gorgeous. But he doesn't seem to notice she's there. He stares at me with a deep intensity, and despite my vow not to let him get to me, I feel my pulse quicken.

"Hey, Beck," she says, her voice soft and silky. "It's been a while. Thought I'd say hi."

He doesn't move, his eyes staying on mine for another moment. "Hi Jess, it's good to see you," he says finally, looking polite but uninterested. Luckily Jess can read a room. She tells Beckett she'll see him around and then saunters away.

"Part of your harem?" I ask, raising one eyebrow.

"Maybe. I can't recall. There are just so many of them."

I glare at him. He glares right back. My jaw is clenched so tightly there's a pulse in my cheek.

"What do you want, Beckett?" I'm getting tired of his hot-and-cold routine. I can't figure him out. I know Beckett the businessman all too well: he's a force in the hotel industry, a focused and determined vice president who has kept the Liberty Hotel in the top 10 for the past 3 years. He's arrogant, but well-respected. Beyond that, Beckett Taylor is a mystery. He keeps his private life just that.

"You're cute when you're irritated." He's staring at my mouth. I huff out a breath. I'm annoyed that I'm letting him get to me.

*Up. Your. Game. Jules.*

"And you're a pompous ass who could benefit from a handful of CBD gummies."

Enjoyment sparkles in his eyes. "I think you like pompous asses."

I balk. "Can't stand them."

"I think you like a man who takes charge, who knows what he's doing," he says, then leans in closer, so close that his lips almost brush my ear. "A man who knows what a woman likes."

I close my eyes, my skin on fire at the closeness of him, as if a spark has ignited deep inside of me. What does he want with me? Why is he teasing me like this?

"Are you saying you know someone who fits that description?"

He pulls back and grins. "You look nervous. Are you feeling flustered, Jules?"

"I'm not nervous." Lies. I am, at least a little. Beckett's wit is quick, I have to be on my toes to keep up.

He cocks his head to the side. "That's what you're busy

telling yourself, but the flush of your cheeks is saying something different."

My cheeks suddenly feel like I'm on fire and I silently curse myself for not being able to hide my emotions. It's just… he sets me off balance. He makes me feel like I'm coming unglued. It's him in his dress shirt, with the sleeves rolled up his forearms. It's the vein that runs the length of his corded, tan arms. I wish he'd put his suit jacket back on. It would make this easier. My eyes drift down to his trousers, snug around his flat stomach. I wonder what's behind the fly.

"My eyes are up here," he smirks, and I flick my attention back to his face, my blush deepening even further. This man oozes confidence. I hate that he makes me feel inferior to him. I really need to walk away.

"Why did you come over here, Beckett? What do you want?"

His eyes flare. "Are you always this uptight?"

I laugh. "Trust me, no one has *ever* called me uptight. Haven't you heard? I'm the life of the party."

A slow smile crosses his face, and he looks like he's skeptical. What would he know about a good time? He wouldn't know fun if it walked up and smacked him on the nose. God, I'd love to knock him down a peg.

"Is that so?" He laughs. "I'm sure your posh charity events and country club brunches are a pile of fun."

I frown, annoyed by the comment. Beckett doesn't know the first thing about me. *Screw him.*

"Is that what you think I do with my spare time?"

"Am I wrong, princess?"

I glare at him.

Suddenly I feel another set of eyes on us and turn to see Grayson, his expression pained. Grayson studies me for a second before trying to diffuse the situation. "Hey guys, play nice. Should we check out the dessert buffet?"

What I would like to do is shove the entire dessert buffet up Beckett's ass. I take a deep, calming breath and the survival instinct in me kicks in, telling me to get out of here, as far away from Beckett Taylor as I can. Sierra must have noticed my face changing colors because she's back at my side, a concerned look on her face.

Beckett exhales. "I—"

I glare at him, my quivering bottom lip betraying my emotions. "You've said enough. Please stop. I'm done. Sierra, I'll catch you later."

I give him one laser-pointed look and then turn towards the ballroom doors, barely able to keep myself from screaming. I practically run all the way to my room, where I slam the door behind me and flip off my heels. I am so done with that man.

After changing out of my dress and getting ready for bed, I ease between the sheets, happy to be in my room and far away from Beckett Taylor. I say a silent prayer that he chokes on a mini pavlova or falls face first into the chocolate fountain.

Chapter Four

B eckett

My eyes follow Jules as she storms out of the ballroom and disappears into the hotel. *Dammit.* I didn't mean to hurt her.

That's not me. I'm not that guy. I just wanted a reaction out of her and I'm not even sure why. Guilt consumes me. I need to apologize to her—if she'll even talk to me.

"What the hell did you do to her?" Grayson asks.

"Yeah, what *did* you do to her?" Sierra asks. We don't know each other well but I've met her at various work events and often seen her with Jules.

"We were bantering and… fuck, I guess I took it a little too far." I let out a breath and drag my fingers through my hair. "I fucked up."

"Epically," Grayson agrees. "She was pissed. Whatever you said to her must have been—"

My jaw tenses. "I know," I say, cutting him off. "I was there, but thanks for pointing that out."

I could kick myself for letting my insecurities get the better of me. I know Jules' story. I've met her family.

They're Reed Point royalty and have more money than they know what to do with. I know plenty of people like the Bennetts, and I know that they don't have time for a guy like me, born on the wrong side of town to a single mother and a dad who couldn't be bothered to stick around.

Besides all that, the girl flat out hates me. She thinks I'm an asshole for taking that celebrity wedding out from underneath her. She thinks I ran the Seaside's name through the mud. *Fuck.* This is such a mess.

*I'm sure your posh charity events and country club brunches are a pile of fun.* Jesus. Did I really say that?

"I need to go," I mutter, but Sierra stops me.

"Hold up. Not a smart move. She didn't look like she wanted you anywhere near her." I wince at her words. "I'll handle this," she says. "Grayson, it was nice to meet you."

"Wait. Before you go. Can you tell her I'm sorry?"

"You can tell her yourself tomorrow, Beckett. But I'm not sure she'll actually believe it. She knows you think she's just riding her father's coattails."

It feels like I've been sucker-punched. "What the fuck? Why would she think that?" I'm shocked to hear that Jules believes I think that poorly of her. "That couldn't be further from the truth."

"Look. She worries what people think." Sierra pauses as if she's already said too much. "This isn't my place. I think you two need to talk. Finally put whatever this thing is between you to bed."

I nod then watch Sierra walk away. She's right. This has gotten out of hand.

A part of me is pissed that Jules would think I'm that big of an asshole, but I'm also bothered that she's been carrying that weight around. Wondering how she's perceived, worried that people like me think she hasn't earned her place at the table. I've never put myself in her shoes and thought about what it would feel like to work for your father's company. It has its perks, but it can't all be easy.

Grayson looks at me with concern and hands me a glass of champagne he's nabbed from a passing waiter's silver tray. "You're a good guy, Beck. Talk to her. Apologize. You can fix it."

I wonder if I should go find Jules, but my gut tells me Sierra is right. I can talk to her in the morning, when we've both calmed down. Another wave of guilt crashes over me. I'm not a dick. I was trying to rile her up, but upsetting Jules is the last thing I wanted to do.

An image of her in that red dress with her soft, pink, pouty lips flashes through my mind. Yeah, I noticed how hot she looked. I couldn't keep my eyes off of her all night. There's something about her. She's... special. Confident, smart and sexy as hell. And completely out of my reach.

I shake my head, trying to banish all thoughts of her creamy skin, the curve of her collarbones and the tiny tattoo she has on her wrist—the one I'm dying to trace my tongue over. She and I are never going to happen. And that is probably for the best. I need to stay focussed on my career, not on a woman. My mom and Bean depend on me.

"Beck, did you hear me?" Grayson asks, interrupting my train of thought. "What was that all about? It's not like you to get into it like that with someone. Especially a woman. What happened there?"

"She doesn't think very highly of me and I think I just made it worse." I sigh, rubbing one hand over my face. "We had a run-in over the Bayer wedding a while back. She had the contract signed, then the bride changed her mind at the last minute and wanted to go with us. Jules thinks I had something to do with it. She thinks I tried to trash the Seaside's name."

"Why would she think that?"

"I don't know, but I didn't do it. I would never. That's not how I do business. You know that."

"I do."

Jules is incredible at what she does. I admire her. She's smart and she works her ass off. I remember listening to her speak at a conference and being so impressed. Her ideas were relevant and creative, and she spoke with confidence, commanding the room.

I keep glancing at the doors to the ballroom, hoping she'll walk back through them. My jaw clenches, my hand tightening around the stem of the glass I'm holding. I feel like a jerk. She's probably in her room crying and that bothers me.

"Listen. I'm not the best guy to be handing out advice but if you really want to apologize to her, why don't you do something nice for her," Grayson suggests.

"Like?"

"That isn't my wheelhouse, you know my track record with women. But you're a smart guy. I'm sure you can think of something."

Grayson's right. I need to fix this. I spot a waiter carrying a tray of fruity desserts and I think I may have an idea to show Jules that I'm not the giant asshole that she thinks I am.

# Chapter Five

*J*ules

A knock on my door at 7:30am surprises me. I tug on the tie of my plush hotel bathrobe and open the door to find a hotel staff member standing there with a cart covered in plates of breakfast treats, juices and hot drinks. *Huh?*

"Good morning, Ms. Bennett. Can I set this up in your room for you?"

"Um, okay. I'll take it, but I didn't order breakfast," I say, stumbling to the side as he pushes his cart past me. He removes the tray and sets it on the bureau then looks at a slip of paper he has stashed in a drawer in his cart.

"I've got the right room, so it's yours. Enjoy," he says, as I scramble through my purse for a couple of bills for him. He sees himself out while I look at the fresh fruit, sourdough toast, yogurt and granola. I notice a note with my name on it, so I pick it up and read it.

*I'm sorry for what happened last night. It was never my intention to hurt your feelings. I made sure they left off the mangoes because I know you hate them. I'm sorry. Beck.*

How does he know I don't like mangoes? That part is kind of cute, but I'm not sure how to feel about this. It's a sweet gesture, but it doesn't erase the fact that he was a total jerk to me.

Sierra texted me last night about an hour after I left the party, wanting to know if I was okay. She asked me to meet her for a walk on the beach. I declined, not wanting to accidentally run into *him*. I wanted to be left alone to stew. She said she understood but wanted me to know that Beckett felt bad and said he was sorry. *Good. He should be.*

I'm still mad at Beckett, but that won't stop me from enjoying this breakfast. Pulling over the desk chair, my gaze flits to the note. I grab it and stuff it in my purse, then pour myself a cup of peppermint tea. Then I kick my legs up onto the bureau and dig in.

At my third seminar of the day, I stare at the digital whiteboard, but my mind is elsewhere. The night before I left for Miami, I babysat my nephew Hudson so my brother Liam and his fiancée Ellie could have a date night. Ellie is four months pregnant with their second and is completely miserable. Pregnancy, she grumbles any chance she gets, does not agree with her. Hudson is two years old and is the cutest, funniest, smartest toddler on planet Earth —in my slightly biased opinion.

Sierra elbows me in my side. "You're daydreaming again. Snap out of it. You just laughed out loud."

Whoops.

"You're lucky I'm taking notes," she says, tapping her pen to her notebook.

"Do you think there will be a test at the end of this? Because I've got news for you... there won't be," I tease, unwrapping a slice of banana bread I had stashed in my purse and taking a bite. I can feel Sierra's eyes on me.

"What are you doing? You're not allowed to eat in here," she whisper-yells at me.

"Please, what are they going to do? Arrest me? Stick me in the corner and make me write 'I'm sorry I broke the rules' 30 times on that stupid whiteboard?"

She narrows her eyes at me, but then they suddenly go wide, and I have a sinking feeling as to why.

"Guess who just walked in? I'll give you a hint. His name rhymes with Wreck-it."

I roll my eyes at her, then follow the direction of her gaze. My spine stiffens the second I spot him. Beckett has taken a seat at the far end of the room. He looks... good. His thick hair is styled in a perfect, messy look that works with his vibe. His blue button-down matches his eyes. I allow myself to stare for a moment longer, a million thoughts running through my head.

*I should probably forgive him. He looks good in that shirt. He looks really good in that shirt. I need to stop staring.*

I force my eyes away and pop a bite of my loaf into my mouth but I'm annoyed to find myself still thinking of him. I hate to admit it, but Beckett hasn't been far from my mind all day. I'm not sure what to do with him. Unable to stop myself, I look his way again. He takes a long drink from his water bottle, the column of his throat flexing, and I'm mesmerized. He catches me staring and I quickly turn my face back to the front of the room, embarrassed at having been caught.

"I think you should give him a chance to explain," Sierra says. "And if you don't like what he has to say, then at least you tried."

I shrug. "We'll see."

"Listen to me, Jules. I know a lot of things," she says, tapping her skull.

I laugh. "A lot of things. I'll keep that in mind."

Thirty minutes later, the seminar is over and I'm packing my things into my bag. Sierra left me to run to the restroom before we head out for a quick coffee. I'm just about to leave the table when I stiffen at his smoky voice.

"You aren't an easy one to track down. Three conference rooms later and I finally find you."

Maybe he should take the hint. "What do you want, Beckett?" I say without looking at him, a snarky tone to my voice.

"To talk."

The tougher side of me, the one that's been bruised and battered by men, wants to tear him to shreds, let him know I'm unaffected by his hot guy persona. Then there's the other side that just wants to forgive and forget. Like my mom always says, "The first to apologize is the bravest, the first to forgive is the strongest and the first to forget is the happiest."

"There's nothing to say," I snap in annoyance. "I'm sorry you wasted your time looking for me. Enjoy your day."

"Jules, please," he says, reaching for me, his hand clasping my forearm gently. My skin tingles at his touch and I inhale sharply, looking down at his hand. Again, there's that sensation. Every time we touch it's as if a current travels between us. My focus shifts to his eyes and I find him looking at me in astonishment, like he felt it too. He swallows and moves his hand away, then scrapes his fingers through the stubble on his jaw. "Let me apologize. I was an ass. I feel terrible. I don't know what came over me. I didn't sleep last night I was so upset over it. It's... you make me... nervous."

I laugh. "*I* make *you* nervous. Come off it. An armed robber at your front door wouldn't make you nervous. How do you expect me to believe that?"

A muscle in his jaw twitches, a sign that I'm getting to him. Is it terrible that I get some satisfaction out of frustrating him? Probably. Whatever.

He takes a half-step closer.

"I don't expect you to believe anything I say, but I promise you I don't lie. Look, I was a jerk. I didn't mean it."

Tension hovers in the air between us as we lock eyes, and I lift my chin, refusing to be the first one to look away. Beckett's big blue eyes search mine. He opens his mouth like he has something more to say, but then closes it.

I study his face and instead of seeing an egotistical asshole, I see sincerity. I've always thought of him as self-obsessed and underhanded, but I wonder for a moment if maybe I've rushed to judgment when it comes to Beckett. My opinion of him stems almost entirely from that one disastrous deal. The truth is, I'm tired of battling him. I can just forgive him and politely move on. We don't need to be friends.

"I'm past it, Beckett. Truce?" I keep my voice perfectly neutral.

"Truce," he nods. "Maybe even friends?"

I smirk. "Don't push it. See you around."

I hike my bag over my shoulder and head for the door, not waiting for Beckett. I exhale when I reach the hallway, already wishing I'd stuck around so we could have talked a little more.

Later that day, Sierra and I sit poolside at the hotel restaurant, sipping our drinks and soaking up the afternoon sunshine. After the last seminar of the day, we agreed to skip cocktail hour and have a late lunch together instead.

Placing my glass back on the table, I grin at Sierra. "He seemed like he was into you."

"Really?" She fiddles with her coaster. "He is so freaking cute. You don't know if he's seeing someone?"

She's referring to Grayson. She's crushing on him. *Obvious.* I shrug. "How would I know that?"

"Because you're friends with Beckett."

I frown. "Um, I'm not *friends* with Beckett. We can barely stand one another. I assumed that was obvious."

She looks at me.

"What?" I say, noticing the glint in her eyes. "Don't start. I may have forgiven him, but that's as far as it goes. We are not friends; more like frenemies."

She laughs, her fingers tapping the table. "Listen, call it what you want, but you two have chemistry. Beckett can't keep his eyes off you. He's always watching you." She leans across the table. "And it doesn't hurt that he looks like that really hot guy from *The Tudors.*"

"Henry Cavill?" I ask.

"Yes, him! The dark hair and blue eyes are—" she pinches her fingers and her thumb together, kissing them, and tossing them away from her lips in a dramatic fashion. "Chef's kiss."

I shake my head. Beckett is good-looking, but Henry Cavill-level? Not a chance.

"Oh, come on, Jules. Admit it. You think he's hot."

"He's fine. I guess he has nice bone structure, if that floats your boat."

"Whatever." She shrugs, smiling. "Then I guess it won't matter to you that he's sitting over there."

My head whips around in the direction of Sierra's gaze, but I can't see Beckett. She narrows her eyes at me as she takes a sip of her drink. "Gotcha! I was right. You should have seen your face. You like him."

I throw my napkin at her. "Do not. You are such a pest. Now what are we going to do about you and Grayson?"

"Well, first we need to find out if he's single. If he is, I make my move."

"Just like that, huh? I wish I had your confidence."

Just then I spot Beckett and Grayson walk through the patio doors. Beckett has changed into shorts and a gray t-shirt that's pulled snugly across every muscle in his chest. He's wearing sneakers, like he's on his way to the gym— why do I think that's hot? Is athletic gear my kink now?

Grayson sees us first and raises his hand in a hello. Beckett gives me a shy smile, which is different for him. He's trying to make things okay between us; I'm not sure if that's possible.

Grayson says something to the hostess, who then leads them over to the empty table next to us. FML. I touch the small tattoo on my wrist that is there to remind me to stay calm, grounded, and remember to breathe.

"Hey," Grayson says, taking a seat. "Looks like great minds think alike. Enjoying the sun?"

"This weather is perfection. So is my daiquiri," Sierra says, sipping from her drink, her eyes sparkling now that Grayson's here. It's cute.

"Have you ordered?" Grayson asks.

"Not yet, but I'm getting hungry," Sierra says, then turns to me. "How 'bout you, Jules?"

"Definitely."

A few minutes later when our waitress returns to take our orders, Sierra and I are still undecided. She wants the nachos and I want calamari.

"Sierra, I'll split the nachos with you if you want?" Grayson asks.

"Okay." She looks at him and then up to the waitress and there must be hearts in her eyes. "But that's going to be tricky if you're—" she points to their table, "over there and—"

"Good point." Grayson grins, then turns to our waitress, who looks like she'd rather be somewhere else. "Would you mind if we joined their table? Girls, that cool with you? It might be easier."

She reluctantly agrees, then takes the rest of the boys' orders—I swear they get one of everything on the menu—before drifting away.

Great. I inwardly groan at the thought of being in Beckett's company for an entire meal. A truce is one thing, but this is pushing it. I glance in his direction but can't read his expression. I'm sure he's not any happier about the situation than I am. I take a deep breath and try to put things in perspective. I'm sure there are worse things than having a meal with a guy you can barely tolerate: a flat tire, a raging migraine, being forced to watch *Star Wars*. I will survive.

Sierra shoots me a pleased-with-herself look. In response, I give her a look of my own that says, you-will-pay-for-this-later. I sigh and say a silent prayer that our food comes fast so that I can hightail it back to my room to raid the minibar and watch a movie.

The boys leave their table and squeeze in around ours. Beckett sits to my right and I squirm in my seat, feeling the energy shift in the air around us before my eyes meet his and I straighten my shoulders. I can do this. Act cool. Be easy-breezy. Dig deep, Jules.

"So, no Parker this trip? He couldn't make it out?" Beckett asks.

I shake my head. "Not this time. He's in St. Lucia with his wife. They're expecting their first baby and wanted a trip away before life gets crazy."

Parker is the second oldest of my three brothers, the only one who works with me at our father's company. He left Reed Point after college, moving to New York to run the Seaside hotel there, but then moved back to the coast when he reconnected with Olivia, his high school sweetheart. They got engaged, got married and now they're about to become parents. A storybook romance, complete with their happily ever after.

Liam is the oldest in the family. Unlike Parker and I, he didn't join the family business, instead pursuing a career as a lawyer. He's a straight shooter, a quick thinker, and—if I'm being honest—can be more than a little moody sometimes. He's softened since meeting Ellie, his fiancée. Not that he'd admit it. Liam and Ellie have a toddler—my nephew, Hudson—and one more on the way.

Then there's Miles. He's two years older than me and has lived in Los Angeles since becoming an actor. I still can't quite get my head around the fact that my brother is a legitimate celebrity, with a resume of box office hits a mile long. The list of women lining up to meet him is even longer, but he only has eyes for his fiancée, Rylee. He and Rylee have three or four houses all over the world—I've lost count—but they spend a lot of their free time with Rylee's family in Tennessee.

"I didn't hear the news," Beckett says, sounding genuinely happy about it. "Congratulate Parker for me. That's exciting for him. He'll make a great dad."

I look at him, perplexed. It's not the answer I expected. I thought it would be more along the lines of, "Poor guy, his life is going to be over" or, "Better him than me." For the second time today, I find myself wondering if maybe I don't know Beckett as well as I think I do. I've never imagined him to be thoughtful, endearing or soft around the edges.

I brush it off. I learned a long time ago not to get too taken in by charming guys. But whatever. Who cares? My heart is ice.

That's what happens when you get screwed over by love time and time again. You want no part of it.

Once upon a time I had a type: bad boys. I liked the excitement, the thrill, the overt masculinity was like an aphrodisiac. But eventually that excitement wore off and I got tired of the don't-give-a-damn attitude. So instead, I tried the opposite, and dated a nice guy. Alex was a sweet, smart, nerd-type who was studying to be a doctor. My brothers never understood the attraction, but he seemed like the type of guy I *should* be with. Safe. Solid. Not guys like Beckett, who may be attractive in a dozen different ways, but who also have the ability to shatter your heart into a million tiny pieces when they decide you aren't enough for them. It turns out the nice guys can break hearts too. I learned that the hard way when Alex dumped me after a few years together. Said I was *a lot.* Fuck him.

The four of us make small talk—mostly Grayson and Sierra, who seem to have just about forgotten that Beckett and I are at the table with them—until our food arrives. We pass around the plates of appetizers, loading up our plates.

"Thanks," I say with a smile when Grayson passes me the platter of Kung Pao chicken. I fork a few pieces onto my plate then pass the dish to Beckett, a pleasant expression painted on my face. See? Look at me. I can play nice.

Another round of drinks are ordered as we all dig in. There are only a couple of awkward moments of silence as we eat, but Sierra and Grayson keep the conversation flowing. They seem to be really hitting it off.

"Has anyone left the hotel yet?" Grayson asks before stuffing a nacho into his mouth.

"Not I," I say, blotting my mouth with a napkin. "There's been no time, but I'm not leaving until I have one of those Nutella milkshakes from Sweet Spots on Ocean Drive. I get one every time I come here."

"What's so good about them? Romance me," Beckett says.

*Romance Mr. Wonder?* Not a chance. "Well, for starters, they're filled with gobs of Nutella, vanilla ice cream, and brownie pieces. Bonus, they're served in these really cute mason jars. You really haven't lived until you've had one."

"Wait! That sounds familiar. Did I see that place on *Sal Eats Here*?" Beckett asks.

"Yes! I love that show. You saw that episode?" I say, sort of in disbelief. A guy like Beckett Taylor surely does not watch the Food Network.

But apparently, he does. "That episode, along with every other one. Sal knows what he's talking about. Did you see the one where he went to the pizza place in Arizona?"

"The Italian man with the two sons who are infamous for the—"

"Lady Zaza pizza," we both say in unison. "Yessss!" we both say again.

Beckett tips his head back in laughter while I watch him a little stunned. We have something in common? More than that, we're getting along. This actually feels like a nice conversation rather than a lead-up to me wanting to strangle him.

I run my teeth over my bottom lip, thinking back to his apology and then to our conversation in the hallway when we first arrived. It feels like Beckett has let down his guard on this trip. It's definitely a new side of him, and I like it. He seems almost… charming.

Still, it doesn't mean I want to be his friend.

"You two have weird taste in shows," Grayson says. "Watching some dude eat crazy shit at restaurants you'll probably never go to? They're not even entertaining. *Succession* is entertaining, or *Ted Lasso*. Now *that* guy is cool."

"That's because you eat like a frat boy. Your favorite foods are nachos and hot wings." Beckett says, nodding at the mound of nachos Grayson has piled on his plate.

"And I still look like a God."

"Uh-huh," Beckett says, rolling his eyes. "You must be tired from fighting off the 50-somethings all weekend."

I stifle a laugh while Sierra mimics a mic drop, knocking her drink over while she's at it. The liquid spills over the table.

"Now look at what you've done," she says, setting the glass upright, mopping the spill up with a bunch of napkins.

"What *I've* done?" Beckett laughs. "I didn't spill your drink. You're the one that's going to get us kicked out of here."

I help Sierra mop up the drink with my napkin, laughing. As much as I was dreading this, it's actually turning into a good time.

"We're going to Sway tonight," Grayson announces once the chaos has settled. "You two should join us."

"Sway?" Sierra asks, eyes fixed on Grayson. She's been acting all starry-eyed over him for the entire meal.

"Yeah, it's a new Miami hotspot. A club. They supposedly have the best drink list. A friend of mine from back home went the last time he was in Miami and said it's insane. It will be fun."

I raise my drink to my lips, unsure of what to say. I never turn down a night out, and I *have* heard of Sway. I'd be lying if I said I didn't want to check it out, but it means a night out with Beckett. When I set my glass down on the table, Sierra is staring at me with a pleading look in her eyes. How am I supposed to say no?

"You guys should come," Beckett says, before tossing back a drink.

"You down?" Sierra asks.

"Why not?" I shrug. I can take one for the team and you never know, maybe there will be some hot men there.

I notice Beckett's lips curve up into a small smile before he rearranges his face so that it's expressionless.

"Meet in the lobby for seven?" Grayson asks.

"Works for me," Sierra says. "We could—"

"Ouch!" An instant, sharp, burning pain makes me shout. My hand moves to my chest as I notice a wasp zip away, leaving a swollen, red welt just below my collarbone. The pain quickly sharpens, and I rub my chest as a cold sweat breaks out over me.

Crap.

Holy crap.

I have a severe allergy to wasp bites. The last time I was bitten was at my best friend's 14th birthday party. I broke out in hives and vomited all over my plate of birthday cake. Since then, I carry an EpiPen with me wherever I go.

"Shit. You got stung by a wasp. Are you okay?" Beckett asks.

My chest and both arms are already itchy and the skin

from my neck down to the waist band of my shorts feels like it's on fire. I'm not fine at all. My throat has gone dry, swelling, and I can't quite get any words out. I nod and close my eyes, mortified. I hate that this is happening in front of *him*.

Then it gets worse.

# Chapter Six

Beckett

"She doesn't look okay. Jules, aren't you allergic to wasps?"

Sierra is right. Jules can't stop scratching herself and her chest is an ombre splatter of pink and white hives. She reaches down to her bag and it dawns on me that she's probably trying to reach for her EpiPen.

"Do you have an EpiPen in your bag?" I ask, scrambling out of my chair, picking up her purse.

She nods, and says yes, her voice weak. "Okay, I'm going to go into your purse to find your EpiPen, so please don't get mad at me for rummaging through your things."

"It's okay," she manages, "There's nothing incriminating in there. I'm very allergic."

Shit!

Fumbling through her purse, I locate the pen quickly. Thanks to a first aid class I took a decade ago, I know how to use one.

"I got you, Jules. Hang on. Breathe. You're going to feel better real soon," I say, removing it from its packaging and placing the orange tip against the center of her thigh at a right angle. Thank goodness she's wearing shorts. I push the tip into her skin. After several seconds, I remove the pen and massage the area while Sierra hands her a glass of water. Grayson watches with panic in his eyes.

"You doing okay?" Her hand grips my thigh and I have one hand on the back of her chair while I use my other to continue to massage the injection site. I swallow, realizing that in the process of helping her, we've gotten very close. My face is inches away from hers and I let my eyes fall on her soft, pink lips. Damn, she smells so good…pretty and light, like fresh rain and a field of flowers. Looking at her, I almost forget where we are. I want to kiss her, right here and right now.

I like the feel of her skin under my touch. Her grip on my thigh feels good too. I hold my breath, blink. I want more than our hands on each other. A lot more. I grit my molars, reminding myself she's just been bit by a wasp.

She nods, then looks down at her hand on my thigh, removing it quickly like she's afraid to get burnt. The sharp movement knocks me out of the temporary spell I was under and my sanity returns. I sit back in my chair and take a long sip from my water glass.

"Geez, that was scary. Are you sure you're okay? You're still scratching your arms," Sierra says from across the table, a worried expression on her face.

"Much better. I'm sorry to cause a scene," she says a little out of breath. "Thank you," she adds, her gaze landing on me. "You were so calm. I appreciate you jumping into action like that and helping me."

My stomach flutters.

"It was nothing. I'm just happy you had your EpiPen on you. I guess you never leave home without it."

"I try not to."

My eyes travel to her chest. The bite still looks swollen and angry, but on the bright side, there's been an improvement.

"Eyes up here, Mr. Wonder," she says playfully, staring back at me. *Mr. Wonder?* What the hell does that mean?

"Hurt, but still sarcastic," I say. "I'm impressed."

She laughs, "Oh good. Wouldn't want to disappoint."

The table has gone quiet. I can feel Grayson and Sierra's eyes on the two of us. I'm sure they're just as surprised as I am that Jules and I are getting along. The two of us sharing a meal and not once wanting to murder each other? Call it the 8$^{th}$ wonder of the world, it's that crazy.

I stare at her. Dammit, I need to stop. Her thick, honey-colored hair falls over her shoulders. Her eyelashes are so long that they flutter against her cheeks, and from this close I notice the details of her eyes: dark green around the iris, gold around the pupil. They look like a Monet painting. She's captivating.

She pushes back her seat. "Can you excuse me for—"

"Let me help you." I'm out of my seat with my hand on her elbow before she can finish the sentence. I don't know what it is, maybe it's that she fascinates me, but I feel an intense need to take care of her, to make sure she's okay.

"I'm fine, Beckett. It's just a little wasp bite. I can walk to the restroom on my own." She grabs her purse and goes.

I frown, taking my seat. Grayson reads my face, raising one brow with a stare that seems to see right through me.

*You like her,* his eyes say.

*Fuck right off,* mine say in response.

"You have superpowers, Beckett. Who knew you had mad EpiPen skills?" Sierra says. "That was impressive.

Thank God you were here, I just froze like a deer in headlights."

"It was nothing," I say, glancing in the direction of the washrooms. "Maybe you should check on her. I'm worried she might be lightheaded, or sick to her stomach."

Sierra cocks her head, giving me an inquisitive once-over. "You're right, I should. I'll be back."

Sierra walks across the patio at what seems like warp speed. Grayson, meanwhile, appears to be distracted by the view of her walking away. He's definitely checking out her ass. Once she's out of sight, he turns his attention to me with a know-it-all expression.

"What?" I demand, not even needing to ask what he's thinking. "It was a medical emergency! Should I have just sat there and watched her lose consciousness?"

He sits up straighter in his chair, skepticism written all over his face. "You have a thing for her. You've been staring at her all day, Beck. For minutes at a time. You've got it bad for Juliette Bennett. I wonder what her father would think of that."

I already know what Michael Bennett would think of that: Not much. But it doesn't matter, because I do *not* have a crush on Jules. Just yesterday we couldn't stand each other. Hell, I think she might still feel that way. I was only being a nice guy, doing the right thing. "You have an over-active imagination, Grayson. I don't 'have it bad' for her. I just didn't want her to pass out in my hot wings."

"Okay, great. Then you won't mind if I take a shot." I freeze. There's a thumping sound in my ears. He's bluffing.

Grayson shakes his head, laughing.

"Joking," he says with a pleased smirk on his face. "But you should have seen your face."

I ignore him, checking for signs of the girls across the

patio when my phone vibrates with a text, and I slip it from my pocket and swipe open the message.

> I've got tickets to the Yankees game. It's
> next Saturday if you want to go. Or if you'd
> rather, you can take a friend.

The message is from my dad. My jaw tenses and my fingers clench my phone. I stare at the screen, going to a dark place in my mind, then have to make a concentrated effort to steady my breathing. Fuck it. He isn't worth it.

Six months after I was born, he left. He didn't give my mom a reason, but it didn't take long for her to figure out why. He left her for another woman—one he had been seeing behind my mom's back for over a year. The asshole got the other woman pregnant around the same time and he chose them in the end.

As if that wasn't bad enough, he didn't even have the decency to move his happy family out of town. Every so often we would spot them while we were out running errands and Mom, Bean and I would have to stop whatever we were doing and go home. My mom didn't trust herself enough not to lose it, not make a huge, messy, public scene. I wouldn't have blamed her if she did. I'll never forgive him for abandoning us.

When I was younger, I used to wish for my parents to get back together. All I wanted was for us to live together, one happy family. But that dream died as I got older and realized that my dad was never coming back. He had made his choice. We didn't matter to him. That become painfully obvious. He made half-hearted attempts to keep in touch, but a text or a voicemail every six months is no substitute for a dad who is actually around. It was obvious that he had forgotten about us, and I worked hard at forgetting about him too.

I've ignored most of his texts and calls for years—I have no interest in helping to ease his occasional guilt. After a while, the messages stopped all together, but he's back at it these days. He wants to talk. He wants to see me. No thanks. My allegiance will always be to my mom.

"Did you just say *fuck* to yourself?" Grayson says. "Are you talking to yourself now?"

I didn't realize I said that out loud. My jaw pulses. Why do I let him affect me like this? You'd think that after 27 years I'd be past this. I mean nothing to him, so why do I allow him to make me feel this way?

"You good?" Grayson asks, a puzzled look on his face.

"Good as motherfucking gold," I say, shaking it off, stuffing my phone back into my pocket.

"You sure about that? It looked like whoever that was on your phone really pissed you off."

"It's nothing new." I rub the nape of my neck. "By the way, are we really going to Sway with Jules and Sierra? Fuck man, it feels like a double date. You really didn't think that one through."

"Or maybe I did. They're both cool and fucking hot."

"One of them hates me."

"Hate-fucking is hot. You could try it. Besides, it didn't seem that way to me. Not after you saved her life, Prince Charming. I think she's warming up to you."

I shake my head then look up to see the girls walking back across the patio to our table. A fluttery sensation fills my stomach when Jules' eyes meet mine.

She slips into the chair next to mine looking much better, but still not herself.

"Felling better?" I ask.

"A little." She clears her throat. "My skin feels like it's attacking me. It's still itchy as heck but don't worry about me. All of this concern and getting along is weirding me out. This doesn't feel right. You and I argue. We take jabs at one another. Let's go back to that."

I laugh, leaning my elbow on the table. "Would you prefer it if I insulted you?"

"I think so." She half-smiles and looks down at her plate.

Grayson drops his fork, making a clanging sound against his plate. "You two should skip dessert and just tie the knot already. You act like an old married couple."

"Zip it, Grayson," Jules quips. I bark out a laugh.

The 4 of us spend the next 30 minutes finishing our appies. We talk about the conference, a speaker we all admired, social media trends. Jules looks tired. She's trying, but her spitfire personality is noticeably toned down.

Our waitress brings us the bill, which I pay, while we finish our drinks and enjoy the last of the day's sun.

"I'm going to head up to my room," Jules says, scratching her chest. "I'm going to have to bail on tonight. I never say no to a night out, so you know I'm feeling rough."

"Then I won't go either," Sierra tells her. "I'll stick around and keep you company."

"Sierra, no. Please go. I'm a grown woman and I don't need anyone to look after me. I'll be fine."

"Are you sure you're okay?" I ask.

She waves me off, standing from the table. "I promise I'm fine. I just need to lie down. I'll be as good as new by the morning."

Her deep green eyes hold mine, those eyes that make me weak. I wish she wasn't running off. I could walk her to her room. Run her a hot bath. Tuck her into bed.

*Not smart, Beck. Stop. Now.*

Jules turns and walks away, and I watch her go. Each step she takes makes me feel as if I've lost something important. It's silly, I know, but I can't help it. I can still smell the scent of her on me, feel her smooth, creamy skin under the tips of my fingers.

"Jules," I say.

She turns around to face me. "Yes?"

"Can I text you later to see if you need anything? I'll get your number from Sierra."

She studies me, her expression hesitant, as if she's unsure, as if she wants to say yes but she's scared. Given our track record, it makes sense.

"It's really not necessary, Beckett. Go enjoy your night."

I nod. "You sure?" I ask.

"If you ask me again I'm going to think you're stalking me."

I laugh. The girl is funny even when she's not at 100. I feel off balance. Having had her that close to me, my hands on her thigh, her body so close to me…it's felt hard to breathe ever since.

*Snap out of it.*

I never should have sat with her. I should have steered clear of her on this entire trip, but as soon as we started bantering on day one in the lobby, I didn't know how to stop.

Jules pivots, heading for the door, weaving her way through the patio tables. And then she's gone.

And maybe I'm a little gone too.

On my balcony a few hours later, I watch the vacationers in the pool below soak up the last few minutes of golden hour. The sky is a watercolor of pink and blue and yellow. The breeze feels good on my skin. I'm supposed to be downstairs in the lobby in half an hour but instead I'm here, trying to stop my thoughts from drifting next door to Jules. I keep hoping she'll step out onto her patio so I can make sure she's okay. I keep wanting—no, needing—to see her again.

Something in my gut has been nagging at me and I know exactly what it is.

It's her.

I was fine before her. Totally fucking fine. And now, thanks to Jules, I'm all wound up.

I wonder what she's doing now. She didn't look so hot when she left the restaurant. Okay, maybe that's the wrong choice of words. Jules always looks hot, but it did look like that allergic reaction took a lot out of her.

Pushing up from my chair, I go back inside and lock the patio door behind me. I brush my teeth, throw on a pair of pants and a shirt and take the elevator downstairs to the lobby, where I find Grayson and Sierra waiting for me.

"Hey, you two. I'm going to sit this one out. You guys have fun. I'll see you in the morning."

## Chapter Seven

Jules

My eyes pop open at the knock on my door. I sit up slowly, checking the time on the clock. It's seven o'clock, which means I've been lying in bed for over an hour. The itchiness and pain are still there, but thank God the headache is gone. I force myself out of bed, catching a glimpse of my tired eyes and still-splotchy chest in the mirror.

I pad to the door in my sleep shorts and tank top, no bra, my hair piled on top of my head in a messy bun. I pull the door open, expecting to see Sierra. Instead, I'm mortified to find Beckett standing in the doorway, a Gatorade in one hand and a bottle of Benadryl in the other.

"Beckett. What are you doing here?"

"What kind of neighbor would I be if I didn't at least come and check on you?"

I stare at him, not quite believing that he's here. I watch his eyes widen as he takes me in, lingering on my messy bun, down to my bare shoulders. I quickly move to hide most of my body behind the door, remembering I'm half-naked and in my pajamas.

"You gonna let me in, beautiful?"

I frown. "I'm not any fun tonight. And stop calling me that."

He looks amused as I reluctantly step aside to let him in, crossing my arms over the thin tank that shows more than anyone should see. *Crap!* This is so embarrassing. He walks past me, and the door slams shut behind him. I quickly slide back into bed, pulling the covers over my chest. It's as if he can read my mind when he says, "Don't worry, I didn't see anything. Now, let me get you a cool cloth and get this Gatorade into you."

"Why do I need a cold cloth?"

"Because you look hot...I mean flushed. Stop questioning me and do what I say."

"I thought you'd be out with Grayson at Sway. I'm fine, Beckett. Go have some fun."

He ignores me, disappearing into the bathroom. "I'm not feeling it tonight," he says over the sound of the tap running. "Besides, I was worried about you. I wanted to make sure you're okay. No casualties on my watch, beautiful."

There's a boyish grin on his face when he returns to my bedside and places the cold washcloth on my forehead. He looks relaxed, handsome, and it's hitting me smack dab in that spot right above my ribcage. I close my eyes. I must have a fever.

"Thank you," I sigh. "That actually feels good."

"Told you so."

"You're surprisingly good at this."

"What? You didn't think I could take care of someone?" He picks up a glass from the bedside table and fills it with Gatorade. I notice his fingers—long and slender with short, nicely groomed fingernails. I wonder what they would feel like on my skin. Would he run the tips gently over my flesh or grip my skin hard, like he can't get enough?

"It comes naturally, I guess, looking after someone. My sister has…she has Cystic Fibrosis. And since I'm really close with her and my mom, I'm used to helping out. Her name is Bean. I call her Jelly Bean."

My heart snaps in my chest. "How old is she?"

"She's 19 now. Eight years younger than me," he says, handing me the glass. I take a sip and the cold cloth slips, so he reaches out and readjusts it. *So sweet.*

"That must be tough. It can't be easy watching your sister struggle. I'm sorry."

He half-smiles. "Don't be. She's never let her illness get her down. She's pretty amazing. I bet you would like her."

"I bet I would too."

"Should I put on a movie?" he asks nonchalantly, grabbing the remote from the dresser. He's wearing light gray sweatpants and an MIT T-shirt. This look on him is doing crazy things to my brain. I bet he's toned and muscular under that shirt, with rippled abs and smooth, soft skin. I doubt I'll ever know, but a girl can dream. Visions of him pushing me against my hotel room door and ravishing me flicker through my mind. A rush of heat ripples through me. I put a stop to that immediately.

"Jules, a movie?"

Shit, I spaced out. "Sure."

Beckett motions to the edge of the bed. "This okay…if I sit here?"

It's a terrible idea, but how can I say no? The man could be out enjoying the Miami nightlife, but instead he's here, trying to make me feel better. Besides, it's a hotel room—it's not like there are endless seating options.

"It's okay," I say, pulling up the duvet a little higher on my chest. "So, MIT, huh? Did you go or just buy the merch?"

He pats the area on his chest in front of his heart. "You wound me, beautiful. Do I not seem smart enough to go to one of the top universities in the country?"

I laugh. "Well…"

"Give me that Gatorade back, and the washcloth too. I'm offended."

"Please no. Not the washcloth," I tease. "I take it back. You are the smartest person I know. There's nobody smarter."

"That's better. And to answer your question, yes, I went to MIT. Graduated summa cum laude, I'll have you know. I'm very smart, Jules."

"I get it now. The reason for your inflated ego, it's because you're a smarty-pants."

"Yes, yes I am," he says flexing his bicep. "I have muscles too."

I shake my head. "So why aren't you out with Grayson at that club?" I ask, removing the now room-temperature cloth and setting it on the nightstand. "You're missing out on a plethora of women who would I'm sure fall all over themselves for a chance at Mr. Wonder."

He cocks a brow. "Mr. Wonder? That's the second time you've called me that."

"Never mind that. So?"

He shrugs. "I told you. Wasn't feeling it. Grayson went with Sierra instead. Don't make it into a thing."

I'm tempted to push it but decide to let it go when he cues up the movie and fluffs two throw pillows behind his back, making himself comfortable. I guess we're doing this. In bed, together, with me half-naked.

"I guessed that you'd like *When Harry met Sally*," Beckett says when the movie begins.

"I'm surprised. I didn't take you for a chick-flick junky. I thought maybe *The Terminator* or some Dwayne Johnson movie."

He laughs. "I've watched my fair share of girly movies with my sister. She likes my company when she's feeling crappy. Now come on, beautiful. Are you going to talk through the entire thing?"

I laugh—turns out that happens a lot when I'm with Beckett. Who knew?

We settle into the movie, me under the duvet and him on top of it. Beckett agrees with Harry that true friendship is impossible between a man and a woman, while I argue that sex doesn't always have to get in the way. We both agree the "fake orgasm" scene is chef's kiss.

"He's charming," I say, explaining Harry's appeal. "It's why Sally falls for him. Men should take a page out of Harry's book."

"So then…have *you* fallen for any charming guys?" he asks.

I frown.

"Tell me," he says.

"I thought maybe I'd found 'the one', but he ended things. Said I was *too much*. My entire family never could understand why I was with him in the first place, they thought he wasn't exciting enough for me. He studied a lot and didn't like peopling. It was an argument to get him to leave his house. I guess Alex just felt safe. Exciting isn't always the best choice. I can see now that the breakup was for the best, but at the time I was pretty upset."

Beckett's face turns hard. "The guy's an idiot, Jules."

"What?"

"The guy's the dumbest of dumbos to let a girl like you

get away." His eyes lock on mine. I tilt my head, considering his response.

*Does he really mean that?*

"It doesn't matter now. I'm over it. Besides, he showed me what I *don't* want in a relationship, so it wasn't for nothing," I say. "Your turn."

"My turn?"

"To tell me about the one that got away. I told you about my stupid ex-boyfriend, so now it's your turn."

"Fine. Her name was Isabel. I met her at university."

I nod. "And…"

"And we dated for a year." My eyebrows shoot up. I'm surprised he's had a relationship that long. I'm also surprised we're opening up to each other like this. It feels like something has changed between the two of us.

"Why do you look so shocked?"

I shrug. "I didn't know Mr. Wonder had it in him. You know…to commit. I've seen the way women look at you. I'm sure there are a plethora of women who would like to—"

"You think I'm handsome," he interrupts me, sitting up next to me. "Admit it, Jules. You think I'm hot."

And I'm smiling. Beckett is…funny.

"In your dreams," I say, shaking my head. "And don't put words in my mouth. I never said that. Stop trying to fish for compliments. You won't get any from me."

"Oh, come on. Just one. Tell me one thing you like about me."

"Have you lost your mind?"

"Nope," Beckett says. "Just one. Then *I'll* tell you something I like about you."

He gives me an encouraging nod. Then he taps his wrist. "Tick tock, Jules. And don't be afraid to really lay it on thick."

"Ugh, fine. It's your eyes. They're so blue. They remind me of the deepest part of the ocean."

His eyes hold mine as tension sizzles in the air between us. He takes a deep breath before looking down at his hands in his lap. Shit. Did I say too much?

He looks back at me, his expression different now. There's a need in his gaze that makes my breath hitch. This feels dangerous, but I can't stop. I feel pulled towards him.

"My turn," he says. "If I had to pick just one, I'd say it's your honesty. And the way you never apologize for it. You call things the way you see them. That, and you're really beautiful."

My cheeks heat. I'm pretty positive he notices. "Hence the nickname?"

"Hence." His lips press together. His chest rises and his eyes darken.

"I see."

He opens his mouth like he wants to say something, then closes it again. My heart beats triple time. It pumps so hard, I'm sure he can see it beating right through my chest.

"Jules…" he says softly.

*No. Yes. Dammit, I don't know what I want him to say.* I like having him here, he makes me happy. But I don't need a man to do that, I was perfectly happy before any of this started between us. Honestly, I don't even know what *this* is.

Beckett gives me a hard look. Flustered, I reach for the Gatorade on the nightstand. "I need something to drink. I'm thirsty." I sip from the glass, ignoring the fact there is a tremble in my hands. In my peripheral vision, I can see his head dip, his hands raking through his hair.

"Better?" he asks carefully.

"Yes," I lie. I flip my gaze to Harry and Sally sitting on

the airplane. "The cuddling scene. I love this part. We should…um…watch the movie."

He gives me a curt nod, then sits back against the pillows. "Yeah, I guess we should."

The room goes quiet, but the tension between us is still there. I suddenly realize that I don't even know what Beckett was about to say.

It doesn't matter. I don't need a guy like Beckett messing with my heart.

A little while later, my eyes start to feel heavy and I slip into sleep and into a dream of a beautiful man with dark brown hair and aquamarine eyes and a smile that makes me feel fuzzy. I think I feel a warm hand on my forehead, and the brush of soft lips against my temple. Then I hear the sound of a door closing, and I fall deeper into sleep.

# Chapter Eight

J ules

I wake not to the sound of the alarm that I forgot to set, but to my phone's ringtone. I bolt upright in bed and fumble for my cell on the nightstand.

Seeing that the call is from my dad, I swipe to answer it, glancing at the clock as I do. 8:10am. *Shit.* I'm late for my first seminar of the day. Juggling the phone against my ear, I pull a skirt and blouse from the closet as my dad asks me how the convention is going.

My parents and I have always been close—so close that I've only been out of Reed Point for three days and they're already checking in. I can hear my mom in the background, no doubt busy making breakfast for Hudson, who is with them for the day. I should be hauling my ass downstairs right now, but I can't resist taking time for a quick chat.

"Liam dropped Hudson off this morning on his way to Bloom. Your brother is helping Ellie assemble some new furniture she bought for the shop."

Liam's fiancée Ellie and my sister-in-law Olivia have been friends since they were kids, and now they co-own Bloom, a flower shop with a couple of locations.

"You should see our little man, Jules," my dad gushes. "He gets cuter every day. He's walking all over the place."

"It's not possible he could get any cuter than the last time I saw him," I say. "Give him a smush for me and tell him his Auntie JuJu misses him."

"I will," he promises.

"Hudson, you monkey!" I hear my mom call out in the background. "What did Mimi say? No drawing on your dog!"

I choke back a laugh. Liam must have dropped off his Golden Retriever, Murphy, too. Poor Murphy is Hudson's favorite playmate. My nephew is the cutest little trouble-maker: light brown hair, deep chestnut eyes and a cheeky grin that helps him get his way.

It sounds like my mom has her hands full, but I know she wouldn't have it any other way. She thinks "Grandma" makes her sound old so she's Mimi instead, but being a grandmother brings her so much joy. With Liam and Ellie expecting their second child and Parker and Olivia expecting their first, she'll soon have a bunch of kids to spoil.

"I'm sorry, sweetheart, I need to run," my dad says. "Murphy is going to look like a zebra if I don't help your mom stop this now."

"It's fine, Dad. Say hi to Mom for me. I'll see you both when I get home."

"Safe travels, Jules. I love you."

After ending the call, I whip around the room, packing my laptop bag, running a brush through my hair and adding hoop earrings and a small gold necklace to complete my look. Giving myself a once-over in the mirror,

I notice the faint red mark from the wasp bite, running my fingertips over the area. I think about last night and Beckett. I had a good time with him. It was better than good… it was spectacular.

He was sweet, funny and thoughtful, and it turns out we have more in common than I would have thought. And the way he took care of me yesterday is enough to crack my heart wide open. There's something about him that excites me, and the truth is I do like him. Enough that it makes me nervous.

With a sigh, I slip on my ballet flats, grab my bag and open the door, wondering if I'll see him in the hallway. When I don't, my lungs deflate in disappointment.

I shake my head. How is it possible that after only two days with the man, I've developed a craving for him? This ache inside of me wanting more? I haven't wrapped my head around what has happened between us yet. I've been too busy trying to convince myself that I haven't been affected by him. But I know that's a lie.

Walking the narrow hallway to the elevator block, I will myself not to think about Beckett.

I'm not thinking about how sweet he was last night or the fact that he loves his sister fiercely or his stupid smile that is hotter than hell. I'm so focused on *not* thinking about Beckett, that when I step out of the elevator and turn the corner I walk straight into a man's hard chest.

Beckett.

"Woah," he says, lightly grabbing my elbow to steady me.

In the aftermath of our little collision, my bag slides down my arm and knocks the cup of coffee he's holding, splashing it across his button down. *Great.* I inwardly groan at my inability to ever look cool around him. If it's not one thing, it's another. Either I'm cursed or this is just the effect

Beckett Taylor has on a woman. Whatever it is, my cheeks flame with embarrassment as a result.

"Oh my goodness, I'm so sorry," I say, taking a step back. He looks down at the mess on his shirt. I want to find a rock and crawl under it.

Beckett's six-foot frame towers over me as I reach into my bag for something to help him clean his shirt. I find a couple of napkins and hand them to him.

"Beckett, I feel awful. What can I do?" I say, looking at the mess I made on what is really a very nice shirt. It fits him perfectly, like someone designed it specifically for the width of his biceps and his deliciously hard chest. He looks like a professional athlete—his frame long and lean and powerful. He's too busy blotting the ruined fabric to notice me staring, so I take a few extra seconds to appreciate the view.

He looks up at me and grins. "It's fine. I never liked this shirt anyways. I have plenty more in my room. Don't sweat it."

Can he see the horrified look on my face? Probably. He's watching me with a curious look in his eyes.

"You okay? Why such a hurry?"

"I slept in. I guess I forgot to set my alarm before falling asleep." My face scrunches in embarrassment for what feels like the 40th time in the two days I've spent with this man. "And on that note, I'm sorry I fell asleep on you."

Beckett chuckles. "If I wasn't so sure of the fact that I'm fantastic company, I might have taken it personally."

He smiles. That smile…it's ridiculously gorgeous.

*Think of something to say, Jules.*

"Everybody thinks they have good taste and a sense of humour, but they couldn't possibly all have good taste," I blurt out. It's a line from last night's movie that suddenly popped into my mind.

"Ah, so you didn't sleep through the last half of the movie, Harry," he says. The man is quick.

"You recognize it, Sally?"

He winks. *Fuck, he winks.* There is a flurry of butterflies in my stomach. "I wasn't the one who slept through the entire movie."

"I didn't sleep through the *entire* movie." I still like pushing his buttons which isn't helping the flurry of butterflies in my stomach. "I'm sorry, I shouldn't keep you. I'm sure you want to run up to change that shirt."

His gaze tips to the stain on his chest, but a second later it's back up to me. His expression is soft, almost vulnerable. It's a side of Beckett I've rarely seen. "I'm not in a rush," he tells me.

"Beckett, you smell like a dark roast."

He laughs. That damn laugh of his, the way he grins like a schoolboy, his eyes crinkled at the corners. My skin tingles and something dangerous tugs at my core. He's managed to get to me, even though I know I shouldn't let him.

"Yeah, I guess you're right. I should change it," he says, running his fingers over the stubble of his jaw. "I'll see you around?"

"Yeah, I'm sure you will."

He nods his head, winks and walks towards the elevators. My eyes stare at his ass that looks good in those pants. His slim waist and broad shoulders aren't so bad either. The man clearly works out. Before he disappears, he looks over his shoulder with a small smile. I smirk at him and he laughs.

The rest of the day is spent in seminars. Sierra and I jammed as much as we could into our schedules, which allowed us only a quick stop by the buffet lunch that's been set up in the hotel's banquet room. I caught a glimpse of Beckett and Grayson, but we didn't have time to talk.

I'm finally leaving the ballroom at just past five o'clock when Beckett comes out of a meeting room across the hall with an up-to-no-good grin on his face.

"Hey," I say, meeting him in the middle of the hallway. "Nice shirt." It's a gray polo and he's changed his pants as well, now wearing fitted black jeans. He takes me by surprise when he says…

"Come with me, let's get out of here." There's a playful look in his turquoise eyes.

"Where are you taking me?"

"It's our last day here and you haven't had that Nutella milkshake."

I glance down at my skirt and ballet flats. I'm a little overdressed for milkshakes, and my feet will ache walking in these shoes, but I've always believed you need to life live, to jump in with both feet. Today that means milkshakes. Besides, they *are* one of my favorite things in the world.

"It's my treat. Let's go before someone sees us and drags us into the closing seminar. I can't take another one today," he says, lacing his hand in mine pulling me toward the lobby doors.

My heart is beating right out of my chest. Part of me finds his spur of the moment move exhilarating, but there is another, smaller part that is annoyed that Beckett has this pull over me.

We make our way to Sweet Spots, walking the busy, palm tree-lined streets. The sun is beaming, and we haven't let go of each other's hands.

The walk takes around half an hour, past the bustling hotels, restaurants and bars of South Beach's always busy Ocean Drive.

We finally arrive at the small shop and join the line that

is almost out the door. Eventually we order two Nutella shakes then find a seat near the window.

A server wearing a pink apron and a baseball cap carries our shakes to our table. "Enjoy, you two. If I can get you anything else, just holler."

"Are you ready for the best thing you've ever tasted?" I ask him, before sucking the straw between my lips.

"I'm down."

I watch Beckett take a long sip through his straw and give him a knowing look when his eyes flare wide then shut closed in bliss.

"I told you so."

"You did, and you weren't exaggerating. It's award-worthy," he admits, going back for more. "No wonder there's a line out the door."

"It's always like this. I've heard they also have the best beignets with berry cream, but I always stick to the shake," I say, dipping my straw into the whipped cream and running my tongue across it. When I do it a second time, the cream misses my mouth, dripping to my chin and down my hand.

We both laugh as Beckett hands me a napkin. I wipe my mouth while he reaches over the table to dab at my wrist.

"I like the anchor tattoo. Does it have a special meaning?"

The tattoo on the edge of my wrist is small, a black anchor around the size of a nickel. "Stability. An anchor gets firmly planted into the ocean floor and gives the ship the stability it needs to not drift off in any direction. It reminds me to focus, which I'm sometimes not good at. I've always been a bit of a handful. I got it when I was 18. I think my dad cried."

"Does it help…the tattoo? Does it help you stay focused?"

I shrug. "Sometimes. I can be impulsive so no, not always. Maybe that's the other reason I got the tattoo. I wasn't always very good at thinking things through. I had to forge my mom's signature just to get it because I technically wasn't old enough."

One brow arches. "So, you're a rebel?"

"Ooh yes, bad to the bone," I laugh. "It's funny, none of my three brothers have tattoos. I'm the only one."

He laughs. "Classic last child syndrome."

"I guess." I shrug. "I've just never worried what other people think. If people like me, that's great. If they don't, that's fine too. I never want to feel like I need to impress anyone. I grew up around some very wealthy and influential people who were obsessed with keeping up with the Joneses. They kept up with appearances even when the whole world knew their lives were turning to hell. Thankfully, my parents aren't like that. I know you don't know my dad well, but if you spend even five minutes in the same room with him you can see the type of man he is."

"I've never heard a bad word spoken about him."

"Good," I say with a smile.

That same vulnerable expression I saw on Beckett's face this morning returns. "So does this mean you don't hate me anymore?"

I exhale. "I never hated you. You just weren't my favorite person."

"Oh, I'm pretty positive you hated me," he chuckles. "Did you forget about kicking over the Ficus tree in my office and then calling 'I hate you' as you stomped out?"

I cover my face with my hands in embarrassment, peeking through my fingers. "I was hoping you forgot."

"How could I? It was cute."

"Me losing my mind on your faux Ficus tree was *cute*?" I feel my cheeks burn.

"You're a firecracker, Jules. I thought it was hot as hell."

*What?* The flush that started in my cheeks spreads throughout my whole body. I clear my throat. "It wasn't the best side of me. I'm still not over how I acted. I swear I'm not normally that crazy."

Inquisitive eyes take me in. I wonder if he's enjoying this as much as I am. This… thing between us.

"Hey, I like your crazy," he insists. "You have conviction. You stood up for your family. I admire that so much. Jules, you know I never said—"

"Wait." I stop him right there. After these past few days with Beckett, I know that he didn't say the slanderous things about the Seaside that I thought he did. He doesn't need to defend himself. "You don't have to say it, Beckett. I know."

"I just would never. I want you to know that."

And I do. But I find myself wanting to know more about *him*. What makes him tick? What does he do in his spare time? I start with, "Tell me about your family."

He thinks for a second, like he's weighing every word, wanting to get them right. "It's just me and my mom and my sister. I have a step-dad too. We're really tight. They depend on me. They need me, and that goes both ways. So I work hard to make sure I can take care of them. I always have." He pauses, rakes his hand through his hair, shifts in his seat. "My dad isn't around. It's a long story."

I want to ask more questions, but I sense that his confession was already more than he normally shares. I decide not to push for more.

"I had no idea, Beckett. That seems like a big responsibility. Who takes care of *you*?"

"I'm a grown man, Jules. I don't need anyone to take care of me."

"Not true. Everyone needs someone. You're not an exception."

The second I say it, my body tenses. He doesn't need me telling him what he needs. I'm not his girlfriend. We aren't even friends.

"I could use some real food after all of this sugar," he says, changing the subject. "You wanna hit up a food truck next? Pretend we're on the Food Network and rate our experience?"

"I'd like that. Just let me finish my milkshake. There's no way I'm wasting this," I say, taking a long last sip. Satisfied, I slide my cup aside and look up to find Beckett staring at me. His eyes hold mine, those eyes that are so piercing, so deep and so blue—my new favorite color—that they make me weak.

It feels like there's no one in the room but us. The tension that has always existed between us is long gone, replaced by the beginning of something new.

I breathe deep. My chest rises.

"Jules?"

My pulse quickens at the want I see being reflected back at me.

"I had a really great time with you today. You are…not what I expected. You're so much more." I feel the sincerity of his words in my chest. "I knew you were smart and confident." He reaches for my face and my heart feels like it's beating a thousand miles a minute when his fingers brush a loose strand of hair behind my ear. His eyes darken while his fingers linger there, as though there's nothing more he wants to do than touch me. "But I had no idea I would like you this much."

I'm lost in him, in his every word, in his touch, in the

way a look from him can send a shock of beautiful bliss through my body.

His fingers move away from my face and I want to beg for him to bring them back to me. I feel woozy. Butterflies dance in my stomach.

My eyes drop to his hand, wishing it was back in my hair, pulling at the strands, making me scream his name. I take in his full lips, admiring the curve to his top one, wondering how they would feel pressed against mine.

"What time is your flight tomorrow?" he asks, stopping my thoughts before they can go any further.

"Early. 8:30. I need to get home for a friend's birthday. You?"

"Not until three, but I'm flying to Chicago. Head office for a few days."

"I see."

A serious look skates across his face and I know he's feeling it too. The air around us grows thick, like a warm fog.

I feel unsettled, nervous, something in me warning me not to get too close.

I turn my gaze from him to the window, taking a deep, steadying breath as I watch a couple around my age walk by hand-in-hand. He leans into her, kissing her temple, and she turns to press a kiss to his mouth. He smiles down at her and I'm green with envy.

I want that one day.

I want a love that lasts a lifetime.

I deserve that.

I do.

# Chapter Nine

Beckett

Spending time with Jules at Sweet Spots only made me want more, so I took a chance and asked her to have dinner with me. Thankfully, she said yes. It's our last day together before we head home, and I want to make the most of it.

We head toward the row of food trucks parked down by the beach. Deciding on tacos, we find a table with a view of the ocean. I watch Jules as she digs an elastic out of her purse, tying her long hair up into a ponytail. A few loose strands around her face blow in the warm breeze and she pushes them back off her face. My eyes linger on her long, slim fingers, her nails painted a soft pink. She's gorgeous.

"Need your hair up to tackle a taco? You're not messing around," I say, then slap my hand against the wooden table. "Wait, that's it! I've got the perfect name for our food show: *Tackle The Taco*."

Jules shoots me an are-you-insane look, then busts a gut. "I think we should stick to our day jobs."

I slide three tacos across the table to her. "Let's do this."

I take a bite of the pulled pork taco slathered in guacamole and green salsa, and wow. Fucking wow. My eyes roll back in my head because this is a damn good taco. "A ten," I groan. "Beautiful. Maybe a twelve."

Jules takes a bite and sighs in satisfaction too. "Mmm," she says, stretching out the word for effect. "The tortillas are handmade, and the salsa is extra spicy. Impossible to stop at just one."

"You do seem to be having a moment with that taco," I tease. She's cute as hell. She leans across the table and swats my arm.

"And you're not? You're looking at that taco like you want to date it."

"It's a good fucking taco. So, what's your rating?"

She scrunches her nose and thinks for a second, then licks the corner of her mouth. I have to tear my eyes away from her lips.

"I'm giving it a 9.2."

I laugh. "Just a 9.2? Where did it go wrong?"

"There's pickled onions. I'm not a fan."

"Ladies and gentlemen, we have a taco diva on our hands."

"This is true. I demand a lot of my tacos," she says, before taking another bite. She looks up at me with heat in her eyes.

Or maybe it's wishful thinking.

My heart dips in my chest. Stupid heart. The girl is a Bennett. I am the furthest thing from it. Nothing—I repeat, nothing—will come from this.

After taking a sip of her cola, Jules gets back to chatting. "So, you like to eat. But can you cook?"

"I can. Are you impressed?"

"Very."

"When I was seven my mom married Pete, and they had my sister Bean. Anyways, Pete's a chef, and he would let me help him in the kitchen when he cooked us dinner. He taught me a lot. My specialty is a bacon-wrapped pesto pork tenderloin."

"Sounds delicious. Are you still close with Pete?"

"Yeah, I am. He raised me as his own. He's a pretty great guy, and he treats my mom like a queen."

Jules nods, a warmth in her eyes that's void of judgment. "I'm glad you had someone like him."

She doesn't press for more. The crazy thing is, if she asked about my birth dad, I would probably tell her the whole story. Apart from my best friend from high school, she's the first person that I feel like I could open up to about that.

Jules is so easy to be around. We've talked and laughed all day, and it feels like we've known each other for years. I guess in a way we *have* known each other for years, but not on a personal level. I feel like I have a connection to her. A connection that would have surprised me when I was just a kid from Heritage Heights and the Reed Point kids wanted nothing to do with me.

When I was a kid back in Heritage, I never in a million years would have thought I'd have anything in common with a Reed Point girl like Jules. But since then, I graduated high school with honors and went to university on a full ride. I landed a great job that pays me enough money to live a good life and help support my family. I even bought a condo in Reed Point.

Deep down, though, part of me will always feel like that kid from Heritage Heights.

Jules and I make small talk until we've demolished every bite of our tacos. I lean back, full and happy, and take in the spectacular view of the beach. The sun is just beginning to dip behind the horizon, casting an orange glow across the sky.

I look over at Jules, her skin illuminated by the setting sun. I'm not ready to end my time with her.

"The sun is about to set, and it would probably be weird if we didn't watch it. I mean, it's right there in front of us." I know I sound over-eager, but I don't seem to care. I don't want today to be over.

"You're probably right, that would be weird," she says.

She swings her legs over the bench, rounds the table and sits down beside me. She's kept a safe distance between us, which I'm grateful for. Being this close to her feels intoxicating. It only makes me want her more.

The sun sets in front of us like a scene straight out of a movie, but I'm too distracted to notice. All I can think about is Jules. I've glanced at her a few times, trying not to make it too noticeable. I watch her mouth and the way her tongue wets her bottom lip every so often, and I ache. I want to suck on her tongue, lick it, and then kiss her until she sees stars.

Is that what it would feel like to kiss Jules? Like thousands of shooting stars colliding over the universe?

I see her wrap her arms around herself like she's cold and without even thinking, I reach my arm across the table behind her, my hand brushes her shoulder.

"You're cold. Come here," I say, pulling her into my side, rubbing her shoulder, feeling all fluttery. My entire body goes hot with her body pressed firmly against mine. That's all it takes for me to picture her coming undone underneath me, to hear her saying my name over and over as I push into her. I remember the way her eyes held mine at Sweet Spots earlier, when I tucked the loose strands of her hair behind her ear. Touching her like that, it felt like a tether connecting us, the one and only moment I've ever felt that kind of spark with a woman.

"Thank you. It's a little chilly when the sun goes down."

"Should we go back?" *Please say no.*

"I'm fine. Besides, this is one of the prettiest sunsets I've seen. I'm sort of a sucker for them."

I nod. Noted. "Have you talked to Sierra?" I ask.

She nods, picking at a piece of lint on her shirt. It makes me wonder if she's nervous having my arm around her. Maybe she's liking it as much as I am. "Yeah, I did. I texted her from Sweet Spots so she wouldn't worry about me. We didn't have plans or anything and I think she was hoping to see Grayson anyways."

"I think the feeling is mutual. They've been flirting all weekend. He told me he was going to ask her to dinner. He was worried she say no. I told him he had it in the bag."

"Had it in the bag?" She rolls her eyes, poking me on the thigh. "Wonder, you are such a man."

"Ah, there's that nickname again. Are you ever going to tell me what it means? You know, I might get a complex if you don't."

"Someday, if I feel like it." She wiggles her brows at me. "So, what's happening in Chicago? Why the trip to head office?"

I pause. I haven't mentioned the possible move to London to anyone, not even my mom—I think I'm afraid to jinx it. But for some reason it feels safe to tell Jules. "I'm meeting with the president," I shrug. "He's considering me for a promotion and if I get it I would have to move to London."

"Wow, that's great, Beckett," she says. "How do you feel about the move?"

"It's what I've always wanted. The end goal." I clear my throat.

"Then I'm really happy for you. I hope it works out. I don't see why it wouldn't."

"I hope so. I'd miss my mom and sister, but the opportunity would be too big to pass up."

"It's nice that you're so close to them," she says.

"Always have been. My mom, my sister and Pete live about 20 minutes from me, just outside of Reed Point. Bean and I are really different, but we've always been tight. I was always into sports and she preferred to read and paint. And we look nothing alike: I'm just over six feet and my sister is closer to five-three, but we have the same sarcastic sense of humor. We could re-watch old episodes of *Seinfeld* for days and laugh our faces off."

Jules looks back at me, her eyes warm. "They make you happy."

I smile slowly. I think about that epic argument in my office, about how I thought at the time that she was a stuck-up brat. I had her all wrong.

We take our time walking back to the hotel. It's Saturday night and the streets are alive with musicians and people out enjoying dinner and drinks. Crowded nightspots spill out onto the sidewalk and the place vibrates with energy. I listen as Jules talks about her family. She tells me about her brother Miles, who's a huge Hollywood actor, and the series he's shooting. She gushes over her nephew Hudson, who she clearly adores. She talks about how happy Parker and Olivia are now that they're back living in Reed Point and how her brothers Liam and Miles are both getting married this year. It's obvious from the way her face lights up when she talks about them that her family means everything to her.

A pang wrecks my chest when we reach the door of

her hotel room. We're alone in the narrow hallway and I'm hyper-aware of how close she is to me. My whole body is tense as I wait to see if she rushes to get inside or tries to extend these last few moments together.

"I had fun tonight," she says, her eyes dipping down to my lips for a split second. "I guess it's late. We both have flights tomorrow."

I'm dying to kiss her, but instead I move in for a hug. I slip my arms around her waist and hers wrap around my shoulders. She doesn't let go so I hold her tight, breathing her in.

My pulse surges, and I wonder if I should kiss her. I imagine taking it into her room, where we could do so much more. My dick likes the idea and begins to plump up behind my zipper.

In the midst of my lust-filled thoughts, she suddenly lets go. "I need to pack," she says, looking down at her hands.

"Yeah, I guess I should too."

My voice is a dead giveaway, scratchy and rough. It says everything about how I feel, wishing this night didn't have to end. Wondering if I read that embrace all wrong. Jules seems unfazed, so I guess I probably did.

"Thanks for today, Beckett. I had a lot of fun," she says again softly, her eyes lifting to mine. When they connect, it feels like everything around us goes dim. Like the earth stops revolving. I wish I could stop wanting her, stop wanting something that could never be mine.

"You're welcome. Safe travels tomorrow." I nod but can't seem to move. I don't want to leave her.

She lingers for a second longer and then turns and walks inside, the door closing behind her.

I close my eyes, exhale a breath and I stand there a few moments longer, hoping she'll change her mind. When it becomes clear she's not coming back, I finally walk next door alone, pretending I wasn't the only one who wanted that kiss.

---

I can't sleep for shit. I spend the entire night tossing and turning, itching to see her, replaying every look, every conversation. Knowing she's just on the other side of that wall is torture. I can't stop thinking about her bright eyes or the way her tongue wets the corner of her mouth when she's thinking. Then I'm imagining her tongue licking paths over my skin. My hand grips the sheet as I shove my face deep into my pillow.

I want her.

I fucking want her bad.

Jules is quirky and funny and not at all what I expected, but she checks all the boxes. She's everything I didn't know that I wanted in a woman.

I eventually give up on sleep. It's around 6 a.m. when I scoot out of bed, listening intently for any sign of Jules moving around in her room.

After showering, I quickly change into a pair of jeans, a T-shirt and my Chucks, then head to the lobby to see if I can catch her before she leaves for her flight. I need to see her one last time before we board our planes and head in two different directions.

It's quiet when I walk out into the hallway and stand outside her door. I knock, but there's no answer, so I make my way to the elevator, taking it down 14 flights to the lobby. Frank Sinatra is playing softly through the speakers as I walk past the restaurant. My eyes scan the lobby for her, and my heart skips a beat when I finally spot her just outside the front doors. I stride across the lobby, stepping outside just in time to see her get into a cab. I catch her profile, her long hair down past her shoulders, sunglasses covering her eyes.

I exhale as the cab pulls out from the curb. I was a second too late.

With a final look at the yellow taxi driving away I sigh, realizing I didn't even get her number.

## Chapter Ten

Jules

The parking lot at Reed Point Marina is jammed packed. I snag one of the last spots, parking my Ford Bronco in the far corner, a long walk from the cruiser boat I use when I feel like getting out on the water. The 30-foot Sea Ray Pilothouse belongs to my dad and has been mine to use since I proved I could drive it. There was never any need for formal lessons, I've been on the water watching my dad sail since I was barely able to walk. I've always loved the freedom of the ocean.

When we were kids, my dad would take my brothers and I out on the boat every chance he got. I loved walking the fingers of the marina, admiring the different boats. I learned how to tie lines first, then from there my dad taught me how to get the boat on plane, then how to dock it. We spent every weekend we could cruising to our favorite spots, dropping anchor and swimming or taking the kayaks to shore. My mom would join us some of the time, packing us lunch, reading her books in the sun while my dad taught us to fish or swam in the ocean with us.

Those summers at the marina are some of my best memories.

I breathe in the salty air as I walk to the slip. I've brought my laptop with me, preferring some days to work on the aft of the boat instead of stuck inside my little office. I setup my make-shift office in the sun and get to work.

My fingers fly over my keyboard, but despite the in-box full of emails waiting to be answered, I find my mind drifting to him. Beckett.

I've been home from Miami for two weeks and still can't get Beckett out of my head. God, he's hard to forget. I liked being with him. He made an impression. After I got home, I searched his name online, scrolling his socials. I didn't uncover much besides his penchant for bike riding and a few personal photos of his mom and his sister. The man is seriously photogenic, his mega-watt smile sparkling in every photo.

I try again to push thoughts of him away, needing to get some work done. The conference put me behind. I have a photo shoot to set up for our new website, two weeks' worth of content to plan for our socials pages and an ad campaign I need to approve.

Straightening my spine, I focus on work for the next three hours, until my stomach rumbles and I need to eat. I didn't pack a lunch. The fridge my roommate and I share in our two-bedroom apartment near the beach was empty, unless you count three bottles of rosé and a jar of olives as food.

I pack up my things and hop off the boat, taking in the warm summer day. The way the sun sparkles on the ocean's ripples, the smell of the sea air, the reflection of the blue sky on the surface of the water—everything about this place settles me. I work a lot, always trying to impress my dad. I'm careful to keep up-to-date with media trends, staying ahead of the competition. When I'm not at work I'm with my family or squeezing in a weekly yoga class with the girls. There isn't a lot of down time in my life and some days it feels like I rarely ever sit down. The days I am able to work from the marina are a chance to decompress.

Ten minutes later, I'm stepping through the doors of Dream Bean Coffee. I order a tall frap and a turkey croissant then find a free table. Being able to drive 10 minutes to wherever you want to go without ever having to battle traffic is one of my favorite things about living in Reed Point. It's just big enough to have all the amenities you need, but without the pitfalls of the city. I love its quaint, small-town feel. Living a stone's throw from the ocean is a major bonus too.

Taking a bite of my sandwich, I open my laptop to check my emails. My mouth is stuffed with croissant when I hear someone call my name.

"Jules?"

I know that voice…

I look up to find him standing at the edge of my table, holding a to-go cup and a pastry bag. Alex. My ex.

It's been a few months since I've seen him, but I can't seem to avoid bumping into him. I guess that's one of the not-so-great parts about a small town. The last time was at the drug store, of all places. The time before that was at my office, when he showed up with flowers. He had never bothered to buy me flowers when we were together, so it confused me when he plunked a vase full of carnations on my desk. A week later he sent me chocolates. Two weeks after that it was bath products. He was relentless.

A slow smile crosses his face. He's still so handsome with his dirty blond hair which is trimmed short, he has dark brown eyes and a Roman nose. Beyond the Ken-doll good looks, though, I know now that he's not the man for me. He's serious and overly cautious. A devoted rule follower and mama's boy. The break-up still stings, because I didn't see it coming. For a long time, I thought Alex was the one. Until he wasn't.

My back straightens when he motions to the seat across from me, silently asking if he can sit. He lowers himself to the chair before I have the chance to argue.

"Hey." He sets his cup down on the table, leaning towards me on his forearms. I stare at him, still not speaking. The whole thing feels awkward and I wish he would read the room and leave.

I give him a polite smile then take a sip from my Frappuccino. I remain cordial considering Reed Point is a small town and we did spend two years together.

"It's good to see you, Jules. How've you been?" he asks.

I frown. "I'm fine, Alex. Why are you sitting here?"

"Why am I sitting here?" His brows furrow, and he looks towards the baristas behind the counter, avoiding my stare. "I wanted to say hi. Would it have been better if I saw you, pretended I didn't, got my order and left?"

*Kind of.* I wouldn't have objected to that. Our ship has sailed. Do we really need to be sitting here exchanging pleasantries? Had he bothered to consider my feelings he would know that coming over here to chat was a bad idea. He broke me when he called it off. I couldn't function for weeks.

"I just don't see why we need to do this every time we run into one another. Reed Point is small. We're going to have to see each other. We can just nod or wave and then carry on our separate ways." I arch my brow, annoyed that he continues to want to talk.

"You act like us running into each other is a bad thing."

I cock my head, truly curious. Does he not get it? I was in love with him. He broke my heart.

"And you act like—" I shake my head. "It doesn't matter anymore."

He scrubs a hand over his jaw. "I miss—"

"Don't, Alex. Don't you dare." I inhale a deep breath. Hurt and rejection stab at me, the feelings I worked hard for months to get over. "You don't get to do that to me. I've moved on."

He pauses. "I don't understand what the problem is, Jules. We can be friends. There's no reason why we can't be."

I huff out a breath at his denseness. "Alex, you're wrong. We can't be friends. That's not how a break-up works. You had your chance, and you chose to leave."

His expression turns serious. "What if I regret it? What if I want another chance?"

I clench my coffee cup to stop from saying what I really think. "It won't change a thing. We're over. It's done."

He shakes his head, like he doesn't believe it. But I truly *am* over him. Maybe it's good to spell it out like this, to make him understand that I have no interest in getting back together with him.

"Jules," he pleads, reaching across the table and placing his hand on my forearm. "There's nothing I can do?"

*No!* I feel myself tensing.

"No."

I look away, wanting this conversation to be over, and when I do, I see Beckett standing near the doors of the crowded cafe, his gaze focused on Alex's hand, still on my arm. Beckett's eyes rise to mine and I pull my arm back. He blinks, then turns his head to the menu board above the pastry counter.

"Who is that?" Alex asks, noticing my reaction to Beck-ett, his lips tightening.

"That's none of your business."

He scowls. "Now you're just being mean. We were together for a long time, Jules. Why are you being like this?"

I take a sip of my drink, trying to stop myself from causing a scene. It's not worth it.

"That's not fair," I say, setting my coffee cup down. My eyes stop on the watch he's wearing on his wrist—the watch I bought him for his 30th birthday 3 months before he dumped me. His gaze follows mine, and he moves his hand to his lap under the table.

"Listen, I'm sorry if I was an ass. I truly am. I never meant to hurt you," he says, running his fingers through his blond hair.

I exhale the breath I was holding. "It's fine."

"I think I let the stress of residency get to me. I have so many regrets about how I handled things. I was a dick. I just hope that you can forgive me?"

I hear the heel of his shoe bouncing on the hardwood, a tell that he's anxious. I need to put us both out of our misery. "I can, Alex. I can forgive you," I say, and I mean it. "Now will you stop sending me gifts?"

He laughs. "Point taken… I guess that's it then."

"It is, Alex. Take care of yourself."

"You too, Jules."

Alex finally gets up to leave and a wave of relief washes over me. I turn to where Beckett stands in line and find him watching me. His face is tense, his eyes curious as they bounce from me to Alex, who's on his way out of the café. He picks up his coffee cup from the counter and in four long strides he's standing right in front of me.

Beckett looks gorgeous in a crisp white collared shirt,

slim navy dress pants, a tan belt and matching shoes. His shirt is open at the collar, his hair styled off his face, and his chiselled jaw is covered in a tidy five o'clock shadow. He's breathtaking, and I immediately feel that heat that burns between us. It's still there, searing the air around us. I wish he would stop being so good looking.

I haven't seen or heard from Beckett since that night in Miami, although I haven't been able to stop thinking about him. The apology note he sent with room service that first morning at the hotel is still tucked in my purse.

"I'm not interrupting, am I?" he says. "Hot date?"

"Not exactly. That was Alex, the guy I told you about in Miami. The one who said—"

"You were a lot," he says, gently cutting me off. I exhale a long breath. Beckett nods to the seat Alex just got up from and I motion for him to sit.

"That would be him."

"Everything okay?"

I run my teeth over my bottom lip. "Yeah, everything is fine. There isn't much to say. He asked for a second chance, and I said no. He apologized and it was enough for me."

"Do you wanna talk about it? I'm a good listener. Or maybe you'd prefer a good joke?" Beckett asks, his mouth curving into a gentle smile. It's distracting. He's doing what he can to take my mind off Alex and it's working. "Why are you smiling at me?" he asks.

My skin pebbles. "I'm not sure. Why are you?"

"Maybe because I really want to tell you a story."

"Shoot. What do you want me to know?" I ask, taking a sip from my drink.

"My friend's bakery burned down last night. Now his business is toast."

I laugh, almost spitting out my drink.

"You just *had* to tell me a joke," I groan.

"I'm determined. Did it help?"

Beckett runs his thumb around the perimeter of his cup. My eyes follow, wishing that thumb was on my skin, drawing tiny circles on my abdomen and then trailing lower to…

*Nope. Must stop the pornographic thoughts in my brain.*

"It did, but a Nutella milkshake would have been better."

"We could do that again sometime?" It comes out like a question.

"It's a possibility," I admit, liking the idea a lot. My head spins. A second ago my ex was here asking for me back and now I'm sitting across from Beckett, a man I shouldn't have these tingly feelings for. A man I should avoid. It's one thing having an impromptu coffee together, but an actual date? That would be a very bad idea for so many reasons. For starters, he'll likely be moving to another country in a matter of months. Then there's the fact that we work for rival companies. The list is long.

"So, it's a date?" he asks, amusement in his eyes.

"Slow down, Mr. Wonder. We're friends now. You wouldn't want to mess that up."

"So I've worked my way into the friend zone then?"

"You have. Look at us, getting along. It's a sight to be seen."

Beckett cracks up, but then his expression changes. "Any chance I can work my way up to more?"

My cheeks flame, but Beckett is cool as a breeze. Confident. Beautiful. Charming. He gives me a long look like he's waiting on my answer.

I smirk. A fling could work. One night with a hotter-than-hell man who I'm sure is a God in the bedroom. "Keep it up and you might."

Something flashes behind Beckett's eyes, and he gives me a slow once-over that has me clenching my center between my legs. He gives me chills. My heart flies. Something tells me Beckett Taylor isn't a quitter.

He cocks a brow, and a smug little smile appears on his face. "I plan on it. Pass me your phone."

I unlock my phone and slide it across the table towards him. After adding his contact info into my phone, his cell-phone buzzes on the table. He must have texted himself my number. He glances at it, then slides my phone back to me.

My heart skips a beat. Things have changed between us.

I feel it.

He feels it too.

We walk out together, a warm breeze from the ocean blowing past us when we step onto the sidewalk. Before he walks away, he grabs my hand.

I look up at him, smiling like a fool. His blue eyes shine back at me. "I'm really glad I ran into you."

My hand feels so good in his, but it isn't enough. I want more. Bad idea, I remind myself. "Me too."

Suddenly, my chest is pressed against his, strong arms wrapped around my waist in a tight hug. I inhale his fresh, summer rain scent before we break apart. He smells so good.

He removes his hands from my hips, a sexy smile on his face.

*Don't stop touching me…*

"Bye, Jules."

"Bye, Beck." His nickname slips from my mouth so easily. Acting on instinct, I go up on my toes and kiss Beckett's cheek. His hand moves back to my waist, almost like he wants my body back against his.

I turn to walk to my car, feeling his eyes on me the entire way. I shake my head and let out a breath.

Later, I'm in my kitchen eating ramen when my phone lights up with a text. My mouth tips up in a smile and my heart races as I read it. It's from "Mr. Wonder." *That bugger.*

> Mr. Wonder: When can I take you for dinner? And not spontaneous street tacos, Jules. I mean a real date where I pick you up.

I reply quickly, before I can spend too much time thinking about all the reasons we shouldn't.

> Jules: Ask me. I probably won't say no.

> Mr. Wonder: Friday night. Can I take you somewhere fun?

He ends the text with a praying hands emoji. Doesn't he know my answer is a yes? An absolute, for sure, yes.

> Jules: Friday night works.

> Mr. Wonder: Looking forward to it. Send me your address. I'll pick you up at 7. Night, Jules.

> Jules: Night, xo

I set my phone down on the counter and think about his blue eyes, the way they find mine and hold them. Then I imagine Beckett and I on a date, then him kissing me goodnight, then maybe more…

## Chapter Eleven

**B**eckett

I wake up cold, yanking the duvet up as far as it can go over my bare shoulders. I rub my hands together under the blankets, wishing I hadn't forgotten to turn off the AC. I hate to be cold. It reminds me too much of my childhood growing up with nothing, of the heating bill that sometimes went unpaid. Until my mom married Pete.

Growing up in Heritage Heights wasn't all bad. There were always plenty of kids around to play with, and we were mostly left unsupervised while our parents were working long shifts. I spent a lot of time riding my hand-me-down bike around the tiny town with friends or playing rugby after school. On weekends I would ride my bike into Reed Point and White Harbor Beach. It was one town over, but it felt like a different world. With its gated communities and manicured lawns, the place reeked of money and status and everything we didn't have.

Us Heritage kids were never invited to the parties there, but the beach was fair game. With hulking white bluffs and fine, almost white sand, we would go there to escape. We avoided the rich kids from Reed Point. A few of them were assholes, but whatever. We were tough and knew we could handle any one of them if it came down to it. It was our real-life *Outer Banks*.

I saw how hard my mom worked during those days as a single mom, taking extra shifts at the grocery store and just barely making ends meet. She's had a lot of tough days in her life, none worse than the period after my bio dad left, breaking her spirit and her heart. But eventually she moved on and she met Pete, the most right-minded man I know. After they got married, he became my dad. They had Bean a few years later and soon after that my sister got her diagnosis, another tough day for my mom. Cystic Fibrosis is progressive and requires daily care, so my mom eventually had to quit her job to take care of her. Thankfully, Pete made enough money to get us by. We weren't rich by Reed Point standards, but we had a home where we felt loved and wanted.

Pete is the one who would stay up late to help me study, or throw a ball around when I needed to blow off steam. He taught me how to change a tire, how to cook a good steak and file my taxes. He taught me how to be a good man.

My bio dad, on the other hand, showed me what I *don't* want to be. I've often wondered how he could leave his own son so easily, just up and walk away like that. When he did that, he taught me the hardest lesson: that loving someone and losing them is incredibly painful. For that reason, I've kept my heart guarded, everything surface level. It's easier that way. No one gets hurt.

But... I can't stop wanting something with Jules.

Even though I know a relationship isn't going to work.

Not when I'll have to leave soon. Not when I don't ever get too close.

Something is happening between us, though, and I don't know how to stop it.

When I walked into Dream Bean Coffee and saw Jules sitting with that guy, my heart went from beating to running a 10-mile marathon in my chest.

I thought she was on a date. The way the guy looked at her, he was clearly into her. Then I noticed his hand on her and I wanted to burn the place down. That's one of the reasons I know I have it bad for this girl.

That was four days ago, but it's felt like an eternity. I'm itching to see her tonight. I couldn't stop myself from asking her out, even though I knew it was probably a terrible idea. Getting caught up in something right before I may be moving to a different continent isn't smart. But I don't care. I think about Jules constantly, wondering where she is, what she's doing. Is she thinking about me too? Will she change her mind and get back together with Alex? The guy's studying to be a goddamn doctor, how the hell am I supposed to compete with that?

I tear away the covers and sit on the edge of the bed, scrubbing my face with my hands.

An hour later, I'm riding my mountain bike through the network of trails that local bikers have built in the woods. Riding is something I've never stopped doing, going from the streets of Heritage Heights on my Spiderman bike to the $15,000 Santa Cruz that I splurged on when I made VP. It not only keeps me in shape, it's my sanctuary —downhill riding clears my mind, keeps me in the present moment. I've grown addicted to the speed and boost of adrenaline I get when I barrel downhill.

My legs push the pedals, all of my muscles engaged, and my heart rate elevates as I work to stay balanced adapting to the terrain. My core is on fire. The forest crunches under my tires and the skyscraper trees pass by in a blur. The early morning fog is a blanket over shady glades. I take it all in. Only a few more months of this view before I could be in London, working my ass off at my new job. I push those thoughts aside.

At the bottom of the trail, I stop for a water break. I chug from the bottle, both feet on the ground straddling my bike, the air cool against my sweaty skin. I chuck the bottle back into my backpack then start the 15-mile ride to my condo near the beach.

Just after seven, I knock on Jules' door. She opens it looking like the definition of a summer day, wearing a pair of skinny jeans and a tight white top, her hair swept partly back in a braid. The golden strands in her hair are the color of the sun, her lips the color of raspberries. I can't look away.

And even though I vowed that I wouldn't let myself *feel* things for her tonight, I already am. She's special, different from any girl I've ever met. She's a magnet that draws me to her.

I stand here, drinking her in, wondering if her heart is beating as hard as mine. "Hey."

"Hey, you," she says, a blush creeping over her cheeks. "Am I dressed okay? It's hard to know what to wear when you have no clue where you're going."

"As long as you aren't afraid of giant, hairy spiders you should be okay."

Her eyes flare. "What! Aren't most people?"

"I'm only kidding. Come on, let's go."

She laughs and walks towards my car, my eyes

following her the entire way. I snap out of my brain fog and jog to her, opening the passenger door of the car. Once she's settled in, I slip into the driver's seat and pull out of the driveway, taking the first turn onto First Street, the main drag in Reed Point. We pass restaurants and bars all packed with people as we leave the bright lights of town behind us.

"I'm thinking something a little different than just dinner in a restaurant. Sound okay to you?" I take her in, from the skinny jeans that hug her body just right to the top she's wearing that ties in bows on her shoulders. She looks out the window, giving me a few seconds to admire her smooth skin, still kissed by the Miami sun.

"Somewhere different sounds good. Are you going to tell me where?"

"Nope. I'm a vault. You won't get it out of me."

"That's fine. I love surprises."

I smile. "Has anyone ever thrown you a surprise birthday party?"

"Every year when I was a kid. It became the running joke of my family: how are we going to surprise Jules this year? My birthday is in July, but for my 21st, my family surprised me in May because they knew I'd be expecting my friends and family to jump out at me from behind a couch and yell surprise."

"July, huh? That's coming up soon," I note.

"Yup, July 16th," she answers, dragging her teeth over her bottom lip. I file that date away in my mental Rolodex as we drive towards the bluffs, the part of the beach that's usually quiet, with the exception of a few beach houses scattered here and there.

"That's in three weeks."

"It is. So, I'm assuming there will be a party in my honor any day now."

"Really?"

Jules' chest rises and falls with silent laughter. "No. Now that my mom is a grandma, Hudson is the only one getting elaborate birthday parties."

We're now out of the city and it's quieter, darker. "Are you taking me somewhere where they won't find my body? Tired of competing with me?"

I laugh, raising one brow like I'm up to something. "Hmm… you got me."

Shifting gears, I drive us to one of my favorite spots. We turn down a gravel road, the tires of my SUV kicking up rocks. She breaks out into a smile when I park the vehicle.

"The beach?" Jules asks.

I nod and shift the car into park. "Yup. I remembered you like sunsets. I packed us dinner and thought we could build a bonfire."

"Oh."

"Is that okay?"

Her gaze captures mine. "I love it, Beckett. It's the best idea."

I exhale slowly, relieved, and she laughs. It's been a while since I really wanted to impress a girl. I hope I don't fuck this up.

I grab a couple of blankets, my duffle bag and a basket from the trunk, then lead Jules down a grassy path to the beach. The fresh smell of the ocean and the sounds of cicadas fill the air around us. The sun sits low in the sky, sinking into the horizon.

We find a vacant fire pit, and I spread the two blankets out on the sand. We're alone for the most part with the exception of three guys a ways down the beach, close enough that I can hear murmurs of their conversation, but far enough away that it still feels secluded.

Jules sits down on one of the blankets as I start the fire, then I lower myself down next to her and open the basket.

She peeks inside. "Did you pack all this yourself?"

"I did." I start unloading the bottle of wine, two glasses, an Asian noodle dish with vegetables and chicken that I made before picking her up, some strawberries and chocolate chip cookies.

"You did all this today after work?" she asks, taking the plates and forks I brought and arranging them in front of us. "This looks incredible."

"I did good?" I ask sheepishly, opening the wine bottle. "It's been a while since I've planned a real date."

She looks a bit speechless. "It's better than good. It's perfect."

"Do I need to worry that you're going to spill this on me?" I joke, passing one of the wine glasses to her with a cheeky grin.

"I'm going to need you to forget about that if we're going to be friends."

*Friends? Fucking Fantastic.*

Maybe it was just a slip of the tongue. Would she really say yes to a date with me if she felt nothing more than friendship? My guess is no.

"I'm not sure I can. I can still see your face after you body checked me in the lobby. You were mortified when my coffee met my shirt."

She shakes her head, "I was. All the more reason to pretend it never happened. Now, pass me some noodles. Let's see if they're a 10."

I feel a ridiculously stupid smile plaster itself on my face as I dish out the noodles onto our plates. We sit and eat, listening to the waves crash against the shore. We talk about work, food, our hobbies. I tell her about my addiction to mountain biking, she tells me how she loves to sail.

Jules describes in great detail the days and nights spent on her dad's boat in the summers, sailing to the marina a couple of towns over, reading on the bow. It feels like we're making up for lost time. I want to know everything about her.

"Wait," Jules says suddenly, cocking her head at me. "You know my birthday, but you never told me yours."

"October 20th," I tell her.

She thinks for a moment. "That makes you a Libra, then."

"Is that a good thing?" I ask, twirling a forkful of noodles from my plate.

"It means you're extroverted, friendly, charming, a creative thinker. But you hate confrontation. You work to attain balance and harmony. And bad manners are also your biggest turn off."

I arch a brow. "You know an incredible amount of horoscope facts. Do you moonlight as an astrologer on weekends?"

She tips her head. "What can I say? I'm a zodiac nerd."

"So, July 16th…I think that makes you a Cancer, right? Do Libras and Cancers go well together?"

"Like oil and water," she shrugs. "Two of the worst signs you could put together. Destined to be a total trainwreck."

"What? Are you joking?"

She laughs and runs her hand over her braid. "Yes, I'm joking. They actually get along quite well, although you wouldn't have known it by the way we started."

"Yeah, we were a mess for a while there." I look out at the view and then back to her. Our eyes meet. "I'm glad we're…good."

"Me too."

I realize I'm still staring. I have zero chill with this girl.

The sun sets and the stars slowly appear, and we watch the changing skyscape from our shared blanket, our faces illuminated by the glow of the bonfire. Two hours have passed in a blur. We've spent it talking and laughing and I don't think I've ever had such a good time with a girl. Unless you count our non-date in Miami. I'd forgotten what it feels like to learn new things about someone, to sit and chat and keep wanting to learn more. I feel completely at ease with Jules. It dawns on me that the anxious feeling I've been carrying around with me about the potential London job offer vanished as soon as I picked her up at her place.

The fire blazes, but it's gotten chilly, so I reach into the duffle I brought and grab her my sweatshirt. "Here, put this on. It will warm you up."

I watch as she sits up to pull my hoodie over her head, and we both laugh when she struggles to get it all the way over. I can't help it when I lean into her, tugging the fleece gently over her head, so close to her now we're nose to nose, my gaze shifting to her mouth. That sizzle between us—that burning heat that's been scorching since our last night in Miami—is more than I can take. I want to run my hands over the braid in her hair; I want to trace her pouty, bottom lip with my thumb, then again with my tongue to see if she actually tastes like raspberries, the color of her lips; I want to bury my face in her neck and inhale her scent, the one that reminds me of orange blossoms. This is the closest I've ever been to her and I'm teetering on edge. I need to kiss her as much as I need air to breathe, so I lean in a few millimetres closer, watch her lips part. Mine part too but we're interrupted by voices beyond our fire pit. It's a sobering reminder that we're not alone.

Jules clears her throat and I sit back on the blanket.

Moment lost. Part of me wants to punch the guys wandering by in the throat, but it's probably for the best. Jules and I don't make sense.

There's an awkward silence between us—the first and only one of the night—so I try to ease the tension by digging into the basket for the cookies and strawberries and offering them to her. She takes one of each and moves closer to the fire to warm up.

"Come here. I'll keep you warm," I say, without giving it a second thought, and she does. She sits between my legs, her back resting against my chest. The moon is bright, casting a glow over the water. We sit together, her warm body nestled into mine. And it's bliss.

"This was the perfect night," Jules says, echoing my thoughts. "Thank you for planning it."

A beat of silence hangs between us. My hand brushes along her arm. "I asked you on a date because I like you, Jules, and I've missed you every day since Miami."

I can't see her expression, but God, I wish I could. I do hear the hitch in her breath though. It's enough to make me stop breathing.

"You have?"

"Every. Single. Day." My fingers are still running the length of her forearm and she hasn't pushed them away. "Why do you sound surprised?"

"I don't know. I didn't think I made a very good first impression. Well, I guess it would be second impression."

"You're always making an impression on me, Jules, in a good way. A very good way. Like I said, I like you. There's always been something about you that I'm drawn to."

"You know we are a bad idea, right?"

"Yeah, I know." My hand stops moving over her arm, but I let it rest there. "But I've never been any good at not following my heart."

"Me either," she says resting her hand on my thigh. "This was a good night, Beckett."

I allow my fingers to brush over hers. It isn't much and not nearly enough, but it still feels so damn good. She flips her hand over and tangles her fingers in mine.

"I'm just trying to get the girl."

And when we finally pack up to leave, I walk back to my car with her hand laced in mine, wishing the night would never end.

## Chapter Twelve

**J**ules

Beckett's hand is in mine the entire drive home. He unclenched them briefly to open my car door and tuck me in then reached for my hand as soon as he started the car. My body has been in a constant state of butterflies ever since.

My head is spinning after our date as well, replaying every word he said to me. *"I've missed you every day since Miami."* After that, the night became blurry. Once the words set in, I felt elated. I missed him too. Every single day. As hard as I've tried to forget it and move on, I haven't been able to get our time together in Miami out of my mind. Beckett makes me happy. He puts the biggest smile on my face whenever I'm with him.

And he plans the most amazing dates.

Everything about tonight was perfect. I'm used to fancy restaurants with elaborate menus and Michelin star chefs, but given the choice, I'd take a picnic on a beach with Beckett any day of the week. I wonder if somehow he knew that or if he just took a chance on a fun, casual date and got lucky. Either way, I loved it.

Which gets me to thinking about what ifs. What if I ignored every reason why dating Beckett is a terrible idea? What if I forgot about where he works, and the fact that he may be leaving for London? I could, couldn't I? A quick fling before we go our separate ways. It could be that simple.

But in my heart, I know that it's anything but simple. I know that a quick fling with Beckett wouldn't be enough. He may be interesting and funny and charming and gorgeous, so gorgeous that he makes me nervous sometimes, but if he does get the job in London that means we'd only have just weeks together. Then he'd be boarding a plane for a new life in a new city and I'd still be here, missing him and broken-hearted.

Not only that, I also can't just forget the fact that Beckett works for our biggest competitor. I don't want to do anything that could jeopardize my relationship with my family. And for what? A couple of weeks of really hot sex?

I glance down at our hands, still locked together, then back at him. I take in his profile in the glow of streetlights. The curve of his nose, his angular jaw, the slant of his cheekbones. It takes everything in me not to straddle him in his seat.

His SUV eventually pulls down my street and a minute later we're parked just outside my door. He rounds the car and helps me from my seat, then stands in front of me and even though I've been with him all night, the sight of him takes my breath away. In his light gray jeans, black sweater and Chucks, he's the sexiest man I've ever seen. His hair is doing that messy-styled thing and the stubble on his face makes my hands itch to touch him. I let my gaze drift over him until it meets his eyes, which are blazing back at me with heat. My pulse races. We've been dancing around these embers smoldering between us for days.

"Jules, I—" he stammers over his words.

"What is it, Beck?"

He looks up at the sky before looking back at me, "I want more than just tonight with you. I want to date you. I don't care about where you work or where I work. I want to be the guy who gets to hold your hand. I want to take you places, to kiss you goodnight."

My hand flies to my mouth. I'm completely taken off guard. I don't know what I expected him to say, but it wasn't any of that.

"I'm sorry if that was too much," he says. "The truth is, I've had feelings for you since Miami. I wanted to kiss you then. I keep thinking about kissing you now."

Tension builds in the air all around us. He's staring at my lips like they're all he's ever wanted.

"Beck... when your eyes find mine, I get lost. I can't think, I forget where we are. All I can think about is you. It's like the whole world disappears and it's just us and all I can think about is being close to you."

"Jules—"

"I mean it. I've never felt insane chemistry like this." My back is against his car. My heart races—not because I'm nervous, but because I know he feels the same way. Then my breath catches as Beckett's eyes fall to my lips again.

"I wish you would kiss me."

The words are barely out of my mouth before he's moving toward me. His hands brush over my shoulders, down my arms. I shudder. It's the softest touch, but it's enough to light me on fire. We're both panting. He cups my face in his hands and the warmth of his fingers over my cool skin feels like that moment when you step into a hot bath and your skin tingles.

Then my eyes close and he kisses me, my back pinned against the cool metal of his door. A breathy sigh escapes my lungs while his hands thread around my neck.

Beckett groans as his mouth meets mine, his lips soft and sensual, tempting me as his tongue begs for entry. I open for him, needing everything he has to give me. The kiss deepens as his tongue finds mine, searing me to my core. And all I can think about is *more*.

More.

Finally.

More.

I sigh against his mouth and he makes a guttural sound that I feel everywhere—my heart, my soul, my bones. His hard body pressed against mine only makes the fire he is lighting inside of me burn hotter. His hands roam from my face down my neck, so painstakingly slow that I'm not sure I will survive. I want his hands on my chest, my thighs, my ass, everywhere all at once.

He takes my mouth softly, his tongue continuing to control mine, until his kisses turned harder and greedy, and when he tilts his head to deepen the kiss even further, he groans. I feel the sound he makes, and it turns what started out as sweet into something hot and fiery and borderline illicit. His mouth owns mine while my fingers cling to his shoulder blades like I never want to let go. And I don't.

I couldn't care less that it almost feels hard to breathe.

I couldn't care less who is watching us from their window.

I only care about this kiss, and Beck, and never coming up for air.

He keeps kissing me, his hands framing either side of my neck, controlling the pace. Matching him kiss for kiss, my fingers tighten over the muscles of his back through his sweatshirt, unable to get close enough.

Beckett breaks the kiss with eyes dazed and full of lust, his breathing just as labored as mine.

"I don't want to stop," he whispers.

"Then don't," I say, my forehead against his.

He tilts my face up to his and kisses me again, one hand firmly grasping the nape of my neck, the other on my hip under my shirt. His fingers stroke my bare skin. His tongue expertly finds mine, stroking and sucking while my heart flies from my chest. Kissing Beckett feels like taking a chance on something sweet and good and exciting. Most of all, it feels right. Like we are exactly where we belong.

His hand moves from my hip to my ass, pulling me into him, his hard length pushing against my stomach. He groans again when my back arches into him, craving the friction, needing to be as close to him as I can.

"I've wanted this… this with you… every day since that night in your hotel room," he admits, softly kissing down my neck and then back up to my jaw. The open mouth kisses are so slow and gentle, surprising me. I run my hands up over his firm pecs to his throat, threading my fingers through his hair at the nape of his neck.

"Every night?"

"I haven't stopped," he murmurs against my lips. "You in my bed."

He pulls back and the heated look in his eyes feels hot enough to set me on fire. I exhale hard. "Your weight on top of me…"

*Fuck.* I want that. I want it now.

"My mouth tasting every inch of you…"

"Same. Same here," I breathe, pulling his lips to mine with the grip I have on the back of his neck, and we kiss and kiss in the darkness, making out in the parking lot until I remember where we are.

I drop one last kiss on his lips before reluctantly pulling back. "We should stop before we put on a real show for my neighbors."

"You're right, we should," he sighs, his hands lingering on both sides of my face.

It feels unfair that the night is ending. I search his eyes, looking for answers about where we go from here and what tonight means, but I can't read them.

"I'll walk you to your door."

He laces his hand in mine as I lean in closer to his side, enjoying the last few seconds of being together.

"I don't want to say goodnight, Jules, but I think it's for the best. I'm having a hard time keeping my hands off you."

His smile is sweet, replacing his usual cocky one, his thumb gently brushing across my hand held firmly in his.

"I had a great time with you. Thank you for everything."

"Night, Jules," he says when we reach my door.

"Night, Beck." He drops a kiss to my lips. He's still holding my hand as he steps backwards, finally letting it drop as he turns to leave.

"Beck," I call his name. "Your sweatshirt."

He's at his car when he turns to face me. "Nah, keep it. I like it better on you."

One side of his mouth tips up in a hint of a smile, then he opens the car door and slides in.

I'm left standing at the door to my apartment, every nerve in my body tingling as I remember how good it felt to kiss him.

"That was some kiss." My roommate Bella gives me an

expectant look as I close the door behind me. A smirky-smile on her face.

My hand is on my lips, I'm sure my hair is a disheveled mess, and I'm still lost in Beckett-land. I look at her, unable to mask the silly smile on my face. That was the best kiss of my life. I feel high remembering it, knowing it will keep me up at night for the next two weeks thinking about it.

Bella makes a face like she's dying to know every single detail.

"Please tell me you didn't see all of that," I say, kicking off my shoes, flopping on the couch next to her.

Bella is around my age, but unlike me she is even-keeled, level-headed and extremely organized. She's also madly in love with her boyfriend, Jack, whom she met at the accounting firm where she works as an office manager. Bella and I met at a party at a mutual friend's place three years ago, hitting it off right away. When I decided it was time to move out of my parents' place, she asked me to move in with her.

"Oh, I saw it all. I thought you were going to rip each other's clothes off right there in the parking lot. And by the way, you could have told me the guy is stupidly hot. He looks like Henry—"

"Cavill," I finish for her, shaking my head. "Not you too."

"Jules, how did you not drag the guy in and let him devour you in your bedroom? Missed opportunity if you're asking me."

For the next 20 minutes, Bella interrogates me about the details of my date. I'm trying desperately to play off my feelings for Beckett, but it's no use. Bella knows me. She was there when I fell in love with Alex and she was still there when he broke me into pieces, mopping up my tears and eating junk food with me to cheer me up.

"I know you. You wouldn't have kissed him like that unless you really like him."

I'm not sure there's a point in denying it. The date was incredible. The beach, the bonfire, the picnic dinner—the entire night was all perfect. The kiss had been jaw-dropping. It was a dream date.

"We'll see where it goes from here," I say, pulling my knees up underneath me, trying to play it cool. "Which I don't think will be far."

"After that kiss, I'm pretty sure he's not going to be blocking your number or regretting the noodles he slaved over the stove to cook for you."

I roll my eyes, but I'm too damn happy to actually mean it. "It's not that simple," I murmur. "He works for our biggest competitor. How the hell would that work? Can you imagine Beckett, myself, and my father sitting around a dining room table together at Christmas?"

"It would only be awkward if you let it. Besides, your dad would understand. Let's face it, Michael Bennett is the nicest guy on the planet."

I shrug. "You've never done business with him."

"You're right, I haven't. But I'm still very confident I'm right."

"There's more." I cringe. "He's being considered for a new position at the hotel. Which would mean moving to London for a big president job."

Bella's grin disappears. "He might be doing *what?*"

I give her the rundown on the job offer and the potential relocation overseas.

"That is bad timing. Geez, Jules, I'm sorry. I'm not sure how you'll navigate that one."

"It's fine. It was only one date. Let's not get ahead of ourselves. It could all fizzle out by tomorrow."

She chuckles. "You keep telling yourself that."

She gets up from the couch. "I'm going to bed," she says. "I need my beauty sleep. Jack is picking me up and taking me to Cape May tomorrow. But maybe we can plan a double date for next week." She winks, sauntering down the hallway to her room.

"Not. Happening. I told you it's going to fizzle."

"Whatever, Jules," she says, sounding unconvinced. "Nighty night."

As soon as I'm alone that warm, fuzzy feeling is back in my chest and I'm left trying to catch my breath.

When I fall asleep a little while later, Beckett's smile is the last thing I see.

# Chapter Thirteen



**B**eckett

I have no memory of my drive back home after leaving Jules' place last night. I must have been on autopilot, too busy thinking about that kiss. I haven't been able to get it out of my mind. Somehow, I made it home safely and fell into bed with a smile on my face. Last night was one to remember.

I stand in the shower, close my eyes under the warm spray and let the images from last night rush through my mind. Best kiss ever. Best date ever.

I've been on enough dates to know that last night with Jules was different, better than all the rest. I'm already eager for a second one. And believe me when I tell you— I've dated a lot. But I've never found someone I've liked long enough to want a real relationship with other than Isabel and even then, I knew she wasn't the one. There was never that spark, that can't-go-a-second-without-thinking-about-the person kind of feeling. Until now.

I linger in the shower just a little bit longer, remembering my favorite moments of last night. Jules' back against my chest by the bonfire, her hand in mine the entire drive home and then that kiss. That fucking, earth-shattering, mind-numbing kiss that made me feel…

I'm feeling things I've never allowed myself to feel and it's scary as hell.

I try to shake away the thoughts, to bury them. Letting people in is not something I've ever allowed myself to do, but spending time with Jules is making me think that maybe it's time I tried. Take a chance on something good. I can't guarantee what the future will hold, but I can give it a shot. I only hope she wants to take a chance on me.

I'm stepping out of the shower when my phone buzzes on the bathroom counter with a text from my mom.

*Morning, Beck. Don't forget about lunch today. Be here for noon? We're all looking forward to seeing you.*

I promised Mom I would stop by for lunch today. It's been a few weeks since I've been by for a visit and I know they're anxious to see me. My mom and my stepdad have never been the type of parents to make me feel guilty if I haven't visited or called for a while, and I'm grateful for that. They understand I have my own life now and I work a lot, and although I know they miss me being around, they support me. They've never questioned my decisions, whether that was deciding to go to MIT or taking the job at The Liberty. Even when I took off on a spur of the moment biking trip across Switzerland and came home with nine broken bones in my body, my mom just took care of me and said it was an experience I would never forget. And after I'd healed, they never even suggested that I stop riding, knowing what it means to me. They just asked me to be careful.

My family and I are close, which is the biggest reason I haven't told them about London. They'll never say it, but I know me moving 3,000 miles away would kill them and until I know for sure I don't want to put that worry on them.

Pete's in the living room watching hockey when I arrive. He's followed every sport under the sun since I was a kid.

He looks up at me when I approach, and his focused, game day expression turns into a smile. "Hey, Beck. How's my boy?"

"Hi Dad." I started calling him dad two weeks after my mom introduced us. I'm surprised I lasted that long. All I'd ever wanted was a dad like my friends had, and Pete treated me like I was his from the second I met him. "What's the score?"

"Oh, this lousy game. The Rangers should all be fired. They're playing like donkeys," he grumbles.

I laugh and bend over to give him a hug. As much as he likes to root for the Rangers, I think he likes to give them shit just as much. "Let me go say hi to Mom and Bean really quick and I'll come and watch the game with you."

I find my mom in the kitchen with her face in the oven.

"Hi Mom," I say, grabbing a potato chip from the bowl on the counter.

"Hi, my baby," she says, closing the oven door, and placing a piping hot lasagna on the top of the stove. "Come here. Gimme a hug."

She wraps her arms around my waist, and I kiss the top of her head. She gives me a once-over. "You good, Beck? You're not working too hard?"

"I'm good, Mom. You don't need to worry about me."

She has her hands on her hips like she's not so sure.

"Where's Bean?"

"She's upstairs. She had a rough morning, but I think she's feeling better. Speaking of your sister, thank you for paying for her medications again this month. You know how much we appreciate it."

"I do, Mom. You don't have to thank me."

Although Bean has health insurance, it doesn't cover everything and living with the disease is expensive. Bean relies on three oral and three inhaled medications daily and it's more than my parents can afford, so ever since I started making good money, I've been contributing to her health care bills. My mom and dad like to fight me on it, but it's futile. I'm happy to do it.

Mom hands me a jar of olives and asks me to open it. She stands watching with a scrutinizing glare as the lid pops. "Honey, you look great. And happy. Are you…"

I shake my head, and Mom blows out a breath.

"Well, you can't blame me for hoping. I just don't like thinking of you being all alone. I want you to find someone wonderful. A girl who deserves you."

It's not the first time I've heard this from my mom. Thankfully, Bean comes to my rescue, walking through the kitchen doors just in time to save me from this conversation. "Sorry," she mouths at me silently, having obviously heard the tail end of my mom's concerns. She knows how I get when Mom starts to pry into my love life. Or lack thereof. Up until recently, there hasn't been much to tell.

"Hey, Jelly Bean." I give her a hug. "You feeling okay? Mom said you had a rough morning."

"I'm fine, Beck," she says, shaking her head. "Stop making a deal about me. You know how I hate it."

I throw my hands up in the air like two stop signs. "Sorry, sorry. It won't happen again."

I know better than to treat my sister like a patient. She's never allowed CF to define who she is. She has a job, she's had a few boyfriends and she's planning on going to college in the fall. At five foot three, her tiny frame and long ,dark-blonde hair make her look young, but Bean is a spitfire who doesn't let anything get in her way.

Her phone rings and her cheeks turn pink when she looks at the screen. Answering the call, she walks out of the kitchen as fast as she came.

"Must be the guy she's been talking to," my mom says while she slices into a garlic loaf. "Her face turns the color of candy apples every time he calls."

"You'll tell me if I need to kick his ass?"

"Yup, and I'll send you his address too," she says, shaking the knife in the air. "But so far, so good. They've met for coffee a few times. He's a sophomore in college. Studying engineering."

I cast a sidelong glance at her from where I'm sitting on a stool.

She takes a sip of her water and swallows before asking me, "Have you heard from your dad lately?"

I shrug. "He's not my dad. Pete is."

"You know what I meant."

"He texted me while I was in Miami. Said he had tickets to a Yankees game. I never texted him back," I say, taking the garlic bread to the table. My mom rubs my shoulder with a sympathetic look.

"What's that look for?"

"It's just my face. No judgement here. You're a grown man, you don't need your mom telling you how to live your life," she says as I follow her to the kitchen table. We all take a seat around the table, which is packed with platters of food. It smells like homemade sauce and garlic bread and my mouth instantly waters.

Bean is in the seat next to me and I take the opportunity to give her the big-bro interrogation as we eat. My mom stays quiet, but I can tell she's listening intently.

"Enough with the third degree," Bean says, swatting

me with her napkin. "You're not exactly an expert. Have you *ever* brought a girl home, Beck?" She pauses for a beat, and I'm silent. "That's what I thought."

"Never a dull moment with these two," Pete says, looking at my mom like he has all he's ever wanted sitting around this small table with him.

I smile, because I know it's true.

As soon as I leave my parents, I call Jules because that's what I've been dying to do all day. She picks up on the second ring and right away I pick up on the hesitation in her voice.

"Hey," I say through my Bluetooth on my car. "I hope I'm not interrupting anything."

"No, I just wasn't expecting you to call. But I'm glad it's you, Wonder."

I laugh at the nickname that I'm still clueless to understand. "Is that so?"

"It is. Now don't go and make me change my mind with your cocky attitude."

I love it when she busts my balls. I'd love her hands on my...

*Jesus, Beck. Stop now with the inappropriate thoughts.*

"What are you up to?" I ask through a laugh.

"I'm at home finishing up some work on my computer. Staying one step ahead of The Liberty as per usual."

"Is that right?" I say in a cheeky tone. "Do you ever take a day off?"

"Do *you*?"

"Of course, I do."

"So then, tell me... what does Beckett Taylor do on his day off?"

"Right now, I'm on my way home from a family lunch. My mom made lasagna. I watched a little hockey with my dad, and I hung out with my sister, grilled her on the new guy she's seeing."

"Hmmm… so you're overprotective."

"Damn rights I am. I'll kick his ass if he messes with my sister." I mean it. "What are you doing tonight?"

"No plans."

"Not plotting a Liberty Hotel takeover?"

"Not right this second."

She's quick, her smart-mouth is such a turn on. And now I'm picturing her straddling my hips, naked together in my bedroom, feeling her ride me, while my hands grip her hips…

*Stop. These. Thoughts.*

"Oh good. I have a job for a few more days."

"At most," she deadpans.

"In that case, any job postings at the Seaside? I'm sort of a big deal in the hotel business. You might have heard of me?"

"No, I don't think so. Doesn't ring a bell."

God, she's fucking cute.

"Back to tonight. Want to go to dinner?" My pulse races, hoping she'll say yes. I haven't been able to stop thinking about her. Last night wasn't even close to being enough.

"Depends. With who?"

"He's charming, tall, handsome and he's very good company. He'll also let you choose the restaurant. He's easy like that."

"He sounds wonderful. What's his name?"

I shake my head with a smile. She's really going to make me work for it.

# Chapter Fourteen

Jules

Goosebumps.

I have goosebumps dotting my arms as I listen to Beckett's smooth voice on the phone. He wants to take me for dinner, but after our banter back and forth and that kiss last night I'd prefer to skip the meal and go straight for dessert. Dessert being a code word for Beckett's body.

I waited all day for a text from him and when one didn't come, I started to think I read our date last night all wrong. After all, when I broke the kiss he didn't complain. He didn't suggest we go into my apartment either. I went over every word we said to each other, over and over in my head, thinking maybe my mind was playing tricks on me. Maybe what I felt last night wasn't mutual. In the end, I convinced myself it must have been a one-time thing for him. A bit of fun.

Then when my phone lit up with his name on the screen, I threw all chill out the window and answered it as quickly as I could.

"He sounds wonderful. What's his name?" I tease when he hints at being tall and handsome and very good company.

"I can do better than give you his name."

"You can?" I ask, confused. Then I hear a knock at my door.

My heartbeat races. I open the door to find Beckett standing on my doorstep with his phone to his ear and his other hand in his pocket. The smile on his face knocks the air from me.

"What are you doing here?" I ask, still shocked that he's standing right in front of me.

"I missed you and wanted to see you," he says. "I hope it's okay?"

Is this really happening?

"Come in, Wonder. It's very okay."

He follows me inside and looks over my apartment. Past the entryway is the living room, with an L-shaped gray couch covered in pale pink and white pillows, an ottoman that we use as a coffee table and a console where our TV sits. Beyond that is the kitchen with its white cabinets and stainless-steel appliances and a small round table with four chairs. My favorite thing about the place is the partial view of the beach from the kitchen.

There are dishes still on the counter from lunch, as well as an opened bottle of orange juice and a loaf of bread that I didn't put away. And if Beckett ventures into my bathroom, he'll find my bath towel on the floor and my makeup scattered all over the counter. I *did* make my bed this morning, I'm not a total animal.

I begin to clean up my mess in the kitchen while he admires the view from the sliding door that leads to a small patio.

"You've got a great view," he says as I close the refrigerator door. "How long have you lived here?"

"A few years. I moved in with my friend, Bella. She's the bedroom over there and mine is that way," I say, pointing in the direction of mine. "It worked out really well. She's easy-going and we get along great, and although it's probably time I get my own place, I would miss having the company. You? I've never asked where you live. Are you in Reed Point too?"

"I am," he says, shifting his weight from one foot to another. "I live on Sycamore. No roommate and not too far from Choices. I moved in shortly after taking the job at the hotel."

He takes a step closer. He smells good. He looks good too. His hair is mussed and he's wearing shorts and a plain T-shirt that fit just tightly enough to remind me of his toned body underneath. The one I still fantasize about after seeing him in only swim trunks at the pool in Miami.

I allow my eyes to rake over him, chastising myself for shamelessly staring at the man, but it doesn't stop me from noticing how good he looks. It's not right the way he puts every other man in Reed Point to shame.

His gaze finds mine as he drops his keys on my kitchen counter and I find myself wanting to move closer. He grins, then erases the distance for me, like he knows how much I want his mouth on mine. His eyes drop to my lips and then he's sliding both of his hands over my neck to my jaw. My skin blazes under his touch. Every inch of me lights up in seconds.

Slowly, Beckett kisses me. A make-your-knees-weak, sensual kiss. My arms wrap around him as he pulls me into his chest. My God, the kiss is heated, and it sears through me when I open for him and he slips his tongue in, searching for mine. My body comes alive for him, the chemistry so strong. It always feels like this when we're together.

I forget everything else as his tongue strokes mine, my heart racing, wishing this moment could last forever. His lips, the hold he has on my jaw and his hard body against mine feels so good.

Beckett knows how to kiss a woman. He's in control, gentle at first then hard and demanding, skillfully sucking on my bottom lip. My body aches for more.

Softly, his hands move from my jaw down my neck, leaving goosebumps in their wake. He pulls back, keeping his forehead pressed to mine. "I couldn't wait another second longer. It's all I've been thinking about since I left you last night."

I exhale, "Me too."

His eyes close for the briefest of seconds then they're back on mine. "I promised you dinner. Where can I take you?"

Where I really want him to take me is to the couch, then to my bedroom and then after that up against the wall, but I play it cool.

"I have an idea."

"Tell me," he says, cocking a brow.

"We could go bowling and eat pizza?"

He doesn't answer me, but instead moves in for a chaste kiss that makes me giddy. When his lips pop off of mine he smiles at me like it's the best idea he's ever heard.

"It's a date."

At the bowling alley, Beckett and I find a lane and then order pizza and a pitcher of beer. An Ed Sheeran song drifts from the speakers, competing with the sounds of families and a few other couples who are occupying the other lanes.

Before leaving the house, I changed into a pair of jean shorts and a light sweater that falls off one shoulder as I tie the laces of my bowling shoes. Beckett is bent over beside me tying his. I don't know why these things have to be so darn ugly.

"What's that face for?" he asks.

"Nice shoes, Wonder," I say, glancing at his rented footwear.

"I better not wake up with athlete's foot tomorrow. Do you think they clean these things?"

I laugh. "I doubt it. I'm pretty sure the teenagers working the rental desk would much rather be spending their time on TikTok than scrubbing some musty old bowling shoes. I mean, can you blame them?"

"You're probably right," Beckett says with a grimace. "Remind me to burn my socks then bathe my feet in turpentine when I get home."

We sit at the monitor, where Beckett takes over the keyboard to type in our scoreboard names. The chairs are small and his knee rests against mine, sending a hiccup in my heart rate. "Wanna go first or would you like me to show you how it's done?"

I mock-roll my eyes at him. "Put me in first. I plan on mopping the floor with you."

"Listen to you. I like your tenacity."

When he's finished typing in my name, I push his hands out of the way and type in his. W O N D E R.

He laughs. "A wager," he says, turning his body to face me. "If I win, you're telling me what that means." He points up to the screen where Wonder is displayed in place of his name. "Oh, and I get to kiss you."

"You can kiss me anytime you want."

"Gimme," he says, reaching for me. I meet him halfway and he kisses me. An open-mouthed kiss that just about puts us at risk of being arrested for public indecency. "Are you ready to do this?"

"Let's."

I grab a ball and walk to the center of the lane. It's been a while since I've been bowling, but when I used to come here with friends, I wasn't too bad. Taking three steps forward, I loft the ball down the lane. It starts off straight, then takes a curve to the left, knocking down three pins.

"Nice one, Jules," Beckett cheers behind me. He's wearing that sexy smirk when I turn around to get another ball. His legs are stretched out in front of him, and he looks at ease and confident. Cocky but charming. His eyes are on me, exactly where I like them to be.

I finish my turn, knocking down three more pins, and when I turn around, I find Beckett still staring, his sky-blue irises pinned on me. My heart rate kicks up three notches.

As he passes me on his way to pick up his ball, he grabs me by my waist and kisses my neck. It's playful, but my body reacts. Even the slightest touch from Beckett and I'm melting like snow on a warm, sunny day.

He grabs a ball and throws a strike on his very first turn—and looks hot as hell while he's doing it. Impossibly, he even looks good in those maroon and brown borrowed bowling shoes. He lifts his eyebrows at me, as if to say *that's how it's done*. And I wonder what else he's good at.

On my next turn, I throw two gutter balls and on the third try I knock down one pin. I glare down the lane at the pins still standing there mocking me. I think the older lady beside me feels sorry for me because she leans over and offers me a few pointers. She's one of those league players who brings her own ball to the alley, so I figure it can't hurt to take her advice. "Throw it like you're angry!" she insists. "Show those pins who's in charge around here."

She must have given me her bowling juju, because on my next turn I bowl a spare.

"Atta girl, beautiful," Beckett says. I turn around and he lifts me in his arms. I squeal when he swings me around, my cheek against his. "You did it."

I giggle, "I did."

Beckett continues his winning streak, a strike every time. Meanwhile, my luck runs out and I only manage to knock down a few pins.

We have one frame left when they call our number at the bar. Beckett jogs over and a few minutes later he's back with our pizza in one hand and the pitcher of beer in the other. We dig in.

"How was your visit at your mom's today?" I ask.

He swallows a bite of pizza. "Good, like any other visit. It's just the four of us, so it's…simple. Nothing too crazy. I don't have a lot of family."

"Do you go over a lot?"

"When I can."

I try to picture Beckett at home with his sister and his parents, but he hasn't painted a very clear picture, so I come up pretty blank.

"My family is great." There's a warmth in his eyes. "I just think they're probably different than what you're used to."

"Because I grew up in a house with three loud and unruly brothers?"

His beer cup covers his smile. "Something like that." Then he changes the subject. "So, out of ten…how is the pizza?"

"Hmmm," I say, tapping my chin. "I think it's reasonably good for bowling alley pizza. It isn't life-changing, but the cheese is good and stretchy so for that reason I give it a seven."

He grins, "Stretchy cheese. I'm not sure I've ever considered the stretchiness of the cheese on my pizza."

"Then you don't know good pizza," I tell him, trying not to laugh.

We're just finishing up our dinner when Beckett's phone buzzes. He digs it out of his pocket and when he looks at the screen his face turns serious, a line forming in between his brows.

"Everything okay? If you need to deal with something, I'll be just fine," I offer.

"Nah, all good. It was just my dad."

"Pete?"

"No. My bio dad."

The look on his face tells me there's more to say, but he doesn't seem eager to talk about it. Instead, moves to sit beside me, his long legs straddling the bench so he's facing me. There's plenty of space, but he leans toward me so that his knee presses against my thigh. "I won the game, Jules. You know what that means. Tell me why you call me Wonder." He pulls me into his chest, wrapping one arm around my waist while the other sweeps my ponytail off my shoulder and he kisses my neck. I shiver.

"Okay, okay… but you have to promise not to get mad at me. I came up with that nickname for you after our incident in your office." He squeezes me tighter, making me laugh and I squirm in his arms. His breath on my neck tickles.

"I promise. Now tell me." I flip one leg over the bench so I'm straddling it as well, facing him. His hands move to each of my thighs and he leans in and kisses me.

I wince, trying not to laugh. "It's short for… Mr. Man Wonder."

He cocks an eyebrow at me, clearly amused.

"I thought you were full of yourself. Admit it, Beckett… in business, you think you're something else."

"That's because I am," he quips back. "I think you have a little of that in you too."

I scoff. "You can be infuriating, you know."

"Me?" he asks, with his hand across his chest.

"Yes, you. You like to ruffle my feathers. Don't act like you don't. "

He shrugs, an up-to-no-good look on his face. "You know…I kinda like it. Mr. Man Wonder. It has a certain ring to it. Maybe I should change the nameplate on my office door."

I roll my eyes. "It wouldn't surprise me if you did."

"You're cute when you're all bothered," he teases with a grin.

"There you go again, pushing my buttons." This is the cocky side of Beckett Taylor that used to drive me mad. Now it's a turn-on. I can't believe how much my feelings about him have changed. Ever since that day in Miami when I got the wasp bite, I see Beckett in an entirely new light. Before then, I wanted to hate him. Now I have to admit I kind of like his cockiness. The way he walks into a room exuding power and confidence. The way he blatantly watches me and holds my gaze.

"I think you like it when I push them," he says, and my skin is on fire.

Beckett's hands move further up my legs until they're almost at the top of my thighs. My mouth is inches from his, my skin tingling under his touch, my heart hammering inside my chest.

"I'm ready to go home now. How 'bout you?" I say, before dusting the softest of kisses over his lips.

A slow smile lights up his face and I notice his Adam's apple bob in his throat. He brings his lips back to mine in another feather-soft kiss and I'm pining for him. "Yeah, I'm ready too."

Beckett drives twice the legal limit back to my house, his hand on my thigh the entire time. My pulse under my skin beats rapidly, and fuck…I want him so bad. I'm done trying to resist this, trying to control this intense need for him, because I can't. I want him more than the air that I breathe.

When he parks the car, he frowns.

"Your roommate, Jules."

One corner of my lip tips up. "She's away for the weekend with her boyfriend."

Beckett smiles like a kid on Christmas morning, then looks at me in a way that makes me feel like he's staring into my soul.

Then he opens the car door and breaks the spell.

And I can't wait to find out what happens next.

## Chapter Fifteen

**B**eckett

I pin her against my car, kissing her until we're both breathless, unable to wait. It's 20 feet to her apartment and I'm not sure I'll make it. I want her so bad that it hurts.

Who knew bowling and eating cheap pizza was such incredible foreplay? I'm used to seeing Jules in the boardroom and while she always looks professional and perfectly put together, I couldn't take my eyes off her tonight. The way her ponytail swayed when she stepped onto the lane or how she crinkled her nose when her ball veered off into the gutter. I even loved watching her make small talk with the older couple beside us, like she'd known them for years. Every little thing about this girl has me tied up in knots.

And seeing her in that off-the-shoulder top and her sexy cut-off jean shorts the night was a special kind of torture. The way those shorts showed off her long, lean legs made me wonder what they would feel like wrapped around me as lay on top of her. Bowling while sporting wood is not as easy as it seems.

I'm done resisting her. Jules Bennett swept me off my feet the first time I saw her. I wasn't ready to admit that to myself then, but there's no denying it now.

Now, we're back at her house standing in her parking lot and all of my brain cells have short-circuited. She's pressed firmly against me, her tongue is in my mouth. It feels incredible.

"I want you, Jules," I breathe, pulling back to look at her.

"I want you too." Her big eyes stare back at me.

I take her hand in mine, pulling her with me, and when we get to the door she fumbles for her keys. My mouth on her neck probably isn't helping.

"That feels so good," she says, her voice all breathy.

The door finally opens, and I have her pressed against it as soon as it closes, anxious for her lips back on mine. My body vibrates when my lips meet hers, and I let out a moan when her tongue slides along mine, back and forth, deeper each time. I kiss her like I've been separated from her for years. But it's not enough. I want to devour her, make love to her mouth. I slant my head to the side so I can deepen the kiss, sucking on her tongue and exploring her mouth with mine.

"The way it feels when we kiss, Jules," I say when my lips leave hers. My body is on fire from the inside, burning out. "It does crazy things to me."

"Beckett…it's so good with you. Never…like…this," she breathes as I kiss my way down her neck, her words lighting a fire inside of me because now I know she feels it too. This intense attraction that I've been fighting since our time together in Miami.

I can't get enough of her smooth skin and the sugary taste of her as I lick a straight line down the column of her neck, then suck the skin right below, leaving a mark. My dick is throbbing. She writhes beneath my mouth, her hand on the back of my head, pressing my lips closer against her skin. I kiss a path across her collarbone to her bare shoulder. Every time her sweater slipped off her shoulder tonight it made me want to kiss and suck on her skin. As sexy as she looks in it, I'm dying to see what's underneath it.

My hands find the hem of her sweater, tugging it up, and she raises her hands for me so I can pull it over her head. I toss it to the floor then concentrate on the black, lacey bra she's wearing, her tits spilling out of the top.

"Jules," I groan, my fingers tracing the line of the fabric. "You're so fucking perfect."

She has a heated look in her eyes, then her gaze follows my mouth as I suck her nipple through the lace. I stare back at her, my hands moving to her back to unhook the clasp of her bra while my mouth continues its assault on her chest. The bra falls to the floor and my mouth latches back onto her, sucking on the stiff peaks of her chest as my fingers travel lower, brushing across a tattoo of two small birds inked on her ribcage. I dip my mouth to her ribs and taste them with my tongue.

Sighing, she tips her head back against the door. A second later, she's reaching for my T-shirt and I help her, lifting it over my head. My skin erupts with sparks when her hands run from my shoulders over my pecs to my abs, like she's cataloging every inch.

"See something you like?" I ask with a bemused expression.

"I don't know where to start," she says, wrapping her hands around my back as I take her mouth again in a punishing kiss. Her bare chest against my bare chest, our hands exploring each other's bodies.

"I like your eyes on me."

"I can't seem to ever look away," she says into a kiss. "Stop being so handsome."

I laugh against her mouth as my fingers find the button of her shorts, unzipping her and pushing them down her legs. She kicks them off…and fuck me, her panties match her black lace bra. My hand tightens around one of her ass cheeks, squeezing, then my fingers play with the hem of her underwear. I slip a finger under the lace then slip it back out and she moans, pushing her pelvis against me, needing more. I'm happy to give it to her. But I'm not in a rush. I plan on taking my time with her, enjoying her, savoring every inch.

"Bedroom. Now," I say, taking control, wanting to lay her out on her bed so I can worship every inch of her. I lift her into my arms, her legs wrapping around my waist, and I carry her down the hallway to her bedroom. I stop at the foot of the bed, letting her slide down my body, over my dick, and it responds by growing harder.

I'm so hard it hurts as she unzips my jeans and urges my shorts down my thighs and sinks to her knees. I kick them off the rest of the way and on her way back up, she runs her cheek over my straining hard-on over the fabric of my boxers. "Fuck," I moan as she stands, then she goes up on her toes and kisses me while her hand curls around the imprint of me through my briefs.

The groan I make tells her exactly how good it feels. I could come right now. I walk her backwards towards her bed, pulling the elastic out of her hair as I do. I lay her in the center of the bed and lower myself over her, her hair spilling out across the blankets. Her blinds are open, allowing what's left of the sunlight to filter into the small room, so I can see her and see us together for the first time. I'm already hoping it's not the last.

I kiss her mouth, then her neck, then down to her

breasts, taking each one in my mouth again. She arches her back off of the mattress and makes this sexy sound that I feel in my bones.

"Feel good?" I ask. My tongue swirls around her nipple in little circles.

Her teeth scrape over her bottom lip and her eyes squeeze shut as she barely gets out the word, *yes*. I give the same attention to the other peak before flicking my tongue over the sparrow tattoos on her ribs once more and then moving lower to the black lace. The only piece of fabric left to take off. I'll fix that.

Slowly, I slide her underwear down until they're on the floor then I appreciate the view. I stare down at her, taking her in. She's fucking perfect. Narrow hips, lean, long legs and ample breasts. Her deep, hazel eyes, framed by thick lashes, watch me. "You slay me, you know. I don't know what I want to do to you first."

"Do something, Beck," she breathes, and I'm loving the sound of my name on her tongue. "Anything. Just do something."

So I do. I kiss up her legs to her mouth while my index finger slips inside her. I add a second and her hand clutches the nape of my neck as she bows her pelvis up to meet my hand.

"Beck…"

"Let go, baby. I've got you," I tell her. She widens her legs and I find the spot that I know she needs, my finger moving in tiny, quick circles as she breathes out hard. In minutes she's stiffening underneath me, crying out my name and gripping the bed sheets. She's fucking beautiful when she comes. Her face is pure bliss, her wide eyes glazed.

Her hand reaches for my jaw and I grab her wrist and

kiss the anchor tattoo, sucking on her skin like I've been dying to since the moment I first saw the ink.

I want to tell her she's mine. The nervous feeling inside me needs to know this isn't a one-time thing between us. It's so much more than that to me, but I can't say the words for fear this could all end tonight if I do.

I quickly forget everything but right here, right now, when she pushes against my chest and I roll over onto my back bringing her with me. My legs part and she kneels in between them.

"Why are you still wearing these?" She runs her hands down my abs to the elastic band of my briefs, tugging them over my hips and down onto the floor in a pile with her underwear. My hard-on springs free, landing on my stomach, and I laugh. "He wants you."

"I want him too," she says, curling her hand around my shaft, pumping her hand up and down my length and then over the head. I roll my hips up off the bed, pumping into her hand. I shudder and my dick hardens even more in her grasp.

She's on her knees between my legs, her big green and gold eyes holding mine, as she strokes me with one hand. Her other hand is on my thigh near my aching groin, massaging me.

Lust rips through me and I'm already so close to shooting, so I sit up and reach for the back of her neck, pulling her down on top of me, her skin against mine. Her hair spills over her shoulders, tickling my chest. "I want all of you, Jules, but if it's too soon I—"

"I want you to fuck me, Beck," she says, and for a long moment, I take her in, just staring in disbelief that Jules Bennett is going to be mine.

I watch her reach for the nightstand and grab a foil

packet from the drawer. Emotion swells inside of me. I want her more than I've ever wanted anything in my life.

She straddles my hips, watching me suit up. "I want you to ride me, Jules, then I'm going to flip you over and take you hard and fast. Sound good?"

Her eyes flare and she nods, then she lines my dick up with her center, slowly sinking down on me until she's all the way seated and I'm filling her completely. Her eyes hold mine and I groan at the feel of her tightening around my thickening shaft.

I'm in paradise.

I'm in her.

And nothing has ever felt better.

Every pent-up feeling I've ever had for her, every emotion that has driven me to madness, releases in this moment.

I want this.

I want her.

I want us.

As long as she will let me.

It's so fucking good that the house could be burning down around us and I wouldn't notice the flames. It feels like there are only the two of us left on this earth, just Jules and I and the hottest, most beautiful thing I've ever experienced.

She rises up then drops back down on me. Over and over. I watch myself disappear inside of her, gritting my teeth, trying to hold on and make this good for her. But it's not fucking easy because she feels so damn good. When I know I'm almost there, I flip her so she's lying underneath me, kneeing her legs apart, her cheeks flush. Her streaked hair spilling out over her pillow. I stare down at her in wonder while I push in.

"You feel so good," I tell her as I ease out and pump back in.

I kiss her fiercely, our tongues swirling together. There's nothing soft about the way my mouth is on hers. It's ferocious and feral and everything I've needed from her since Miami. I want to kiss her everywhere, to know every inch of her body, but this feels too good to stop. So I continue to fuck her, hitching her leg up around my hip, so I'm as deep as I can get, aching to come.

"Don't stop. I'm so close," she says, her hands gripping my ass as I give it everything I've got, taking her over the edge with me. I'm so fucking turned on and determined to make this good for her, thrusting and pumping into her in an intense rhythm.

I pick up the pace and I can feel that she's close. Then with a shuddering cry, she's digging her fingernails into my back, gasping and shouting my name.

*My name.*

I made her feel this way.

I did that.

And when she opens her eyes and stares back at me, there are so many words I want to say to her. Instead, I kiss her, showing her with my mouth how much this means to me. How badly I want her. Want us. Over and over.

I hold her gaze as long as I can, soaking up every second of the intimacy it brings, until I can't hold off any longer and my climax slams into me like thunder. I squeeze my eyes shut and my mouth falls open as I give in to the pleasure that takes hold of me, shuddering through the vibrations. Pulse by pulse, I go over the edge until I'm spent and sated, collapsing limply over Jules.

"Beck…"

"I know."

"It was—"

"Fucking incredible." I take the words right out of her mouth, my lips hovering in the crook of her neck.

We lie together on her bed for a while until I finally drag myself away from her, needing to take care of the condom. When I return, she's still lying on the bed, one arm above her head, the other over the blanket pulled across her bare chest.

"Will you lay with me?" she asks, our eyes locked in the dimly lit room. I see the vulnerability I feel in that moment reflected back at me in Jules' eyes and I realize that we're both aware of all that has changed between us. We crossed that line, one that we'd been skating on for a while now, and all we can do is wait and see if there will be fallout.

"I'd love to."

I crawl under the covers and pull her onto my chest. We're both still, naked, and she has one leg hitched over mine. I draw her closer to me and it takes everything in me not to climb on top of her and fuck her again.

"Will you tell me about the tattoo on your ribs?"

"Do you like it?" she asks.

She tilts her head so she's looking up at me, her fingertips drawing lines across my chest.

"That feels good," I murmur. "And yes, I like the sparrows very much. Tell me what made you get them."

She shifts her weight so she's lying against me on her stomach. I push a few loose strands of her hair behind her ear and wait for her to say more.

"Sophomore year, I got the sparrows for my best friend. One representing me, the other for her. Her name was Charlie." She swallows and I run the tips of my fingers over her arm. "Our families were close, and we grew up together. They lived on the same street as us, we went to the same school. We were all on a ski trip together when it happened. She died in an accident. I wasn't there but I was supposed to be. It was devastating to lose her."

"I'm sorry. I can't imagine."

"Thank you. Anyways, when we got back to Reed Point there was a sparrow on our doorstep, and I felt her… I mean…I felt Charlie all around me. I know it sounds crazy—"

"It doesn't sound crazy at all. They say people come back to you in different ways after they pass. Sometimes in dreams. In your case, as a sparrow."

She nods. "No tattoos for you?"

"Not yet. You never know…maybe one day."

"Beck…." She eases up on her elbows and looks at me, her sated eyes mirroring mine.

"Yeah?"

"Do you want to stay here tonight?" she asks.

"Do you want me to?"

"Stay." She yawns against my chest and then snuggles into me.

I hold her as close to me as I can, then kiss the top of her head and wonder how we've come this far in only a matter of weeks. But as far as we've come, there's a weight there, too. It's the heaviness of being with Jules, who I have no business being with, of London and of something more that I know we are both a little afraid of.

But none of that needs to be worked out right this second.

Instead, I allow myself to just enjoy this perfect night with her.

# Chapter Sixteen

**Jules**

I'm a trainwreck when I wake up the next day.

"I hate mornings."

Beckett laughs beside me. His long legs are tangled in mine, one muscular arm flung over my torso. "You do?"

"They're awful."

Beckett pulls me into his side, laughing into my neck. "Even with me here?"

I groan. "You're helping, but coffee would speed up the process."

"Do you always wake up this homicidal?" he asks, hitching his leg over my hip. His dick is soft, and it's pressed against my backside.

"You act like it's not totally obscene to wake up before seven."

"I think most people do wake up before seven."

"Not normal ones," I moan into my pillow.

"Okay, let's get you some coffee," Beckett says, twirling a strand of my hair around his finger.

"And a shower too."

"I can handle that." He kisses my shoulder, then sits up in bed. I reach an arm across the mattress as he stands and give his bare ass a squeeze before he gets out of bed. He fishes his boxers from the pile of clothing on the floor and slips them on.

"Thank you," I call out, before shoving my face back into the pillow.

Ten minutes or so later, he pads into my room with two mugs in his hands. He passes one to me and takes the other one with him to the opposite side of the bed. I sit up, pulling the sheet over my bare chest as he climbs back under the covers. Instantly the air in the room grows heavy, like we're both suddenly aware of the fact that we're lying naked together in my bed.

I take my first long sip of coffee and feel my mood instantly start to improve. It gets even better when my eyes focus on Beckett's body, only covered by the bed sheet from the waist down.

As my eyes linger on his rippled chest, I find myself thinking—for the first time in my entire adult life—that maybe mornings aren't so bad after all. Waking up next to Beckett feels good.

His eyes follow my gaze to his chest, then he smirks. "Want to touch it?"

Shaking my head, I choke out a laugh. "You would like that way too much."

"You're right, I would," he says from behind the rim of his mug.

I roll my eyes. "Shame that I'm not going to then."

"I bet I can change your mind."

He very easily could, and therein lies the problem. I slept with him only a few hours ago, and I already want more. It takes everything in me not to kiss him senseless.

It's unfair how amazing he looks this early in the morning, his hair perfectly mussed and his eyes bright and blue. He's all chiseled abs and confidence and it's frying my brain, so I steer our conversation to safer territory.

"What are your plans today?"

"You mean after our shower?" he asks, one eyebrow raised. *How the hell does he do that?*

The temperature in the room spikes to sauna levels and a carousel of filthy shower fantasies run through my mind. "Yes, after that."

"I'm meeting a friend for lunch."

"Oh," I say, straightening my spine. *A friend?* I tamp the jealousy down immediately because I'm not that kind of girl. Besides, Beckett isn't mine. And I have plans today anyways.

"Zane is his name." Beckett smiles a crooked grin, obviously having caught a glimpse of my resting-jealous-as-fuck face. "The guy I'm meeting at Catch 21 today."

I mentally smack myself upside my head at my ridiculous jealousy. Did I really think Beckett would take a girl on a date right after spending the night with me? I guess stranger things have happened, but I know him well enough to know that he's not a dick.

"What about you?" he asks.

"I have dinner at my parents' house. My brothers, and their wives—okay one wife, one girlfriend—are coming too. Well, except for Miles and Rylee… he's filming in L.A."

Beckett sets his mug on the side table and turns on his side to face me, his arm bent under his head, the tips of his toes running the length of my calf. "What's it like having a famous brother?"

"Not much different than my other brothers except I see him a lot less," I say. Miles lives in L.A. with his fiancée and is always filming. "But I'll be seeing both Miles and

Rylee in a few weeks at a charity gala my parents are hosting. Rylee is Miles' fiancée and she's the cutest thing."

"Your brother is the man. That movie where he plays the arrogant ass lawyer is legendary."

"And the furthest thing from Miles. There's nothing tough about him." I shrug. "Liam is the hard-ass. He's a lawyer, a demanding one and he can come off as pretty intimidating when you first meet him. But he'd do anything for the people he loves. I'm probably the closest to him."

"Liam's the one with the baby?"

"Yup. And he's expecting baby number two around the same time as Parker and Olivia are having their first."

"Your brothers are really adding to the family."

"Yeah, they are." I smile, thinking about my little bud, Hudson, and the new babies who will join our family just a few months from now.

"And where do you fit into this picture?"

"Definitely not pregnant, if that's what you're asking."

He shakes his head and covers his face with his hand. "I didn't mean that. I meant, is there pressure for you to get married and have babies?"

"Sometimes," I admit, because if I said no I'd be lying. "Mostly from my mom. She just wants me to be happy. My brothers though, think I should be locked in my bedroom until the day I get married to a guy they've handpicked for me. All three of them will threaten bodily injury on anyone they think isn't right for me."

He flashes me a look like that isn't something he needs to worry about. "Scandalous."

I laugh but can't ignore the tiny ache in my chest at the thought of Beckett meeting my family. Unfortunately, I know that kind of relationship isn't in the cards for us.

"You're full of jokes, huh?"

"You like my jokes," Beckett says, rolling over so he's on top of me. He kisses along my jaw and I widen my legs for him. My heart pounds in my chest as he looks down at me. He's hard now and his erection is pressed firmly between my legs. I'm not prepared for the intensity in his eyes when he runs his erection up the length of me, asking, "Do you want this, Jules?"

The question is filthy, and it drives me wild as I ready myself for what I know is going to be incredible.

Beckett doesn't disappoint when he takes me rough, his big, strong body controlling mine, his desperate groans and mumbled dirty words echoing through me.

And when it's over, he lifts me from my bed as if I weigh nothing and carries me to the shower, turning the faucet to get the temperature just right, tucking me in against his chest.

And it suddenly feels like so much more than one night. A hookup never spends the night after sex or drinks a cup of coffee in bed while talking about their family. And now this, him and I under a spray of hot water together, it feels so intimate, soap suds spilling down our bodies.

My heart thuds in my chest, and I want to ask him what's next, but I don't. Instead, I close my eyes and pin my lips together to stop myself from saying the words. But they're right there, begging to be asked: where do we go from here?

He steps back and reaches for my body wash and I let my eyes rake over him. I couldn't look away even if I tried. We just spent the entire night naked together, but this is the first time I'm really seeing all of him. Water drips down his chest over his firm pecs. There is a dusting of fine, dark chest hair that ends at his abs, then starts again in a glorious, delicious happy trail that leads to what he's packing. My God, his dick is gorgeous. It's long and thick and already hard again, pointing up towards his abs, the tip almost at his belly button when he's fully hard. I moon over his sculpted body, his defined abs and that deep V that has me salivating.

I draw in a deep breath and tilt my head to the spray of water, feeling Beckett's hands slip over my shoulders.

"It's your body wash," he says, suds under his hands. "This fucking scent on you has been driving me crazy."

"Is that so?" His soapy hands massage my shoulders, then move down my arms, as his nose runs the length of my neck inhaling me. My skin erupts in goosebumps despite the warmth of the spray. His mouth presses the faintest kiss over my earlobe.

"So fucking crazy."

I turn around. I almost beg. "Kiss me, Beck."

He clasps my waist with one hand while the other moves to the nape of my neck, and it feels so good when his lips find mine. The kiss is indulgent, long and slow like we have all the time in the world. Like we have forever. I could spend all day here with his hands roaming my body, his incredible mouth nipping and sucking mine. He moans as my hands travel up the grooves of his abs to his chest and it excites me, loving that he makes sounds like that with me. I want to remember that sound tomorrow, when I'm alone and wondering where he is.

When we break the kiss, Beckett looks at me with a playful gleam in his eyes. "How's that?"

I can't find the words because what I really want to say to him right now feels like too much. But I try. I rise up on my toes and his face dips down to meet mine. His eyes are filled with vulnerability and heat all at once. "I've never had better."

Beckett looks blown away. "Jules?"

I swallow. "Yeah?"

"Feel free to kiss me like that anytime."

I let his words sink in, lowering my eyes to hide the emotions swirling inside of me. I want that so badly, but I know there's so much standing in the way.

It's an excruciatingly sad thought when we could be something so good together.

---

"Something's going on with you."

Ellie, my sister-in-law, sits up straighter on the couch and looks at me with a curious expression on her face. "What's up? Spill it."

It's Sunday evening and we're all sitting in my parents' living room. My brothers Parker and Liam are sprawled on the floor with my nephew Hudson, attempting to teach him the finer points of golf. They're convinced he could be the next Tiger Woods, despite the fact that he's more interested in licking the ball than in putting it. Ellie and Olivia, meanwhile, are busy giving me the third degree.

"Nothing's up," I insist, hoping the blush I feel creeping up my cheeks doesn't give me away. "I'm just tired, I didn't get a lot of sleep last night."

"And that is exactly our point," Ellie says. "We just need you to fill in the blanks for us. Who's the guy keeping you up all night?"

I roll my eyes, but Ellie's not having it. "I'm waiting," she tells me, absentmindedly running a hand over her pregnant belly.

"We both are," Olivia chimes in with a grin. The two of them are best friends, business partners *and* partners in crime. And soon they'll be new moms together too. It's cute seeing them go through their pregnancies together, though their experiences couldn't be more different. Olivia is loving every second of her pregnancy, while Ellie just moans and groans about how everything hurts, and the fact that she has to pee all the time.

"I'd rather not be here for the conversation about my sister's sex life, thanks," Liam huffs. "But Jules, you better not be back together with Alex. I hated that guy."

"Well, you have no say in who your sister dates," Ellie scolds her husband, before turning back to me. "But please say it's not Alex."

"It's not Alex."

"Aha! So you're admitting there *is* someone?" Ellie teases. She's relentless.

"Fine. I admit there's someone, but that's all you're getting for now. It's…new," I reply, digging my heels in.

A memory of last night, with Beckett in my bed, floods my mind. The sounds we made when he was buried inside of me, the feeling of his mouth on my skin. My heart races just thinking about the way he took his time undressing me, worshipping me with his mouth. Alex never did that, always in a rush to get off so he could get back to studying. But Beckett was different. Last night was definitely the most sensual night of my life.

I'm snapped back to reality when the plastic toy golf ball hits me in the ankle and Hudson leaps into in my lap trying to chase it. I squeeze him around his middle and kiss the top of his head and then he's gone as quickly as he came.

"*New* is not an answer, Jules. Who is this guy?" Parker asks, flipping the switch to protective big brother mode.

He's amazing, I want to tell them, and I've never felt like this before. And he has the most beautiful blue eyes I've ever seen. But none of that matters because I can't have him. Oh, and by the way, you know him. He works for our competitor. *Geez.*

Parker would have a complete conniption if he knew that the guy in question is Beckett Taylor. He's known of Beckett for as long as I have and is very familiar with his ball-busting methods of getting a deal done. How he sweeps into a room, all charm and charisma and big-dick-energy, and can land a deal you've been busting your ass on for weeks in mere minutes. It's infuriating.

I squeeze my eyes shut, mentally chastising myself. I know better than to cross company lines, but I did it anyways. And the really crazy part? I would do it all over again, knowing how good we are together.

I open my eyes to find the entire room staring at me.

"What?" I ask, suddenly self-conscious.

"Wow. You've got it *bad* for this guy," Olivia says.

I look away before my expression adds even more fuel to their little gossip fire and quickly change the subject.

"Tell me the latest with the wedding," I ask Ellie, whose attention is now on Hudson and trying in vain to persuade him to drink some water.

Her big hazel eyes flicker with excitement. "Everything is coming together. I spoke to the hotel and confirmed the rooms are all booked and the JP we liked has agreed to marry us."

Liam and Ellie are finally getting married in Hawaii on New Year's Eve. It'll be two kids later and two years longer than Liam had hoped when he popped the question, but Ellie didn't want to walk down the aisle when she was first pregnant. And then she got pregnant again six months later. Liam has made Ellie promise she's walking down the aisle in December, no matter what, pregnant or not. He's anxious to finally make her a Bennett.

"You know, there's still time to fill in your plus one card, Jules," Ellie says with a sparkle in her eyes. "A *new* man on a tropical island, that sounds pretty hot."

"That's enough, Ells," Liam growls. "Not an image I need in my head."

I flash her a not-gonna-happen look, then stand up. "I'm going to see if Mom needs help in the kitchen," I say quickly, needing a change of scenery.

I find her leaning against the counter, staring at her phone. "Hey, Mom."

She puts down the device and takes off her glasses, her brows knitted.

"You okay, Mom? You look like there's something wrong."

She wrinkles her nose. "Just a lot going on with the gala, but I will get it all sorted. Have you found a dress?"

"I have. It's yellow, of course." My favorite color since I was a kid.

"I wouldn't have expected anything else. I know you'll look beautiful." She smiles, then raises her eyebrows hopefully at me. "Will you be bringing a date?"

"No," I say quickly, wanting to end this line of questioning before she really gets going.

My mom frowns, then studies my face like she's done since I was a kid. "Look, your dad and I are so proud of you and how hard you work," she says, reaching for my hand and squeezing it affectionately. "But honey, make sure you work just as hard at being happy."

Then she wraps her arms around me in a hug. "I love you, baby."

"Love you too," I say into her shoulder.

She kisses my cheek and then turns to check on dinner as my dad walks in to get a drink from the fridge.

I sink onto a barstool and watch my mom shoo my dad away from the stove, where he's threatening to dip his finger into the mashed potatoes. I smile at their little routine, the same one I've been watching since I was a kid.

My parents knew instantly that they were meant to be, and all these years later, they're still crazy about each other.

I want that for myself.

But, that's not all I want.

I want the rival.

I want Beck.

Now I just have to figure out a way to have it all.

# Chapter Seventeen

Beckett

I'm at my desk responding to emails when my assistant pings me with a message. My boss, Marco, wants to see me in his office. A nervous energy flows through me knowing how close I am to nabbing this job.

I loosen the knot of my tie and a cold-sweat washes over me. If I was a betting man, I'd bet the house on this being the meeting I've been waiting for.

Marco is on the phone when I quietly knock on his office door. He glances up at me and then nods to the chair across from his desk. I take a seat and wait patiently while he wraps up the call.

"Beckett." He smiles, over the rim of his glasses. Marco has been a mentor and someone I've looked up to since I started at the Liberty. He's tough but fair and even in his 60s, he's the first one here in the morning and the last one to leave. I know because we clock the same hours.

"Hi. You wanted to see me?" I ask tentatively, my heart racing, palms sweaty.

"Yes, let's talk."

I brace myself. Marco watches me for a moment, then leans forward, forearms on his desk. "I've been singing your praises for ages, Beckett. You're a hard worker, you're smart and you're a natural born leader and I like that about you. The team here loves working for you and that's a sign of a good VP."

He pauses and I shoot him a small, appreciative smile while I scratch my finger around the bezel of my watch. Getting this promotion would mean a lot more money. I could pay Bean's medical bills and really set myself up for the future.

But I can't get a read on him. Marco always keeps his emotions guarded—he's got one of the best poker-faces I've seen. I wait, not quite sure where this is going.

"I want you to know that I've appreciated your patience during this process. I know the wait can't have been easy." He clasps his hands together on the desk and smiles. "The job is yours, Beckett. And although it pains me to see you go, I know this is what's best for you. The guys in London are damn lucky to have you."

Marco leans back in his seat and I finally feel my shoulders relax. I've been waiting for this my entire career. My job has been my sole focus, it's the only thing I've cared about besides my family. It's the first thing I think about in the morning, and I'm reviewing contracts and numbers right before I lay my head down at night. It has been my life, and this is the pay-off for all of that work. I'm anxious to know the details. "Thank you, Marco. I appreciate the opportunity. So, what are the next steps?"

"I'll need you in London for meetings by the 21st. We'll put you up in a hotel until you can find a place—HR can help you find a suitable apartment. My best guess is they'll want you the following Monday in the office ready to work."

*That's in five weeks.*

*I will be the president of hotel operations in the United Kingdom in five weeks.*

"Congratulations, Beckett," Marco says, standing and holding his hand out to me across the desk. "We're going to miss you around here."

I shake his hand and thank him again. I'm beyond happy when I walk out of Marco's office, proud that I've accomplished the goal I set for myself, that my dream of London is right here in front of me.

Jules is the first person I want to tell.

As soon as I'm back in my office I take my phone out of my pocket and fire off a message.

> Beckett: Please tell me you're free tonight.

> Jules: And if I wasn't?

Fuck, she makes me smile. It's been three excruciatingly long days since I woke up in Jules' bed and in that time I've only seen her once. We met for lunch at a Thai spot, where we rated the green curry a 10 and agreed to disagree on the pad Thai. I thought her 9.4 was generous. She, naturally, argued.

> Beckett: I'd miss the hell out of you.

It feels vulnerable to admit that, but it's the truth so I send it anyways.

> Jules: Fine, I'm free. Where are you taking
> me, Beck?

Dammit all to hell when she calls me by my nickname. It lights me up.

> Beckett: I'm in the mood for something nice. Catch 21?

> Jules: So fancy for a Wednesday. This is my excited face...

She sends me a selfie and I smile as soon as I see it. She's sitting at her desk so I can only see her from the waist up. Her hair is pulled into a tight bun and she's wearing a white blouse with the top two or three buttons undone, a pearl necklace and bright red lipstick. Her smile is meant to be a happy one, but I see a sexier-than-hell powerhouse. Jules is hot as fuck.

I stare at the photo, my skin tingling. Then I type out a response.

> Beckett: You must be trying to kill me. Or get me fired. Do you have any idea how hot you look?

> Jules: I'm happy you think so. I can only imagine what you would think of the black stilettos I'm wearing with my skirt. ;)

*Fuck me.*

> Beckett: It would only be considerate to send a photo.

I glance at my door, making sure it's closed. This suddenly feels like a private moment, and part of me feels like I'm breaking company rules by sitting here texting Jules Bennett of The Seaside. Any hesitation flies right out the window when she sends me another photo with the caption, "For your eyes only."

I click on it to see her long, toned legs crossed at the knee, a black skirt that's fitted to her thighs and a pair of four-inch black heels that make my mouth water. Before I have a chance to type back, she sends another message.

> Jules: I'm assuming you'd like me to wear the stilettos tonight?

She must be a mind-reader.

> Beckett: And the skirt. But after dinner the only thing you'll be wearing will be the heels.

I'm so turned on that my pulse quickens as I wait for her to write back.

> Jules: I hope you're a man of your word.

> Beckett: I think you already know the answer to that.

I set down my phone to avoid taking this exchange any further than we've already gone. I can't wait to see her tonight. Then a pain takes hold of my heart as I remember my big news, the promotion. Five weeks with Jules isn't enough. It's too soon for this thing between us to end.

I wipe the thought from my mind. The thing I've worked my ass off for years is finally mine. I got it. I should be on the world's greatest high.

So why do I suddenly feel so uncertain?

---

Jules is making it painstakingly hard, pun intended, for me to walk into Catch 21 without a hard-on. She's wearing the heels, the skirt and the blouse and her lips are painted that red that I like. I'm doing my best not to pull her into the bathroom with me, lock the door and push her up against it. Jules, it seems, is doing what she does best—dialing up every one of my senses.

*How does she look this good after a long day in the office?*

Catch 21 is one of Reed Point's swankiest restaurants. A soft, golden glow from the late day sun streams through the wall of glass accordion-style doors at the back of the room and a warm ocean breeze fills the air.

The hostess seats us at the table I requested, tucked away from the bar area. When you live in a place this small, it's hard not to run into people you know, and I don't think either of us is eager for our dinner date to become fodder for Reed Point's rumor mill.

After our waiter brings us each a glass of wine, I raise my glass to Jules. I want to tell her why I brought her here, to share the news of my promotion, but I can't get the words to leave my lips. Thinking about a scenario that doesn't include Jules is depressing as fuck. I settle for a clink of her glass and a sip of my wine.

We pick up our menus and when I look up from mine, her beautiful green-gold eyes are staring back at me.

"See something you like?" I ask, teasing her.

"I'm drawn to the sea scallops," she deadpans.

I laugh at her dismissal. "I'm thinking a steak."

I'm not used to women who challenge me, but it's one of the things I like most about Jules. Some of the women I've dated in the past have seemed so desperate to make a good impression that I have no idea who they really are. I don't want to be with someone who just looks pretty and agrees with me all the time. I love that Jules is a spitfire, that she's smart and funny and confident, that she can take it and give it back just as good.

Jules sips from her wine looking relaxed and content. Looking across the table at her, I realize that there's nowhere I would rather be. She makes everything more fun, more exciting.

"So how was your day?" she asks, and I know this is when I should tell her about London.

"Like any other Wednesday," I say instead, immediately feeling like an asshole. "How was yours?"

"Better now. I had plans with a bowl of Mr. Noodles and my couch tonight if you hadn't asked me to dinner. But don't worry, they said they'd take a rain check."

I cock my head. "Jules Bennett eats budget, convenience store soup?"

She laughs and the sound of it makes me happy. "I also like boxed mac and cheese. I know, it's scandalous."

I snort. "Who are you?"

We continue to talk over appetizers and dinner, chatting easily, avoiding the topic of business. We talk about her favorite shows, about growing up in Reed Point and our hobbies. She tells me she wants to sail with me and that sounds perfect. The entire night is perfect. Just about.

Jules and I have just ordered desserts when a familiar voice calls my name from a few feet away, making me start. "Beckett, I thought that was you."

I freeze like a deer caught in headlights, then I turn to face my bio dad.

What the hell do I do now?

My back stiffens as my dad approaches the table. It's been a year at least since I saw him last, but he doesn't look much different. He has thick, salt and pepper hair and his eyes are blue like mine. He reaches his hand out, as if to clap my shoulder, but then seems to think better of it and pulls it away. It's awkward, like it always is.

"How are you doing?" he asks, his face flicking from me to Jules and back again.

My jaw flexes. I hate that he's here. I hate that he's getting this small, uninvited glimpse into my life. I flip my gaze over to Jules, who I know is trying to figure out what the hell is going on.

"I'm fine. You?"

"I'm good, Beckett." His expression is cautious. "I left you a message recently, not sure if you got it. But I'd love to have lunch with you one day, or maybe we could go to a game."

"I'm busy with work."

He flinches. "Right. I figured as much."

He taps his two fingers against the table and frowns, the silence between us heavy in the air. "I won't keep you then. It was good to see you. If you change your mind, you've got my number."

He says goodbye and heads in the direction of his table and it's not fast enough. His wife looks uncomfortable as hell in the seat across from him.

When I return my gaze to Jules, she's watching me with a puzzled look on her face.

"You okay?" she asks.

"Yeah. I'm fine. That was—"

"Your dad?"

I study her expression. "How did you know?"

"You have his blue eyes. There's a strong resemblance between the two of you."

I'm not sure what to say to that. I would much prefer to look nothing like the man. We sit in silence for a moment while I try to carefully choose my words. Jules reaches over the table and takes hold of my arm and for the first time since I heard my dad call my name, I feel like I can breathe again. I can't explain it, it's just her effect on me. This woman is everything I've ever wanted with her great big heart and tenacious spirit. She gives me a sense of hope, she energizes me, she's turned my world upside down.

It's never felt easy for me to tell my story, it's always made me feel too weak when I do. For that reason, I never share it with anyone. But sitting here with Jules, I want her to know. I trust her enough to tell her my deepest, darkest secret without hesitation. It comes out so easily it surprises me.

I swallow. "He left us six months after I was born for the other woman he was seeing," I explain. "And it took a toll on my mom. It broke her."

For a second, her eyes close, then when they open again they're filled with compassion and I'm flooded with relief. I've never talked about this part of my life because I don't want to be pitied. I don't want anyone to look at me like they feel sorry for me. The truth is, I grew up with a mom who would have moved mountains to give me the life she thought I deserved and later on with a stepdad who wanted me to be his. My life was good. Is good. There's no need for anyone to pity me.

But the way Jules is staring back me, it's as if she understands me without judgment, as if she truly sees me and not just a guy whose dad didn't love him enough to stay. I've had to work really hard over the years to change the way I see myself. The thing is, it's hard to feel any other way when the pain is so heavy it feels like it's suffocating you.

"I can only imagine how awful that must have been for your mom," Jules says.

I nod. "It gets worse. The woman he left my mom for was pregnant with my now stepsister and he married her and bought a house in Heritage Heights a few blocks from us. I felt so fucking bad for my mom every time we had to run into them."

"That's…awful," she says, her expression showing her shock. It looks like she might have more to say, but instead she takes a deep breath, shaking her head slowly. "Your stepsister. Do you have a relationship with her?"

I shake my head. "Not really."

"And your dad?"

"I saw him once or twice a year when I was a kid, then the summer after I graduated high school he started calling and texting again. I typically don't respond."

"Have you thought about hearing him out? I mean… for your sake, not for his. It might help."

I shake my head. "Nah, I'm not interested."

Jules bites her bottom lip, looking towards the bar like she's deep in thought.

"It's fine, Jules. You can ask me anything."

It's not a question. "You and your mom must be close."

"I would do anything for her, just like she did everything for me. I got a job as soon as I could to help pay the bills. I put myself through college on a full ride. I told myself I would make sure she had everything she would ever need, if my father wouldn't. We were his loss."

Jules reaches across the table, putting her hand on mine.

"I don't know why I'm telling you all of this," I say with a laugh, trying to lighten the mood. "Let's change the subject. I'm ruining our date."

"You're not ruining anything. I love that you shared this with me. I had you so wrong, Beck. I find your ability to be open so likeable."

I bite back a smile, but I know my eyes are sparkling. "I'm happy you think I'm likeable."

"I do. Very much."

We're interrupted when the waiter arrives at our table, setting down two spoons and an elaborate strawberry and cream concoction that Jules selected.

She takes a bite, then closes her eyes in pleasure. She looks sated and blissed, the same expression she wore when I was buried deep between her thighs. Her tongue slips across her lower lip, but there's still a speck of cream at the corner.

Before I can stop myself, my index finger reaches for her lip, brushing over her soft, kissable lips. I bring my finger to my mouth and suck off the cream.

Her eyes blaze right through me. "We might want to order another of these for later," she says, her eyes trailing down to the dessert on the table.

Twenty minutes later, my hand is pressed firmly against her lower back and we're walking out of the restaurant to my car, with a strawberry cream cake to-go.

# Chapter Eighteen

Jules

I take a few steps into Beck's modest apartment. It's ridiculously him, all sleek lines and modern touches. There isn't much color; the couches are dark gray, and the kitchen cabinets are a light wood with black pulls. Everything looks brand new and barely lived in, meticulously clean. It's so very Beck.

He walks straight into the kitchen, where he grabs two glasses and a bottle of red that's sitting on the counter. While he pours, I slip off my heels and tour the family room, smiling when I notice a small but thriving house plant.

I look across the kitchen and catch Beckett's eye. He gives me his casual, hot-as-fuck smile. "I didn't realize you have a green thumb."

He smirks and my heart stops beating for a split second. Will I ever get used to his smoldering looks?

He carries the two glasses to the table. "I'm a jack of all trades."

"Is that so?"

"Well, no, not really. But I can keep a plant alive. I can also change a flat tire, if that counts."

I laugh. "I know who to call."

We sit side-by-side on his couch and he hands me a glass of wine. He's put the dessert from the restaurant on the coffee table in front us and this little voice inside of me wonders what we're going to do with it.

I don't have to wonder long when he reaches for the dessert with his finger. I hold my breath and wait to see what he's going to do next. I watch him bring his finger to his lips. It disappears into his mouth, his lips closing around it, as he sucks the cream from his finger.

"So good," he says, as my heartbeat kicks up.

His eyes pin mine and my breath catches in my throat. I'm desperate for him to come to me, the urge to have his hands all over me is fierce. The softer side of Beckett at dinner was surprisingly sweet, but now I want to be consumed by the cocky, arrogant side of him that turns alpha in between the sheets.

I watch him dip his finger into the cream again. This time he brings it to my mouth, and I open for him, circling my tongue around the tip then sucking his finger into my mouth. I make a humming sound, swirling my tongue around in soft strokes.

He moans and I close my eyes with his finger still in my mouth, all temptress. He's eating it up, his blue eyes practically black with lust.

I release his finger with a pop and suddenly his hand is between my thighs, pushing up my skirt. He urges my hips up and then slides my panties down my legs.

He moves to his knees in front of me and pushes my legs apart, crawling up the length of my body until he reaches my mouth. His eyes are laser focused on me when he reaches around to the nape of my neck, grabs hold of the bun in my hair and tips my chin towards the ceiling. "Your hair wrecks me like this," he growls and my skin flames as his tongue drags a line up the column of my neck.

"I'm going to take what I've been wanting all night, Jules," he whispers into the shell of my ear. I shiver at his words.

I reach down to the buckle of his belt and fumble with it while he sucks on my ear. But when he pushes his erection into my thigh, my hand loses its grip and instead I reach around to his hips holding him as tight to me as I can.

"Take everything, Beck. I'm yours to take."

He stops the glorious sucking of my ear and pulls back so he's inches from my face. His eyes are awed like he doesn't quite believe it, but I meant every word. He's the one man I want to be with. This isn't just two people wanting a quick fuck, this is so much more. I want Beckett. I want him now, tomorrow and the next day after that.

He kisses me softly, his tongue delicately tasting mine. It's enough to nearly break me. The kiss tells me everything I need to know. He wants *us* too. He's all in. I can barely catch my breath when the kiss ends, and his hands are roaming down my chest, unbuttoning my blouse painstakingly slowly. Button by button, while my body sparks with need.

Finally, my shirt is peeled off and my bra follows and I'm spinning as I watch Beckett tear off all of his clothes. We're now both naked except for my skirt that he leaves bunched around my waist while he looks at me like I'm fireworks on the fourth of July.

He kisses a path up my body, sucking each nipple into his mouth, nipping with his teeth then licking the spot with his mouth. My back arches into him as my eyes slide shut, gripping his hair in my hands with force.

"Beck…" I whimper.

"Just wait, beautiful. I'm going to make you feel so good when my mouth is between your thighs," he growls and then his face is right there as he promised, invading me completely with one long, tormenting lick.

He grips my thighs, licking and sucking, then adding his fingers until I unravel into pieces. I cry out his name while he consumes me like I'm his last meal until the very last second and I'm boneless under his grip.

My chest is heaving when he pushes from his knees and stands in front of me, his dick in his hand, stroking himself in long, even strokes. "Stand up for me, Jules. I'm gonna make you scream my name."

"You think you can a second time?" I sass, knowing how it turns him on.

"I know I can."

Before I do what he asks, I sit on the edge of the couch so that he's standing between my legs, his dick at eye-level. I take him in my hand and brush my fingers down his happy trail to his base, his hard-on jerking in my hand when I give him a gentle squeeze.

His breath hitches and he looks up at the ceiling as if he's trying to hold on for dear life, his eyes squeezed shut. His shoulders are rigid, his pecs tight, his body rivaling any professional athlete. It's beautiful.

He's hard as steel when I wrap my hand around the base of his dick and wrap my lips around the head. He whimpers.

I lick and suck, my mouth sliding down his shaft until it hits the back of my throat and he groans. I swallow, my hands tight around the base and look up at him, watching him slowly unravel.

"Jules."

"Yes, Beck," I say after one last lick.

"You have to stop. I'm not going to last."

In a blur, he pulls me to my feet, takes off my skirt then bends me over the couch. I can hear the sounds of him searching his pant pocket then foil crinkling as I turn my head to watch him. He rips the packet open with his teeth, watching me while he does it. I know for a fact I've never seen anything sexier in my life. Then he slides on the condom and grips my hips firmly in one of his hands so hard I'll have a bruise. With his other hand he nudges my legs apart, then he sinks into me in one hard thrust. I groan, gripping the fabric of the couch, holding on tight, sensing Beckett is going to be anything but delicate with me. We move together, curing that ache that floods my bones.

"Oh God, Beck." I say, loving the way he feels. "I feel it every second with you."

He pumps into me in a delicious rhythm, in perfect sync, taking charge like I want him to. It's as good as it gets, hard and deep. I feel like I'm soaring.

I'm holding onto the couch as hard as I can when he bites my shoulder, then soothes the skin with his mouth. Goosebumps scatter across my skin while his hand reaches around to the place between my thighs I want him most, circling the bundle of nerves over and over. He sucks and nips the skin of my shoulder while he drills into me faster and harder and deeper.

My skin tingles and pleasure erupts as we free fall over the edge together, falling so fast my vision goes black. Tremors move up the length of my body, my heart trembling on the outside of my chest for Beckett to see.

He moans my name, I feel him shudder inside of me, then he collapses against my back.

The next morning, I wake up to coffee and a caramel apple croissant and Beck sitting on the edge of his bed in running shorts and a snug black athletic shirt. He sips from a Dream Bean cup and rubs the arch of my foot through the duvet.

I sit up and take a sip. "Less murder-y already." I sigh into the lid. "Did you run out and pick this all up?"

"I made a mental note that you are definitely not a morning person so I ran out to get you sugar and coffee. I bought half a dozen croissants in case you wanted to stay tonight too."

"Presumptuous, are we?"

"I prefer optimistic," he teases, moving my foot massage up to my ankle. I take another sip and flop my head back into the pillow. "I like making you happy, Jules. I want to be the guy who spoils you."

My God, this man and the things he says. "You already are."

"And you're incredibly smart and it's such a turn on, and you're beautiful and you give me shit."

I chuckle. "You like that I give you shit?"

"I fucking love it. It's so fucking hot," he says. "And I want you in my bed tonight, right where you are now. I like you here around my things. I hope I'm not scaring you?"

Sitting up, the sheet falls from around my chest, and I go to him, cupping his face in my hands. We're face to face, his hands on my neck. "None of it scares me, Wonder. I like being with you."

He shivers. "I like being with you too, beautiful."

And when he smooths back my hair and kisses my forehead, my heart takes flight and soars. "The plan for this morning. We shower, I drive you home to get dressed for work and I drop you off at your office. Then if your calendar is open, I'll cook you dinner."

He stands and peels off his sweaty T-shirt while I blatantly stare at his sweat-glistened chest, his stiff pink nipples, his abs. He sees my eyes glued to him. It doesn't stop me. His lips curl up in a half smile.

"What will we have?" I ask him. "For dinner, I mean."

"My award-winning bacon-wrapped pesto pork tenderloin," he says, smiling an I-know-exactly-how-to-win-you-over grin. It's working like a charm. "It might help me get the girl."

Too late, I think to myself, I'm already his.

## Chapter Nineteen

**B**eckett

I barely recognize myself.

It's been a week since that night with Jules at my apartment, and I'm sitting at a high-top table with the guys at The Mill, a brewery not far from the beach. I'm only half paying attention to the conversation, my attention instead on the text conversation I have going with Jules. Laughing to myself at her last smart-ass response, it occurs to me that I'm deliriously happy.

I feel happy all of the time. Because of her.

Waiting in line for coffee when the coffee is for Jules is fantastic. Brushing my teeth in the morning next to her, there's nothing better. Checking a text and seeing her name on my screen feels like euphoria. I've always been wary of giving someone too much power over me, because I have never wanted to risk them deciding that they're done and walking away, taking my heart with them. With Jules, though, it's different. It's a risk I'm willing to take.

She's all I think about when we're apart, which hasn't

been often, and when we're together I can't believe my luck. She likes me too. I'm one lucky S.O.B.

Now I'm texting her a photo of my nachos. I've rated them a 9.3, possibly the best I've ever had. Pickled onions, black olives, loads of guacamole. Of course, she has to point out that the stretchy cheese is the reason why they taste so good. This time, I think she's actually right.

Grayson kicks me under the table and gives me a get-off-your-fucking-phone look. "Should we give you some privacy?" he says, nodding at my phone in my hands.

*Fuck. I'm that guy.*

I slide my iPhone into my pocket.

"Can you lay off the dating apps for two hours," Grayson says with a smirk. "And who swipes right on you anyways?"

I flip him off. He laughs.

"Someone who knows a catch when they see one. I'm the definition of what every woman wants. But what would you know about that?" I tease back.

Grayson rolls his eyes while Zane, who is sitting next to me, sets his beer down and says, "I think our boy got laid last night. He's way too fucking cheery."

I crack up. "Is it that obvious?" There's no point in denying it with these guys.

The guys go wild. "Knew it," Carter says, and Grayson flashes me an atta-boy smile. I've been friends with Zane and Carter since middle school and introduced them to Grayson a few years ago. The four of us are like brothers and I always look forward to our weekly boys' night at the pub.

"You haven't been able to wipe that stupid smile off of your face all night. So you *did* swipe right" Grayson says.

"I've never swiped right," I argue. Dating apps have

never been my thing. I prefer to meet someone serendipitously. Call me old-fashioned.

"Then how did you meet her? Tell me so I can find one too," Zane says.

"You make it sound like you're shopping for a puppy," Grayson says, shaking his head like Zane is a lost cause.

I try to skirt Zane's question. Jules and I haven't told anyone about us, and I want to talk to her first about going public before I give the guys the details.

"I met her at a work thing."

Across the table, Grayson stares at me. He tilts his head slightly to the right with a look on his face that says, *I'm not buying what you're selling*, but he leaves it. I can already tell, though, that I have some explaining to do tomorrow at the office. There's been something happening with Grayson and Sierra since Miami, so we definitely have a lot to talk about.

"That's all we get? Come on, Beck. We need more than that," Zane says, like a dog wanting a bone.

"I really like her. There. Give me the gears. I know you want to."

"Not getting the gears from me," Carter shrugs. "I hope it works out. How long have you been seeing her?"

"Only a couple of weeks." I can't tell them the exact timeline, which would add a few weeks to that number. Grayson's smart. He would figure it out in a second. "It's crazy how much I like her in such a short amount of time."

Carter leans back in his barstool. "I don't think it takes long to know you like someone, especially when you have chemistry. You can feel that vibe pretty quick."

I nod, feeling happy that he gets it. "It's just shit timing, though. I haven't told you guys the news."

"You've got news?" Zane asks.

"He sure does. Beck is the man! The motherfucking man!" Grayson announces to the group, drumming his hands against the wood bar table.

Grayson is the only one who knows about London, thanks to a company-wide email that went out this week congratulating me on my promotion. I haven't told Jules yet either and I feel like shit over it.

"I got the promotion at work. I got London."

"Holy shit. Congratulations, man," Zane says, patting my shoulder.

"Thanks. I'm not sure it's sunk in yet. I'm still wrapping my head around the move."

"When are you outta here?"

"In four weeks," I choke out, hoping the guys don't catch the heavy emotion in my voice. "It fucking sucks that I met this girl and now I have to leave."

Zane looks optimistic when he says, "If it's meant to be, it will be."

"Not this time, buddy. But thanks for the glass-half-full pep talk," I tell him.

When the server returns with our drinks, Grayson lifts his glass in a toast. "Let's drink to London and to the guy every woman wants."

"To the ultimate catch," Carter adds, throwing my words back in my face.

"Damn right," I say, then I lift my glass to my mouth.

One drink turns into two, and the guys and I shoot the shit over hot wings and burgers. I'm stuffing a fry into my mouth when my phone vibrates in my pocket.

> Jules: Paying my bill. Thought about you the whole night.

My face heats. It's just a text, but her words feel so

damn good. I hide my phone under the table and type back.

> Beckett: Let me fix that. Come to my apartment. I'll meet you there in thirty.

> Jules: Tempting.

> Beckett: I have the best ideas. So, it's a yes?

> Jules: Will you rub my feet and then feed me croissants and coffee in the morning?

> Beckett: I'd like to feed you something else…

> Jules: You are so naughty.

> Beckett: I am… and you love it.

> Jules: Yes. Yes, I do. See you soon.

Ten minutes later I'm paying my bill when Carter asks, "Sunday good for a ride? You gotta get it in while you still can, Beck. I think your bike riding days are history. Do they have trail riding across the pond?"

"Shit, I didn't think of that. You may be right. We better get out a few times before I go."

I take a last, long sip of my beer, avoiding the reality of my move: leaving Reed Point, my friends, my family. Jules.

I clap each of them on the back before calling it a night. I appreciate their friendship, the fact that they've always supported me and have my back when I need it. And as much as I'd love to stick around a while longer, I want to see Jules more. Brush my teeth at the sink next to her. Spoon her into my side to warm her up when we get into bed and then fuck her six ways to Sunday.

And when I get back home, that's exactly what I do.

---

The next morning, I take Jules to a coffee shop Grayson recommended for breakfast before work. It's about 10 minutes outside of Reed Point so I figure we won't run into anyone we know. Jules doesn't want her family knowing that we're seeing each other. We order breakfast bagels and their dark roast and find a table. The only table left. The place just opened last month, and they've obviously done one hell of a job with advertising.

The floor is a black and white mosaic tile, the counters are a blonde oak and there's a neon sign above the counter that reads *Morning Drug*.

She sits across from me in one of her business suits and a pair of red heels, her hair down in waves around her shoulders. She brings a change of clothes with her now whenever she stays the night.

Jules wiggles her brows. "We could get caught you know."

I arch one brow, giving her a doubtful stare. "You act like that would be okay?"

She sets down her coffee cup after taking a deep inhale of the rich aroma. "After last night and this morning, I'm too happy to care."

I brush my shoulder twice, acting like I'm the man. I delivered her three mind-scorching orgasms so I'm feeling pretty good too. "Good. And I feel the same. It was pretty spectacular. Who knew having sex on top of a washing machine could be that good?"

She tosses me a pretty grin and I'm so fucking happy

until I remember what I need to tell her. I need to tell her about London.

"You know, I came this close to telling my sisters-in-law and two of my best friends about you last night." She holds her index finger and thumb up in the air in almost a pinch. "They know I'm seeing someone."

"They know about us?" I want the answer to be yes. I want her friends to know who I am. There's nothing I want more than for everyone to know that she's mine.

"I just told them things were new, but I didn't say with who."

My shoulders sag a little. "I talked about you last night too. Same thing. Grayson was there so I kept your name out of the conversation because of how it would—"

"Look," she says, finishing my thought. She looks deflated. "It looks bad. I just wish it didn't."

"Jules, there's something else I need to talk to you about," I add, hating what has to come next as I lock eyes with the woman who has changed my whole world in a matter of weeks. My heart is running a 10-mile sprint in my chest.

"Okay," she says, trying to act calm. I feel nothing remotely close to it.

I'm about to drop the bomb, when my eye catches sight of a tall, dark-haired guy at the counter.

"Is that your brother?"

I can only see the back of him but it's obvious it's Parker. I don't know what I was thinking. We live in a small fucking town. We've been lucky but we were bound to get caught sooner or later. *Shit.*

Jules' wide eyes move from me to Parker and back. She nods, but the tone in her voice is surprisingly calm and even when she says, "It's him."

"What do you want to tell him? It's up to you, Jules. You call the shots."

"He'll suspect," she says. "Besides, I'm not going to lie to him. If he asks, we tell him the truth."

"Which is?" We haven't actually had the conversation of what we are to each other and this isn't the way I wanted to have it. But we need to be on the same page if we're going to tell her family about us. There is also that little problem of me moving halfway across the world that will very likely change everything.

She locks her eyes with mine. "What am I to you, Beck?"

"You're mine," I say simply. Maybe this isn't the time to do it, and I'm probably putting the cart before the horse. I'm not sure she would even want to give us a shot if she knew about London. At the very least, though, I want her to know how I feel. She is mine.

I'm this close to saying *And I'm yours if you want me.* But her eyes lift, and she waves, and I know she's made eye contact with her brother.

Five seconds later, Parker is standing beside our table.

"Hey, Parks," Jules says with a slightly strained smile.

There's a moment of awkward silence until I stand and offer him my hand. "Good to see you, Parker. It's been a while."

Parker looks surprised, and I can't blame him. He's probably trying to figure out why the hell I'd be sitting in an out-of-the-way coffee shop with his sister. He looks at Jules, then back at me, then waves a hand between the two of us, "You two are here… together?"

Jules stands. "We were actually just leaving. Need to get to work," she says. "Walk you out?"

In the parking lot, Parker doesn't go directly to his car, but instead stands looking at us like he's waiting for an explanation, and like he may start flipping tables if he doesn't get one soon.

Maybe he won't think it's such a terrible idea that Jules and I are together. Why shouldn't we have the chance to be happy? Jules is his sister, but she's also an adult, capable of making her own choices. I'm done worrying about what others think. I'm done sneaking around. The fact that Jules and I work at competing companies shouldn't matter. We're both responsible, hard-working adults and that's not going to change.

I only hope Parker sees it that way too.

It's time to face the music.

Jules goes first.

## Chapter Twenty

Jules

I thread my fingers through Beckett's hand and kiss his cheek. "Let me talk to my brother. Go to work, I'll call you later."

He squeezes my hand in his and smiles, and that fuels me to have this conversation with Parker. It's the first of a few that I know I'm going to have.

Beckett extends his hand to Parker, who seems to shake it somewhat reluctantly. "It was good to see you. Jules told me about the baby on the way. Congratulations, man."

My brother nods and thanks him. Beckett kisses my cheek and I watch him go down the sidewalk.

"Beckett Taylor, Jules? Seriously? How long has that been going on?"

Wow. He's not waiting a second. "Look, Parks. It's new."

My brother laughs. "He's the guy isn't he? The *new* thing you've got going on."

I rub my finger over the tattoo on my wrist and straighten my spine. "He is. I guess that's obvious."

"Obvious? I'd say so," he says with an incredulous look on his face. "Maybe it was all the cheek kissing and hand holding that gave it away, or the way his eyes were all over you. How's that for a list?"

"Listen, I know it's not ideal—"

"Not ideal?" he says, thrashing his hand through his hair. A car races by us, weaving through traffic and we both look out to the street before returning our attention to one another. "Of all the guys in Reed Point, you had to pick Beckett fucking Taylor? You couldn't have picked a guy that works in finance or a weatherman? He works for our number one competitor, Jules."

I flinch then quickly straighten my spine, determined to make him see that I've thought this through carefully and Beck and I aren't such a bad idea after all. "I didn't choose him, Parks. It just happened."

"How? How the hell did you two start dating?" Parker scrubs the side of his jaw. He's clearly not happy.

I sigh. "It started in Miami, at the conference. No, let's backtrack. We spent time together at the conference, but nothing happened until we got home, and I ran into him at Dream Bean. We just clicked from the start."

His forehead creases. He looks as serious as a heart attack. "Man. Does Dad know?"

"Nobody knows. You're the only one."

My brother shoves his hands in the pockets of his suit pants and looks up towards the sky. "I'm just worried, Jules. I saw what Alex did to you and it was rough." I flinch at the mention of my ex but shake it off. "And Beckett has a reputation. Have you ever seen him with the same woman twice? The guy doesn't do serious. I don't want to see you get hurt again."

"They're not even remotely alike," I argue. "Beckett is a good guy. You would like him."

Parker lifts his eyebrows, skepticism written all over his face. "The jury's still out."

"I'll be careful, Parks. I promise."

My brother opens his mouth to say something, then thankfully bites his tongue. He raises his hands in surrender. "Jules, I'm here if you need me."

"I know."

"Just be careful," he says, his eyes pleading. He's doing the big brother thing, and I can't blame him.

"I told you I would be."

I take a much-needed breath, happy to have the conversation over with. Parker is a protective older brother and although his advice isn't always what I want to hear, I know his heart is always in the right place. He cares about me and only wants to see me happy. The same can be said of all three of my brothers. I expect one more conversation like this with Liam, which will be worse. Then my dad.

For now, I count today as a win and I'll worry about the rest of it later. I have a busy day at the office. I need to be on my game.

"Come on, I'll drive you to work," Parker says, leading me to his car.

Once I'm at the office, I sit at my desk and begin to type out a text to Beckett. I hit send and then hurry to the boardroom, where I have to attend a meeting that was called by my dad. A meeting that ends up taking four hours. And when it's over, my head is pounding, my vision is blurry and I'm nauseous. A migraine: something I've suffered from since I was a kid.

The next thing I know, my dad is driving me home, then later his strong arms are helping me into my bed.

Then the room goes black.

# Chapter Twenty-One

Beckett

Back at the office, I can't sit still. I'm like a caged animal pacing the floor as I wait to hear an update from Jules about her talk with her brother.

I need a distraction, something to take my mind off of the endless waiting, so I walk the hallway to Grayson's office, a stress ball in my hand. When he looks up from his computer, I toss the ball at him and he catches it with the grace of a pro-leaguer first baseman.

"Nice one," I say. He tosses it back, aiming the ball at my head, and I catch it with one hand. "I'm like a cat, buddy. My reflexes are super-human."

"You're something all right," Grayson laughs, sitting back in his chair and crossing one ankle over his knee. "What brings you to my neck of the woods? Oh wait, let me guess... are you ready to spill the beans on your mystery girl?"

I sit down in the chair across from him. "I need your advice."

"Ask Coach Grayson. I got you. What's going on?"

I swallow, readying myself for his reaction, "The girl I'm seeing is… Jules Bennett."

His expression turns astonished. "No shit. The plot thickens. Jesus Beck, did this all start in Miami?"

"Not exactly, but that's where I started feeling something for her." I tell him the rest of the story, starting at Dream Bean where I ran into her and ending with today and her brother.

"Parker Bennett is a legend in this town and the Bennetts are tight. I bet you rattled his cage when he saw you with his little sister. You could have sold tickets to that encounter."

He isn't wrong. Everyone in Reed Point knows about the Bennetts. They're one of the wealthiest families in the city and their reputation is solid in the community. The fact that Miles is one of Hollywood's most famous actors is another reason people stop and take notice. It's another sad reminder that I don't fit in with them.

"Fuck off, can you just be serious?"

He mimes a new serious face, swiping his hand over his expression. "So how did Parker take the news of you banging his sister? I'm guessing not well?"

"I think he was still getting over the shock when I left the two of them to talk. He looked like he wanted to push me into oncoming traffic."

"You think it's because you work for The Liberty?"

"What else would it be?"

I pause. I've been so busy worrying about Jules' family's reaction to our relationship, I haven't even given thought to what my team here at the office would think about it. My boss only gave me the promotion a week ago. Rocking the boat now, so soon, seems like a bad idea.

I sigh. None of it will matter anyways when Jules learns about my move.

As if he's read my mind, Grayson asks, "How does she feel about you leaving for London?"

"That's the thing. I haven't told her."

He shakes his head. "There's your first mistake. You're not being honest. You need to tell her, and you need to do it quick."

I toss the ball in my hand in the air and catch it. "I know."

Grayson isn't wrong. I know that I need to tell Jules about my promotion. I need to tell her how strong my feelings are for her, and that I'm serious about us. Or is it too soon to be having big conversations like that? I'm clearly going out of my mind.

"Damn, you really like her," he says, looking at me with surprise.

"I really fucking do," I agree, scrubbing a hand through my hair. Grayson smiles sympathetically.

"Then the question you need to ask yourself is how bad do you want her? Can you picture yourself without her? And if the answer is no, then I think you know what you need to do."

"And what if London is a deal-breaker for her?"

"Then you need to figure out how much you're willing to give up to get your girl."

---

When I walk back into my office after a late-morning meeting, there's a text waiting for me on my phone. It's from Jules. I sit at my desk and swipe the screen to life with a nervous feeling in my gut.

> Jules: Sorry about this morning. My brother
> isn't normally that grumpy. He drove me to
> work so I didn't have the chance to call you
> and now I'm running into a meeting. I'll call
> you when I'm done.

That's it? That's all she's got for me? I've been waiting for over an hour for her to tell me that everything is okay. And this is what she writes? I'm growing gray hairs by the second.

Thankfully, a second text pops up just as I finish reading the first.

> Jules: And Beck, stop stressing. (I know
> you are ) Everything is okay.

She already knows me so well. With a sense of relief, I flop back in my chair. But I still feel… off.

I have faith that Jules and I can figure out the work stuff. It's complicated, sure, but we can get people to see that we're right for each other. What I can't figure out is how we make a relationship work when we're living in two different countries on opposite sides of the world.

This is a move I've been waiting a long time for. I can't ask Jules to move to London with me—Jesus, we've only been together for a month. Long-distance sounds like a horrible form of torture, but maybe we could try? But with the time difference and the crazy hours we'll both be working, that seems virtually impossible. I rub both hands over my face, frustrated. We jumped the first big hurdle by coming clean to Parker, but a future with Jules seems farther away than ever.

I roll up my shirt sleeves to my elbows and get to work, trying to take my mind off of Jules. I have a meeting with my team later in the day that I need to prep for.

I make it to the meeting, but I'm scattered and a little

grumpy and I know everyone in the room feels it. I'm short with Grayson when he asks me a simple question and he catches my eye from across the room a little later with a what-the-fuck-is-wrong-with-you look on his face.

This sucks.

It's not his fault that my mind is playing tricks on me, hopeful one second then stuck in a fog of doubt the next. It's not anyone's fault but my own for not being honest, for not telling Jules where my heart is. For not figuring out a way to make this work.

Hell, this morning, waking up beside Jules, I had the feeling that maybe my life was changing for the better. And now my mood is in the dumps.

Because the reality is that I have to leave, and Jules has to stay… these are the cards we've been dealt.

When my meeting is over, I know I need to apologize to Grayson. We hang back as the rest of the team files out.

"I'm sorry I snapped," I tell him.

He sets a hand on my shoulder. "No need. I kinda like seeing Mr. Perfect all fucked up over a girl."

I scrub my face with my hands, embarrassed that he sees right through my bad mood.

"I'm grabbing a turkey clubhouse from the deli. I'll get you one too. Food is the cure for everything." He squeezes my shoulder and smiles. "Trust Coach Grayson," he says proudly, walking through the door.

With my apology accepted and food on the way, I do feel a little bit better.

I'd feel a hell of a lot better if I had the answer to my love life.

Wait… did I say love?

———

I'm home still waiting on a phone call or text from Jules. It's 7 p.m. and I haven't talked to her all day, except for the two short texts she sent me this morning. My calls have gone unanswered and my texts remain unseen.

Screw it, I call her again.

"Hey, Beck," she says when she answers, her voice raspy and a little faint. I rest my beer on the coffee table and lean back against the cool leather of my couch.

"Are you okay?"

"I just woke up. Had a terrible headache but I think it's better. I'm sorry I didn't call you."

"Don't be. I'm sorry you felt crummy. Did it come on at work?"

"It did. It sort of hit me out of nowhere. My dad had to drive me home after lunch. It was a doozy. I took some painkillers and he put me to bed. I've been out ever since."

*I wish you would have called me.* I want to be the one who makes her feel better. "Do you get headaches often?"

She stifles a yawn. "More when I was a kid. I guess I've grown out of them for the most part. I'll sometimes get one when I'm really tired or stressed but I'm fine after some sleep and a couple of Motrin. Now I just feel really groggy."

"Do you want me to let you go?"

I hear her yawn and the rustling of pillows. "No, I'm fine. Besides, I've kept you waiting long enough."

My heart springs in my chest. I hope it went as well as her text this morning leads me to believe.

"How did it go?" I take a sip of my beer and wait for her to tell me.

"It actually went better than I expected. He was upset at first, nervous that you would hurt me like Alex did—"

*Fuck.* "I'm not going to do that, Jules. You know that right?"

"I know," she says. "But he's my brother and he worries, that's probably never going to change. We're close, Beck. Me and all of my brothers are. He wants me to tell my dad. He thinks we should tell the rest of the family too… if we're serious about being together."

She moans like she's still in pain.

"Are you okay, beautiful? Can I bring you something?"

"I'm fine, Beck. I should go to bed early and I know that won't happen if you're here."

"You're probably right," I answer, a little disappointed. "I'll let you go and get some rest, but before I say goodbye, I want you to know I'm serious about being with you. You mean a lot to me."

"Me too. It's the same for me. And Beck…"

"Yeah?"

"I want you to meet my family."

## Chapter Twenty-Two

Jules

The next morning, I shower, get dressed, and then drive to my parents' house. I need to talk to them about Beck. Once I made the decision, it was like I couldn't tell them fast enough. I want them to know that I've found an amazing man who's sweet and kind and charismatic, who treats me the way I know they would want me to be treated. Who makes me happier than I've ever been. Who I'm falling for way too fast.

Worry crowds my mind, but I try to bat the anxious thoughts away and focus instead on the sounds of the beach in the distance as I drive towards my parents' house.

Needing a distraction, I crank the volume on an Old Dominion song playing on the radio and turn up the air conditioning. It's a typical hot July day and I plan on making the most of it later with Beckett on the boat. I'm excited to take him out and show him why I love sailing so much. I can't wait to spend the day on the water, just the two of us.

But first I need to convince my dad that I can date

Beckett without it affecting my performance at work. I'm not sure what I will do if he has a problem with us. I can't walk away from Beck, but my relationship with my father also means the world to me. I need to find a way to have Beck in my life, the job that I love *and* the respect of my father. I need to find a way to have it all.

I also need to reign in my emotions before I see my parents—especially my mom. She can read me like a book.

I park my Bronco outside of my parents' house and take one last, steadying breath before going inside. But before I do, I take out my phone to text Beckett. I talked to him earlier this morning to make plans for a boat day, but he doesn't know I've come here to talk to my parents.

Jules: I have a confession.

Beckett: You think I'm irresistible and sexy and incredible in bed? Am I right?

Jules: So right, but that's not what I wanted to tell you. I'm at my parents' house. I'm going to tell them about us.

Beckett: Yeah?

Jules: Yes. Are you okay with that?

Beckett: More than okay. Then you're mine today. I hated not falling asleep with you last night.

Jules: Same here. I miss you.

Beckett: I miss you too. I can't wait to see you. Oh, and beautiful?

Jules: Yes, Wonder?

Beckett: I can't stop thinking of you.

I shove my phone in my purse and realize that I'm smiling, something I've been doing a lot more lately because of Beck.

Hitching my purse over my shoulder, I walk towards the doors of the home I grew up in. At almost 10,000 square feet, the house is bigger than what anyone needs, but my mom has it decorated to feel warm and inviting. There are plush area rugs, large, comfy couches and dozens of family photos on display. When we were growing up, the place was always packed with our friends from school, who knew they were always welcome to come over uninvited. I haven't lived here in a while, but it will always feel like home.

Rather than knock, I open the door and let myself in, following the scent of my mom's baking to the kitchen at the back of the house.

I call out her name and she turns to face me, removing her glasses and setting them on the kitchen island. "My sweet doll! How are you?" she says, walking towards me with a smile on her face, her arms reaching for me.

"Something smells good," I say. The scent of sugar and chocolate wafts through the air. "Are you making cookies?"

"I am. When you called me this morning and told me you were stopping by, I started to bake a batch. I know they're your favorite."

I give her a hug then hear my dad's footsteps behind us. "JuJu...how's my girl?"

He closes the distance between us and presses a kiss to the top of my head. "You look better. How's your headache?"

"Much better, Dad. Thanks."

"I hate to see you like that," he says, smoothing my hair with his hand. "I'm happy you're feeling better."

I smile because it's moments like these that remind me how lucky I am to have these two for parents.

My mom removes a plate from the cupboard and puts a handful of warm cookies on it. The three of us sit around the kitchen table talking about work and the fundraiser my mom is chairing this Saturday night. She has stacks of papers and to-do lists laid out on the island, every last detail no doubt planned out to perfection.

There's a pause in the conversation and my dad looks over at me, his eyes narrowed. "Is everything okay?"

I couldn't hide anything from them if I tried. They know me too well.

He leans forward against the table with a look of concern now on his face. "Juliette, what is it?"

I suck in a breath. "I have something I want to tell you."

"Okay, sweetheart." His voice is gentle. "You know you can tell us anything. We are always here to listen."

"I know." I pause, staring down at my hands, which I'm wringing in my lap.

"Tell us who he is, honey."

My eyes widen like I've just witnessed a car accident. "How did you know?"

Mom smiles. "Sweetheart, you're my baby. I know when you get this way it's usually over a guy. Now, your dad and I are waiting. Who is the man that has you all tied up in knots?"

I feel my cheeks flame. "You're right, I met someone. I like him a lot. He has the most beautiful blue eyes, he's thoughtful and kind and I want you to meet him."

Thoughts of Beckett tumble around in my mind, the

softness of his lips when he kisses me, the way his eyes linger on mine, the way my heart races when I'm near him. The way I know I've found the right one this time.

"Okay," my dad says with a sigh.

My mom glances at my dad then back to me. "Sweetheart, that's wonderful, but why does it feel like that's not really what you came here to talk to us about?" my mom says, a knowing glint in her eyes.

My stomach twists, "It's just… complicated."

"Most things in life are," my mom says. "Can you tell us a little about him?"

"Well, he isn't really a stranger to Dad," I say, shifting my eyes to my father. "You know him. It's Beckett Taylor… from The Liberty."

Dad's brows pull inward. He's quiet for a moment and I search his face for some hint as to how he's feeling but I come up short. He's expressionless. I start to panic, worried about what he might say next.

*He's not right for you.*

*You work for The Seaside. He works for The Liberty.*

*He could never make you happy.*

*It could never work.*

"Well, I don't know what you expect me to say, sweetheart."

I sigh. While I had hoped they might just give us their blessing, I knew it was a long shot.

"I know, Dad. I know it isn't ideal—"

"What do you mean, Jules? Why is it not ideal?" he asks, staring at me in confusion. I'm sure my expression mirrors his.

"We work for rival companies. *And* we compete for contracts. It's a conflict to date a man from the opposing team."

"I guess you could look at it that way," he says. "But do you like him? Does he make you happy?"

"He does," I say fingering the tattoo on my wrist.

My father lets out a breath. "Sometimes we have to look past the hurdle in order to see how we clear it. At the end of the day, all of those details can be worked through. If he makes you happy then you owe it to yourself to give it a shot."

I exhale. "I wasn't expecting to like him so much."

"Love works like that, baby," My mom clucks her tongue. "Sometimes it sneaks right up on you."

I think about Beckett, and how he makes me feel. How being anywhere with him is my favorite place to be. I can't wait to see him later today.

"Do you think about him all the time?" my mom asks, interrupting my thoughts. I nod in response. "And when he walks into a room, do you get goosebumps?"

A smile takes over my face. "Every time."

"Then you need to take that leap," she says, standing from her chair, rounding the table to squeeze my shoulder and kiss my head. "You have to give love a chance, baby."

"Invite him to the gala this weekend. Your mother and I would love him to be our guest. We have room at our table," my dad says beside me.

"I'll ask him, Dad. Thanks."

"My work here is done then," my dad says, getting up from his seat. "I'll leave you two to chat. I have the drum set I bought Hudson just about put together and I want to have it ready for him when he comes over tomorrow."

"A drum set?" I laugh. "Liam is going to lose his mind. You realize there's no way he is going to go for that, right?"

"He's my first grandchild and I'll do what I want," he says with a wink. "I love you, JuJu. I'll see you tomorrow.

And I look forward to hopefully talking to Beckett on Saturday."

He walks away, leaving me with a giant lump in my throat.

I should have known my dad would have reacted like that. Michael Bennett is a good man—he always knows what his family needs. He's protective but not smothering, just supportive and encouraging.

The room is quiet as my mom pours herself a cup of tea and I sit and think about everything my parents just said. It's an easy silence, one I'm used to after years of confiding in my mom. We talk about everything, and she always makes time for me. Not everyone is as lucky as I am to have a mom who listens without judgement.

My mom puts a cup of tea on the table, pushing it toward me, and then sits down beside me. I grab a cookie and take a bite as she looks at me with love in her eyes.

"You worry too much, sweetheart," she says.

I shrug. "I've always been this way."

"You're just like your grandmother. She was the same," she says, then takes a sip of her tea. "Just remember that things have a way of working themselves out."

I nod, gazing off through the kitchen window to the pool and expansive back yard.

"My point is, spend less time worrying and more time enjoying life. If you think he's the one, take a chance. Fall hard."

"How can you say that when you know nothing about him?"

"I know a lot about you, Juliette. And if you think he's great, I trust you."

*Take a chance. Fall hard.*

The words repeat in my mind.

"Now. Don't you have better things to do on your day

off than drink tea with your mom?" she teases. "I'm glad you stopped by. Go enjoy your day, baby."

I grin. I can't wait to see Beck and tell him about my morning. I leave the house feeling hopeful.

I want a relationship with him. I want to bring him to family dinners. I want him to know my brothers, and all of that feels possible now.

But hope can be a scary thing. Sometimes the more we want something, the more excruciating it is when we can't have it.

As I ease my car down the long stone driveway, getting to Beckett is the only thing I want to do.

---

When I pull into the marina, Beckett is leaning against his car, one leg crossed over the other. He's wearing shorts and a black T-shirt, a baseball cap and Ray-Bans—and a smile that does crazy things to my libido. We're in no rush to get back, so we have plenty of time to go for a cruise and anchor somewhere.

He meets me at the trunk of my car with a kiss, catching me in his arms and holding me close to him. I lift his sunglasses from the bridge of his nose, needing to see his blue eyes. I will never understand how the entire world feels like it stops spinning when his eyes meet mine. His turquoise-blues pull me in like a wave crashing into shore.

Whenever we're together, I feel like I'm walking on water and today is no different. I start my day wanting him and end my day the same way. And I want this feeling all the time.

"I missed you last night," he says as I relax into him. His fingers comb through my hair. "You feeling better?"

"I'm fine. No headache. I missed you too."

He smiles a slow smile and bends down to kiss me. It feels good. He smells good. I want more than a kiss.

But this isn't the place, so we pull apart to unload the trunk of my car.

He carries the small cooler I packed, and we walk the dock to my dad's slip. We pass a few people lounging on the bows of their boats, stopping to say a quick hello before carrying on. Beckett follows me, boarding the boat and then helping to get us ready to leave.

Soon, I've backed out of the slip and we're cruising. It's just the two of us. It's sunny and warm, with blue skies overhead—the perfect early summer day.

Beck slides up behind me in the captain's seat, resting his hands on my warm shoulders, both of our gazes on the ocean and the island formations in the distance. I spot my favorite of them, Twin Islands, where I plan to drop anchor.

"I've been coming to that spot right there," I say, pointing to the landmark about 100 yards away, "since I was about five years old with my family. My brothers and I would swim or kayak or play board games with my parents. It's one of my favorite spots in the world. It amazes me how 20 years later it still takes my breath away."

In my eyes, Twin Islands was one of the most magical places I'd ever been. When the tide moves out, it reveals the rocky runway of beach that connects the two tiny islands. On some days, the way the sun lights up the island, it makes it feel like some place far away and tropical.

"It's beautiful," Beckett says, kissing my shoulder, the heat of his body radiating off of him. "Is it where you're taking me?"

"It is. I thought you'd like it."

"I do, but I like anywhere with you," he says kissing my

neck this time. "I also like watching you command this boat. It's sexy as hell. You have a real talent."

I laugh, "A talent is ballet dancing or archery. I'd be terrible at both of them."

"One does require a bow and arrow, which I wouldn't trust you with."

I crinkle my nose. "Hey! You just shoot the pointy stick into the red circle, right? How hard can it really be?"

"Really damn hard. And I believe the pointy end is the arrow and the red circle is the target," he laughs. "Nevertheless, you look good driving this boat. I'm impressed *and* turned on. Thank you for bringing me out here."

"I'm glad you like it. I was hoping you would like boating as much as I do," I say, pulling back on the throttle so the boat can idle. "This is where I'm the happiest and where I like to spend most of my free time, so you enjoying it too is important."

He gathers my hair in his hands, and it feels good. "What else is important to you, Jules?"

*You.*

I pause, taking my time with the question. "My family. My job. A few good friends. Someone to sail with," I say, smiling back at him over my shoulder. "What about you?"

"My mom and my sister; it's important to me that they're taken care of. My job too, obviously. Bike riding keeps me sane and now… you, Jules. You've become so important to me. I want to take care of you too."

My heart beats a little harder at his response.

"You do?" My whole body heats from my face to my toes. I sit up straighter, finding the breeze above the windshield to cool my skin.

"Yes," Beck says. "I want to do things for you. I want to give you things, take you places, share my secrets with you."

"Your secrets?" I ask, turning to look at him. "What kind of secrets are we talking about?"

He hesitates. "I can be closed off with people. You make me want to change that. You're the kind of girl that makes me want to be better."

"You don't need to be better. You're one of the best people I know, and I can be myself with you. It wasn't like that in my last relationship. I gave up pieces of myself for Alex. I became what he needed, sacrificing parts of who I am. I won't do that again. And with you, I don't have to."

He moves closer to me, until I feel his breath against the back of my neck. His arms gently grip the sides of my jaw from behind me, his thumbs brushing softly behind my ears. "You never have to be anyone but yourself with me." He kisses the top of my head. "I hope you've figured that out by now."

His hold on me makes me shiver. "They know, Beck. My parents are okay with us. So much so, they want you to come to a fundraiser they're hosting this weekend."

I glance over my left shoulder at him, my lip trapped under my teeth. He's quiet for a long moment, as if he isn't certain what to say. I wish I could he see his eyes through the lenses of his sunglasses to give me an inkling of what he's thinking.

He swallows before he speaks again. "Is that what you want, Jules? For me to come with you?"

"Of course, it's what I want—but you have to want that too. My entire family is going to be there. My brothers, their partners. It's a lot, and I'll understand if it's too much for you right now," I tell him. "My parents support us. Everyone else will too. And honestly, I would want you to be my date even if they didn't."

He chuckles, kissing the side of my cheek. "I don't need to be convinced. I'm a sure bet when it comes to you.

I want to be your date. Do you actually think I would turn down a chance to be with you?"

I smile, tipping my head up looking for his lips. He reads the cue, and his lips meet mine. Pulling back, I slip off his sunglasses so I can see his whole face and I'm surprised at the expression in his eyes. There's an underlying tension there that I wasn't expecting.

"Jules?" he says, looking at me intently.

"Mmm?"

"We need to talk," he says, and his voice sounds as serious as a heart attack.

My stomach nosedives to the bottom of the boat. Long seconds pass while my heart is lodged in my throat. My family finally knows about us, and they don't object to our relationship. So why is Beck still so worried?

I tell him we should anchor first, and after 20 more minutes of slow cruising I find a suitable spot. I ask Beckett to watch the large tree on the island that I'm using as a gauge to make sure the anchor isn't slipping. He does what I ask of him and we're both quiet as we move around the boat. It's an uncomfortable silence, which I'm not used to with him. My mind runs wild with thoughts of what it could be that he wants to talk about.

When the boat is secure, we sit together on the leather pad at the bow of the boat and I'm not sure if it's the anticipation of what Beckett has to say to me or the cool, crisp air that has the tiny hairs on my arms standing upright.

Beckett lets out a long breath. He scrubs the back of his neck with his hand, then exhales. "I got the job, Jules. The job in London is mine."

# Chapter Twenty-Three

Beckett

My entire body is wound tight as I wait for Jules to say something, a knot quickly forming in the center of my throat. I take a deep breath, trying to read her expression. Hoping for the best.

But she's quiet—too quiet—and it does nothing to ease my nerves. *Shit.* Will she end things between us right here and right now, after we just figured things out with her family? I reach for her hand. "Jules, what are you thinking, baby? Say something."

Her gaze holds mine, her eyes darker than they usually are. We haven't stopped staring at each other since I dropped the news on her. "I'm happy for you. I really am, Beck. Congratulations."

There's an ache in my chest, in my bones, at the thought of us ending. The thought that something so good may be over before it even had a chance to begin. "Thanks—"

"I'm not surprised," Jules continues. "You're good at

your job and I know it's been your dream to land London."

*You're my dream too.*

"I know you understand what my job means to me," I tell her. "Because I know your work is really important to you as well."

She pauses for a second, like she's weighing her words, then just nods her head.

"What does this mean for us?" she asks, bringing us right to the part of the conversation that matters most.

"I don't want to let you go."

I wait with my heart in my throat for what she'll say next. Like a movie reel, our first kiss outside her house flashes through my mind. I'd dreamt about that kiss for weeks before I found the nerve to make it happen. And it blew every one of my fantasies out of the water.

"I don't want you to either," she answers softly, but there's worry in her eyes. "What do you want, Beck?"

An easy smile finds my lips. "I want you," I answer easily. "I want us. You are the most beautiful woman I've ever met. You make me laugh, I feel lighter when you're around. I'm the happiest I've ever been. I want *you*, beautiful."

I take her hand and kiss her cheek chastely, meaning every word.

"I want you too," she says, and I wonder, not for the first time, how the most incredible woman I've ever met wants me too. I've known a lot of women, and not one of them compares to Jules Bennett.

I'm still looking into her eyes when a wave of relief washes over me. That feeling I get when her eyes lock on mine; the one that feels like I'm speeding down a highway, windows down, 300 miles an hour.

Her cheeks flush pink, the way they do whenever she's nervous or excited. The way they do when she sees me.

"I need more of you, Jules. Your mouth. Your body. Your big, beautiful heart," I finally say. "We have some time before we need to figure things out."

"When do you have to leave?" she asks softly.

"In three weeks," I tell her. Jules' face falls.

"That's so soon," she says, then takes a deep breath. "And what will we do then? In three weeks?" she asks, and I wish I had the answer. The truth is, I don't have a clue.

"We'll figure it out together," I say threading my hand in hers. "I don't have the answers right now, but we will figure it out. Until then, I want to be with you. I want to keep doing what we're doing." As soon as the words leave my mouth, I know how much I'm asking of her. This is going to be hard on both of us, but the alternative is too devastating to consider. I have to believe we'll work things out.

"Okay?" I ask, our eyes sharing a brief, vulnerable moment before I smile and bring our joined hands to my mouth, kissing the top of her hand. "Then we'll make a decision from there."

She leans in and brushes her knuckles along my jaw. "I want you any way I can have you," she says. "Just please, Wonder, don't break my heart."

"Never." It's the truth, and I need her to believe it.

I pull her between my legs so she's sitting with her back against my chest. Then I just hold her. The world around us disappears and it's just Jules and me. I'm relieved that she's saying yes to us, but I know that finding a way for us to be together is going to be damn hard. I also know that I will find a way.

I have to.

For the first time in my life, I have everything I've ever

wanted. My dream job, my dream girl. Jules and I are good together and the understanding of that feeds my soul.

"Will you still be my date to the fundraiser?" she asks.

I hold her closer, kissing her hair, squeezing her with my hips. "You sure as hell aren't going with anyone else."

Her green and gold eyes sparkle like the ocean under the sun, a million tiny diamonds reflected in them. I tip my head to the sky, taking in the sea air, the trees, all the beautiful green. I soak it all in. London has always been where I've wanted to be, but I will miss Reed Point and all of this beauty.

"Well, I could go with—"

"Not a fucking chance. You're mine, Jules. No one else's. Do you understand? I don't want another man even looking at you," I say, nuzzling my face into her neck. "We'll arrive together. Everyone will know you belong to me because I will make it obvious, and then we'll leave together, and I'll take you home to my house and fuck you senseless. Understood?"

"I'm yours, Beck. No one else's," Jules murmurs. "I want everyone to know it. And I love it when you fuck me senseless."

And suddenly I can't wait for Saturday night.

"So tell me more about the event you're taking me to."

She starts talking a mile a minute about the Children's Hospital that the gala is raising money for. She's clearly excited about the event, and it's cute as hell. She tells me about the work she's done to help her mom with the evening, the long days her mom devotes to the cause.

"It's impressive, Jules, what your parents do for the charities they believe in. And now what you're doing too. I'm proud of you."

"I want to make a difference, like my parents have. It's important to me to help others, to give back to the community that has supported me for years. My life has been easy, I've never wanted for anything. I just feel like I owe it to a higher power or something like that, to give back as much as I receive. Sorry, I'm rambling. It just means a lot to me."

"You're amazing, you know that?"

I growl into her ear. This beautiful, smart, witty, funny woman is mine and everything about her drives me wild. Her passion, her smile, her intelligence. I love that she's so in charge in the boardroom, but she still loves it when I'm possessive with her when we're alone. And yes, I fucking love being dominant with her, but it's so much more than great sex.

"I think you're giving me entirely too much credit. Hold on… wait here a second, I'll be right back," she says, getting to her knees and going inside the cabin of the boat.

A few minutes later she returns carrying a tray piled with cheeses and meats, olives and crackers. She sets it down on the sun bed between us, taking an olive and popping it in her mouth.

"Dig in," she tells me. "You're hungry, I could hear your stomach growling."

It's so like Jules. "This is incredible. So are you. Thank you."

We spend the rest of the day swimming off the boat and lying in the sun. More than once I have to remind myself to live in the present, not to go down the rabbit hole of worrying about what's to come.

Before it's time to head back to the marina, I pull Jules into my lap and take her face in my hands. I want her to know how much she means to me with this kiss.

Softly, I run my thumbs over the edge of her jaw and press my lips to hers. Gently. I kiss her slowly, savoring her, taking my time. She kisses me back the same way and it feels like a tangle of desire and need and hope. Saying goodbye to Jules doesn't feel like an option, but I know in a few short weeks I may need to do just that.

Until then, I will enjoy her.

Make the most of our time together.

And miss her when I'm gone.

The next day, I stop by my parents' place to have a conversation I haven't been looking forward to. Now that I got the promotion, I need to tell them that I'm leaving. I can't put it off any longer.

When my mom hears the news, she hugs me and tells me she's so proud of me. She insists that the tears in her eyes are happy ones, but I know better than to believe her.

Pete pats my shoulder and asks me all of the important questions: the expectations of my new position, the salary increase, the benefits.

Bean wants to know how often I'll be coming back home to visit.

I'm relieved to have it all out in the open, and I'm thankful to them for handling the news so well. I didn't expect anything less.

I'll miss them, but now that it's official I am excited about the prospect of London. It's a new start and a huge opportunity in a beautiful and vibrant city. I can create the life I've dreamed of.

And then I think about Jules.

It must be written all over my face, because my mom reaches across the table and places her hand gently on my wrist.

"Is everything okay?" she asks, frowning.

"Everything's fine," I tell her, because I know it should be. I just landed the job I've been dreaming about for years. I should be incredibly happy.

"You've got something on your mind," she says, not fooled by my half-hearted insistence that all is well. "Wanna talk about it?"

I scrub my hands over my face. I haven't told my mom about Jules yet because I didn't want to get her hopes up. But I don't want to keep it a secret.

"Yeah, maybe I do," I say. "I'm seeing someone, and I really like her, and it's probably going to have to end because I'm moving."

"You're seeing someone?" my mom asks, and I don't miss the note of excitement in her voice. "How long has it been?"

I clear my throat. "Not long, but long enough to know that she's amazing and funny, really smart and... perfect for me."

"And does this amazing, smart, funny girl have a name?"

"Jules," I tell her. "It's funny, she works in the hotel industry too. Her family owns the Seaside Hotel chain."

Her eyes widen. "Don't the Bennetts own the Seaside?"

"Yeah. I don't know her family well, just through work. But they've invited me to a charity dinner this weekend so I'm hoping to get to know them a bit better then."

She nods. "You're going to go?"

"I am. Jules wants me to be her date."

"Are you sure that's the best decision, Beck? Meeting her family when you're leaving so soon? If things with her really are temporary, you might want to put some more thought into this."

"You're probably right, but I'm hoping we can find a way to make things work." I say, rubbing a hand over the back of my neck.

"Long distance isn't easy, but people do it all the time.

If the two of you really want to be together, you'll find a way. Just be careful with her heart, Beck."

I hate this. I hate that I'm falling for her. I hate that I've grown attached to a girl who can never be mine. Time is moving too fast, and soon I'll have to leave, leaving her behind. And we're both going to get hurt. Just the thought of hurting Jules gives me a physical pain in my chest.

"Mom, I'm so worried, every day, that I'm going to mess up a good thing. What if Jules is the one and I never get another chance again at love? And for what? A job? I have a good job here."

She exhales. "You've been working for this opportunity for a long time," my mom reminds me. "You need to think long and hard about this and decide if you could live with yourself in two years if you gave up on your dreams. And for the record, sweetheart, you're handsome and intelligent and there will be a line-up of women in London who want to date you."

I sigh. "But they won't be Jules, mom."

"No, honey, they won't be Jules."

She pauses, searching my eyes. "Do you think you love her?"

I look down at my hands, then back at her. "I think I do."

"I'm sorry, Beck," she says, with sincerity in her eyes. "I wish I had the answers."

"I wish I met her in London," I grumble, face in my hands.

"You could ask her to move *with* you."

"Yeah, I guess I could, but she's really close with her family. She loves her job working with her dad. She would never move."

"It's understandable," she says, picking a strawberry from the plate in front of us. "Can we meet her?"

"I don't know if that's a good idea, Mom. You've been waiting for me to bring a girl home for 26 years. You'll be just as attached to her as I am."

"Well then, we could nurse our broken hearts together over Facetime." She half smiles and half laughs.

"That sounds pretty awful," I groan. "Any more advice for me?"

"Make your decision with this," she says, pointing to my chest, to the heart that beats double time whenever I think of Jules. "Not with this." She points to my forehead. "It will always point you in the right direction."

I smile at her, grateful, because she's right. I'm used to listening to my brain—hell, I've kept my heart closed off for years. But it's time I change that.

Jules calls me a few hours later while I'm at the grocery store buying tomatoes for the pasta I plan to cook for her tonight. I have my phone sandwiched between my ear and my shoulder while I sift through the pile of Romas for the best ones.

"How did your parents take the news?" she asks. I hear the shorebirds in the distance, the rigging of sailboats. She's working at the marina today.

"They took it fine, I guess," I tell her, filling a plastic bag with tomatoes. "They've known for a while that I've had my sights set on the job, so I think they half-expected it."

The line goes quiet for a second. I put a head of lettuce into my basket and frown. I hate that we're even having this conversation. I hate that it's hurting her.

"I'm at the store buying what I need to make you dinner tonight."

"You are?"

"I am."

"What's the catch?" she asks, a smile in her voice.

"I'm the catch, baby," I say, and I swear I can hear her rolling her eyes.

"You okay to have an early dinner?" I ask her, chucking basil into my basket, then garlic, and finally a cucumber.

"If I don't get a better offer."

"Impossible," I say. "Who could be better company in Reed Point than me?"

"I've always thought Mr. Katz down at the hardware store is kinda cute. Plus, I'm pretty sure he could fix the leaking faucet in my apartment."

I laugh. "He's like 70 years old. And don't worry, Jules, I can fix your pipes."

"I don't even know what that means," she snorts. "But you manage to make everything sound dirty."

"You love it. Okay, get back to work. I'll see you tonight," I tell her.

Ending the call, I slip my phone into my pocket, then immediately stop short.

My dad is standing 15 feet away, staring at me with a surprised look on his face. And now he's heading my way. *Great.*

"How are you, Beckett?" he asks, pulling his shopping cart beside mine.

"I'm fine," I say. "How are you?"

I'm so tired of this loop we're stuck in. It happens every time we run into each other, and it feels like shit. I'm angry. He's awkward. I'm a dick to him. He walks away, shoulders slumped. I leave feeling worse.

I'm tired of it, and I want it to change.

Being with Jules, being this happy, it makes everything else matter less. I don't want to keep allowing this conflict and drama into my life.

My dad's hands grip the handle of the shopping cart so

hard his knuckles are turning white. "I'm okay," he stammers. "I'm fine. I—"

"Listen, maybe we could grab a beer or a coffee one day soon?" I say, a little surprised at my words.

If I'm surprised, my dad is absolutely shocked. He looks like I just told him the earth is flat and aliens have invaded Mars.

"I…yeah…I would like that. I'm available anytime."

"Okay, I'll text you a date and time."

"I would like that," he repeats, knocking his fist against the handle of the cart. "I'm really glad I ran into you today."

"We'll talk soon," I nod, walking away, feeling a nervous energy that quickly fades to relief. Putting my past behind me, coming to some sort of peace with my dad, is something I've needed to do for a long time.

On my way to pick up a box of spaghetti, I wander through the bakery and remember that it's Jules' birthday soon.

I need to think of a gift, to plan something really special for her. I wonder if I should try to take her away for the night. I also wonder if it will be the last birthday we spend together.

On my way home from the store, I watch the beach go by, the restaurants and shops of First Avenue. A month from now, I'll be walking through crowds of people in the busy streets of London. Moving into a new flat, meeting new people. I should be excited, but the familiar knot in my stomach clenches tighter.

I think about curling up to Jules at night in her bed, about bringing her coffee when she wakes up to ease her murderous early morning moods.

Then my mind returns to London, and I wonder if the new job and new life waiting for me there are enough to make me happy. I've wanted to climb the corporate ladder for as long as I can remember. I've always wanted a chance to chase my dreams in a big city, to feel challenged and inspired.

*But none of it matters if I don't have Jules.*

I turn my gaze away from the beach and try to find some perspective. The job in London is meant to be. I need to stop questioning that.

Later that night, Jules and I drink wine on my patio, then we shower and watch a movie in bed. I lean back against the headboard, Jules in between my legs, her cheek on my chest.

I hold her tight, kiss the top of her head, try to memorize what she smells like.

I'm going to miss nights like these.

I'm going to miss her.

## Chapter Twenty-Four

Jules

I must be crazy.

I agreed to three more weeks with Beckett. Twenty-one days, then I'll have to say goodbye and watch him board a plane to London.

And it won't rip my heart right out of my chest because I'm not already falling for him… at least, that's what I'm telling myself.

When Beckett asked me if we could keep seeing each other, *yes* seemed like the only response. But there has been a hurricane of mixed emotions swirling in my gut ever since. Of course, I'm happy for him. His dreams are coming true, and that's what I want for him.

But it hurts like hell knowing that very soon I'm going to have to let him go. I try to convince myself otherwise, but deep down I know that Beckett is going to break my heart when he leaves Reed Point, and I'm going to have to figure out how to put the pieces back together. I'll need to find a way to live without him.

Which will be… well… impossible. I shouldn't have

agreed to this plan, but I like him too much to say no. It's not smart, but it's true. I feel this magnetic pull to him that I've never felt before. I can't ignore it, no matter how hard I try. It's going to be so hard to say goodbye to him, but that's exactly what I will have to do. Beck needs to make the move and I need to be here. And now I need to find a way to live with my decision.

It's the first day in a week that I haven't spent with Beck. We've fallen into a little routine: we wake up together, shower and then he drives me to work with a stop for coffee along the way. After work, we meet for dinner— sometimes at a restaurant, or we cook at one of our apartments or pack a picnic and head to the beach. Later, we fall asleep in each other's arms after the most incredible sex of my life. Some days it doesn't seem real, like I need to pinch myself, every minute better than the last.

Tonight, Beck went out with the guys and it feels strange, not being with him. I'm trying to stay busy instead of moping around my house, so I've persuaded Bella to have a girls' night in. We're in sweats on the couch, face masks applied, digging into a junk food feast.

"What possessed you to buy the rainbow Twizzlers? Everyone knows they're monstrosities. They ruined Twizzlers' good name," Bella says with a grimace, reaching for the Sour Patch Kids instead.

"I like them," I say twirling one in my hand. "It's like eating a rainbow."

"If you like chewing on wax. I swear those things are 95 percent wax, 5 percent some weird chemical syrup. They're gross."

"Works for me," I say, shrugging my shoulders. I bite off one end, make a dramatic *mmm* sound, then wink at Bella. She stretches a foot across the couch we're sprawled over and nudges my leg.

"You're disgusting," she tells me.

"I love you too," I grin.

My phone buzzes, and when I pick it up, I see Sierra's face smiling at me from the Facetime app that's lighting up my screen. I sigh, sitting up to answer it. I know it's time that I face the music and tell her about Beck. I've ignored two of her calls in the past couple of weeks and have replied to her texts with either an emoji or a two-word answer. I've essentially been hiding from Sierra because I don't want to lie to her about Beckett and I, but I also don't want her to tell me what a terrible idea it is to date a guy who works for our biggest rival—the very same guy I accused of slandering my family's business. An accusation I now know is false.

I put the show on pause and accept the call.

"Holy shit, you scared me," Sierra says laughing, her palm over her mouth. "I wasn't expecting to see you slathered in mud like you just lost a *Survivor* immunity challenge."

I laugh. Bella shifts on the couch, so we're shoulder to shoulder.

"I'm here too," Bella calls out, squishing her face into the screen next to mine. "Hi Sierra, can you please tell Jules how shitty rainbow Twizzlers are?"

Sierra scrunches her face in obvious disgust while I roll my eyes and change the subject.

"Don't listen to her. She fell today and hit her head," I tease, casting a sideways look at Bella. "I miss you, girl. How've you been?"

"I'm good, but you would know that if you weren't so busy doing God knows what. Where have you been, Juliette Bennett? I don't remember the last time I talked to you."

"I know, I know. I'm sorry. I've been a little busy," I say. "Also… I'm seeing Beckett Taylor."

*There.* I said it. Ripped it off like a Band-Aid. I hear Bella choking on her Diet Coke beside me as I inwardly turtle at the world's worst delivery.

"What?" Sierra shrieks.

"I know. I'm sorry, I should have told you sooner, but we were keeping it under wraps until I broke it to my dad. I wasn't sure how he'd react, finding out that I'm sleeping with the enemy, so to speak."

"Oh my God, Jules, please don't tell me you broke it to him that way," she laughs, shaking her head. "I'm not surprised, though, that you two are together."

"You're not?"

"Gosh no," she says. "It was so obvious that you were totally into each other in Miami."

"We were not."

"Come on, Jules. Anyone with a pulse could see that something was going on there."

I lean back into the couch with the silliest smile on my face. My skin prickles, and I can still feel the places where Beckett touched me last night.

Bella flicks her thumb at her bedroom door and mouths, *I'll be in my room,* taking the bag of Sour Patch Kids with her as she goes.

"Fine. I thought he was handsome, and I liked spending time with him, but nothing happened in Miami."

"So, when then?" she asks.

"It started two weeks after I got home from our trip." I fill her in on the rest and she listens with her face propped in her hands, eyes wide, eating it up. "I'm just not sure it's the best idea," I say leaning back against the couch and propping the phone against my thighs.

"Why not? It's not because of your dad, is it?" she asks.

Sierra understands how seriously I take my job. She knows about my insecurities working under my father, my need to be taken seriously.

"It's not my dad. He's happy for me." I sigh. "Beckett is up for a position in London, so he could be moving very soon. I already feel like it's going to crush me if he does."

"You really like him, huh?" Sierra asks.

Like might be an understatement.

"I do." I rub my temples with my fingers. "Just say it, Sierra. Say I'm an idiot for falling for someone who could be moving a million miles away. Tell me I'm going to get hurt at the end of this and I must be crazy to put myself through it."

She stares back at me with her eyebrows raised, looking unimpressed.

"What is that look for?" I ask.

"It's the look I think you need to see. You've found someone you really like, Jules. There's always a way to make things work. You just have to want it bad enough. Finding love is the hard part, and you seem to have that part worked out."

"Kinda like you and Grayson?"

She blushes, smiling. It's an expression that I am very familiar with these days. *I can't seem to stop.*

"Don't go changing the subject," Sierra says, eyes narrowing.

"Why not?" I ask, feigning innocence.

"Because I'm not even sleeping with Grayson," she says, her voice dead serious.

"But you *want* to."

She shrugs her shoulders but stays quiet. I stare at her through the phone screen, waiting.

"Fine," she says, finally. "We've hooked up, but it only happened once. Nothing is going to come from it."

"I knew it," I tell her, thinking there must have been something in the water down in Miami. "But why can nothing come of it? Are you sure about that?"

"I'm not sure about anything right now, if I'm honest," she says. "I thought I was happy being single, sow my oats and all of that." She waves her hand in the air. "But now I'm not so sure. Fuck, Jules, I'm a mess."

Sierra and I have talked about this before. I know her position on dating—or, more accurately, *not* dating—and I haven't been able to change her mind on the subject.

Sierra thinks she has her whole life to settle down and get married, so for now her preference is to date guy after guy, have a good time. The last thing she wants is to settle down. And who am I to say she's wrong?

But that was before she met Grayson. He's the total package: smart, driven, *very* good looking, and a great guy. It might be wise to not let a catch like him get away.

We shift the conversation away from our complicated love lives. Sierra complains about this guy she works with who brings tuna fish sandwiches to work every day and tries to sell her on pyramid schemes. I tell her about Liam and Ellie's wedding that is coming up soon, the bridesmaid dress I'm wearing and details of the hotel we'll all be staying at in Hawaii.

I wonder, privately, what it would be like to have Beckett there with me. Would we fly out together? Would he watch me walk down the aisle in my dress, never taking his eyes off of me, not even for a second?

Sierra knocks me out of my daydream when she tells me she has to run. We end the call, and I get up from the couch and walk to the kitchen to get something to drink.

I wonder how Beckett's night is going, then my thoughts drift to the fact that he'll be meeting my family at the gala on Saturday evening. My *entire* family. My stomach nose dives to my toes.

*It's not a big deal,* I say to myself. *They're going to love him.* How could they not?

Bella emerges from her bedroom, flops back onto the couch and gives me a five second warning before she starts up *The White Lotus* again. "Come on," she hollers. "I'm dying to see if Kai gets caught stealing the jewelry."

"I'm on my way."

# Chapter Twenty-Five

Beckett

Jules and I arrive at The Seaside for the charity gala, where we are met with opulence the minute we step into the upscale lobby. Italian marble, crystal chandeliers the size of small planets and gilded ceilings of silver and gold. I have to admit, The Seaside is a gorgeous hotel. Sure, I've stepped foot in here before—you need to know what your competition is doing—but being here with Jules Bennett on my arm is making me look at her family's hotel with new eyes.

The hotel's business model is similar to The Liberty's: highly personalized service, a location in the heart of the city, distinctive architectural features and high-end amenities. It's a destination for travellers who want luxury. The Seaside delivers on that front. My eyes can't help but scour the space, but I remind myself that I'm here as a guest and I need to turn off the business side of me, as hard as that might be.

We enter the ballroom, where we're greeted by a server

in a black suit carrying a tray of ornate finger foods. A well-dressed crowd of Reed Point's elite mill about the space, which is beautiful with its white linen tablecloths, champagne fountains and a stunning custom cocktail bar.

I lace my hand through Jules', wanting the entire room to know she's here with me. She's so gorgeous I can barely stand it. Her yellow dress dusts the floor, and her hair is pinned back into a knot at the nape of her neck. Her eyes are smoky, diamonds glitter in her ears, and her gold heels make her four inches taller and easier to kiss. Jules glows like rays of sunlight. She's the kind of sexy that makes heads turn. She'd look sexy in a paper bag, but Jules in a floor-length fitted gown is deadly.

We walk towards the silent auction tables where most of the guests seem to be lingering. Jules scans the room looking for her parents, spotting them in the corner of the room, champagne glasses in hand, mingling with guests.

Jules squeezes my hand before we make our way over to them, crossing the dance floor. When her mom's eyes land on us, they appear to light up and a smile spreads across her face. She excuses herself from her conversation and walks straight towards us. Her husband—a tall, handsome man in a black tux, follows a few seconds later.

"Jules, you look beautiful, honey," Mrs. Bennett says, hugging her daughter before stepping back and turning to face me. "And you must be Beckett." She surprises me by extending her arms out and pulling me into a hug. "Grace Bennett, Jules' mom. It's a pleasure to meet you."

"It's all mine. Thank you for inviting me," I say. "This is quite the event."

"It only took all year to plan, so thank you. I'm expecting to raise a good amount of money for the Children's Hospital tonight. Now, let me get you both something to drink," she says, motioning to a waiter with a silver tray. She lifts one champagne-filled flute for me and another for Jules. We clink glasses, taking a sip.

"Oh sweetheart, meet Beckett," Grace says to her husband, who has joined us. She rests her hand on his arm. "Beckett, this is my husband, Michael. I believe the two of you already know of one another."

He leans in, shakes my hand in a firm grip, gives me a smile. "I've heard good things about you through the grapevine. You know how the hotel business is. All good things, of course. The Liberty is lucky to have you from what I hear."

"Thank you, Mr. Bennett. That means a lot coming from you. I appreciate that."

"Please, call me Michael," he replies quickly.

I nod, a little in awe that I'm here chatting with Michael Bennett in *his* hotel.

"The hotel is incredible. You have built a franchise I really admire."

"Thank you," he smiles. "I have Jules, here, to thank for a large part of that. She's incredible at marketing. Her mother and I are proud."

I nod, looking down at Jules. I completely understand why she makes them proud—I feel the same way about her too.

Someone calls Grace's name, ending our conversation. She promises to catch up with us later. Jules parents helped put me at ease, but now it's time to meet all three of her brothers. I take a deep breath, mentally preparing myself. All good. It'll be fine. I hope.

Jules spots them standing by the bar, and I look over to find six sets of eyes on us. My heart beats a little faster in my chest as we make our way across the room to them.

Jules' brothers—all tall, built and dressed in expensive suits —stand together, holding tumblers in their hands filled with what looks like whiskey. They look at me like they're trying to shoot daggers at me with their eyes. Next to them are three beautiful women who thankfully seem a little happier to see me.

I'm not worried, I remind myself. I can handle Jules' brothers.

"Jules!" one of the girls says, stepping forward to embrace her. She hugs her as best as she can with her very pregnant belly in the way. "You look beautiful. I love this dress on you. Damn you, I look like a friggin' house, my feet are stuffed sausages in these heels, and I have heart-burn already. I hate being pregnant."

Jules laughs. I'm guessing this must be Ellie, Liam's fiancée.

She confirms it when her eyes turn to me next and she introduces herself before glancing back to the brother I'm guessing is Liam, who looks like he's deciding whether he should murder me with his bare hands or use a blunt instrument.

I glance at the rest of them, each of them staring at me with expressions varying from suspicion to curiosity. They look like they're sizing me up and if I wasn't confident in my relationship with Jules, I might actually be losing my shit.

"This is Beckett," Jules says, acting as casual as she can as she introduces me to Miles first, then his fiancée Rylee, followed by Parker and his wife Olivia.

Olivia smiles, then wraps me in a hug. "We're excited to meet you."

"I'm excited to be here and meet you all as well," I say, downing the last sip of champagne in my glass. A waiter making the rounds takes the empty flute from my hand a second later.

"So, Parker tells me you work at The Liberty," Liam says, cutting straight to the chase.

"Go easy on him, Liam," Ellie tells him, jabbing an elbow lightly into her fiancé's side.

"That's right, I do," I answer with what I hope is a confident smile.

"And are you from Reed Point?" Miles asks next.

I try not to flinch at his question. I may not have grown up in their world, but I've mastered the art of talking my way through any awkward situation. But it's still a reminder that while I have a great job that pays six figures and I own a condo and a nice car, growing up in Heritage means that I'm far from Bennett status. "I'm not," I answer. "Born and raised in Heritage Heights. I moved to Reed Point three years ago, but my family is still there."

"Do you have any sisters or brothers?" Olivia asks.

I tell them about Bean, we talk about their upcoming weddings, then Miles tells us all he's getting another drink at the bar.

"Can I get you one?" he says, lifting his near-empty tumbler towards me.

"That would be great. Thanks," I respond, feeling Jules' hand slide to my lower back. She leans into me, and I can feel the warmth of her hand through my suit jacket.

For the most part, the conversation is going well. Liam looks less rage-y and Parker seems to have warmed up. Miles is a guys guy, friendly, and we bond over Major League Baseball. Most of the time his eyes are all over Rylee anyways, so he's too busy to worry about sizing me up.

"Can I offer you an hors d'oeuvres?" a waiter asks, holding a silver tray of Ahi tuna wontons.

Ellie looks at the tray and frowns.

"What's wrong, Ells?" Jules asks.

"Oh, just another thing I can't eat. Who makes these rules anyways and says pregnant woman can't have tuna?" She narrows her eyes at Liam, who's mid bite into a wonton.

"I saw a waiter with a tray of avocado bruschetta that looked good," I say, trying to help. "I can wave one down for you."

"They aren't avocado, Beck, they're pesto," Jules says.

"They're definitely avocado," I tell her.

Ellie looks confused. "So they're pesto *and* avocado?"

"No, they're just avocado, and they're delicious," I say through a laugh. "I've already had two."

"Avocado pesto?" Parker winces. "It sounds gross."

"The tuna is good," Liam says with a grin at his fiancée, then wipes his mouth with his napkin. Ellie glares at him. "Enjoy it, honey," she tells him sweetly. "It may be the last thing you ever eat."

She groans. "I just want food I can actually eat, and a drink. God, I would kill for a cup of coffee."

"I know," Olivia agrees, her hand rubbing circles on her belly. "I do miss coffee."

"Ellie snuck some of mine this morning," Liam says.

"What are you, the flipping coffee police? I had a sip!" Ellie crosses her arms over her chest like she's pouting.

Liam wraps his arm around her side, pulls her close and kisses her cheek.

"I think the wrong guy went to the bar," Rylee says, watching as guests take pictures with Miles. He seems used to it, stopping to sign a few autographs too.

"I'll never understand why anyone would want a photograph of that mug," Liam says with a smirk as he watches what's turned into a bit of a spectacle.

"Beats me," Parker agrees. Rylee just shakes her head, but I can see she's trying to suppress a laugh.

It's clear from the way that Jules talks about her family that they're a close-knit group, but seeing it up close—their easy banter and obvious love for one another—makes me happy that she has all of these people in her life who have her back.

Fifteen minutes later, Miles finally returns with a whiskey in each hand. He gives one to me, clinks my glass, then brings the amber liquid to his mouth.

"I guess you must be used to that by now?" I say, nodding in the direction of the bar where Miles was just swarmed.

"As used to it as one can be." He shrugs. "It comes with the job."

"Miles, tell him about the time that woman named all three of her sons after you," Parker says.

"Jesus, isn't that grounds for a restraining order?" I say. "That would also be confusing as hell."

Jules is grinning, everyone else is laughing and for a moment, it feels like I fit right in.

I may just be winning her family over.

---

A little later on, we're asked to take our seats for dinner. Ellie and Olivia excuse themselves to the washroom and Jules decides to go with them.

I watch her walk away, weaving between guests, lighting up the ballroom like she's the damn moon. I could stare at her for hours, there's nothing more I'd rather do. In this moment, I can't think of a better way to spend my time. My groin stiffens.

Her brothers and I make our way through the ballroom, Miles patting my shoulder before heading in another direction, stopping again for a photo with a fan.

Liam, Parker and I find our table, which is set for 10. I take my seat and Jules soon slides into the chair to my right. Her parents join the group a few minutes later, but it's not long before Grace heads to the podium and gives a speech about the night's fundraising efforts. Her words are eloquent and moving, and when she's finished the room erupts in applause.

Then waiters descend on the room carrying trays of filet mignon, scallops, braised short rib ravioli and grilled vegetables. As we eat, I answer a bunch of questions from Jules' family. Her dad asks me about graduating MIT, Parker wants to know what trails I ride, Olivia asks about my favorite spots in Reed Point. They seem curious to learn more about me, but they're welcoming and warm and I'm grateful to them for that. Jules' mom even invites me to Sunday dinner at their home tomorrow.

Then the band starts to play, the lights dim, and guests start to fill the dance floor.

"Excuse us, everyone," Jules' mom says, pushing from her chair. Her husband takes her hand and leads her to the dance floor.

"What are you waiting for, Parker?" Liam asks, leaning back in his chair with a smug look on his face. "You know you're dying to get out there and show the 60-somethings your moves."

"Yeah, Parks," Miles laughs. "Don't be so shy. Get out there and show everyone what you learned in middle school PE class. You should have seen this guy, Beckett. The only kid who actually showed up to Mr. Donovan's extra credit swing dance lessons. I'm pretty sure he came home and practiced with Mom in the living room every day after school."

Olivia shakes her head. Parker flips him off.

"Teacher's pet," Liam says over the rim of his rocks glass.

"Missed opportunity, idiots. Who was the guy who had his hands all over the cheerleading squad?" Parker says, leaning back in his chair, crossing his leg over his knee. "Me. That's who."

"Classy Parker," Olivia says, shaking her head at her husband. "And you think you know someone."

My arm is stretched over the back of Jules' chair as I watch her brothers take jabs at one another. They only stop when Olivia drags Parker to the dance floor. Liam and Ellie excuse themselves to talk to a friend, and eventually Jules and I are left at the table on our own. I look at her, smiling my best mischievous grin while I trace my fingers down her spine, landing on her lower back. "I didn't realize how much I love the color yellow until tonight."

She smiles playfully, leaning back in her seat just slightly against my touch. I draw my name with my fingertip over the yellow fabric of her dress, wishing it was her skin under the pad of my finger instead of the silk.

The heat between us is simmering. I'm thinking about later tonight when I have her all to myself. I'm thinking about her dress, whether I want to take it off of her slowly or shred it to pieces, tearing it from her soft skin.

"I see that look in your eyes, Mr. Wonder. You need to behave. My brothers are here, or did you already forget?"

"I don't know why you're acting like I'm being thrown to the wolves," I say. "Your family and I have been getting along just fine tonight."

"They're at a 1500-dollar-a-plate gala," she points out. "They're on their best behaviour. You're not in the clear just yet."

I lean in and press a kiss to her cheek. "I can handle them. Everything is fine."

"Suit yourself," she says with a shrug.

I stand up and pull Jules from her seat, whisking her to the dance floor, where I spin her around in a half circle and bring her into my chest. She giggles then draws her head back so she can look me in my eyes, and I kiss the laugh from her mouth. It's a brief, chaste kiss but I feel it down to my toes.

The band plays "At Last" by Etta James and we sway in the middle of the dance floor to the slow song, her hands wrapped around my neck, mine held tightly to her waist. We gaze at each other, and my pulse quickens. Jules is always beautiful but tonight, in that dress, under the soft glow of ballroom lights, she's breathtaking. So beautiful it physically hurts.

I spin her then bring her back into me, then do it all over again while she smiles and laughs. My hands drift up and down her back and her hips push up against mine while my lips find her cheek or her jaw whenever they can.

"So you can dance too?" she murmurs. "I'm impressed."

"They don't call me Mr. Man Wonder for nothing," I tease.

Jules moves her head up against my chest, places her right hand in mine, the other around my waist, and I nuzzle my face into her hair then whisper into her ear. "Come with me to London."

My heart doesn't just race, it pounds. It's a drum, loud, quick punches that plummet into me. I want her to say yes, but when she freezes and her back stiffens, I'm suddenly afraid of what she's going to say.

Jules pulls back to look at me, opens her mouth to talk but doesn't say a word.

Her eyes hold mine, still bright in the dark, a look of confusion staring back at me. I hold her hips close to me, not letting her get too far. She drops her gaze and swallows, and it feels like hours tick by as I wait tentatively for her to say something.

"I can't leave here, Beck. I can't leave my job, my family, my nephew. I have more nieces or nephews on the way, and I want to watch them grow up."

*Fuck. I'm an asshole.*

"I know, I'm sorry. It was a stupid thing to suggest, but I just…I had to ask. I'm not ready to let you go, Jules. And I'm trying to figure us out."

"Beck—" Jules looks upset and that's not how I wanted to make her feel. We're in the center of the room and even though it's just the two of us talking in hushed tones, it feels like the entire room is listening in.

"I'm sorry. Wrong place and wrong time. I shouldn't have asked you here. Can we talk about this later tonight at my house?" I ask.

My jaw ticks in frustration. I'm an idiot for asking her here. I'm an idiot for putting a frown on her face in front of her family in the middle of such a great evening. I'm pissed at myself for ruining the moment. Pissed at myself for having to leave her.

We've gone still on the dance floor. Jules takes in a deep breath. "I want to be wherever you are, but it's not that simple. I can't just leave my job. My dad depends on me and I'm happy at The Seaside. You of all people should understand that."

"Jesus, Jules," I say, running my hand through my hair. "I know how much your job means to you. I get it, but the thought of leaving you is scary as fucking hell. Let's just talk about this later. Okay? Please."

"We can talk about it later," she agrees, running her

hands down the lapels of my suit jacket. "It's scary for me too. I like you, Beck. I like you a lot."

I inch my body a little closer. "I like you too. More than a lot. I'm falling so fucking hard for you."

I'm crazy about her, and I want to have her for more than just a few more weeks. It makes me feel reckless. I feel an uncontrollable urge to fuck the whole promotion, to walk away from everything I've been working for, to burn the whole thing down and watch it go up in flames. For her. I want to ease this ache in my chest, but I know I can't walk away from what I've worked for my whole life.

"Come here," I say, and she steps closer, her hips lined up with mine. My hand moves to the nape of her neck, my finger running a straight line down the center of her spine. She shivers.

"Kiss me," she whispers, and my heart goes wild in my chest, needing something to hold on to. Something to assure me that this isn't over in a matter of weeks. I need to know there is the possibility of more. I need it like I need air to breathe.

I kiss her, tasting the sweet white wine on her pillowy lips. It's a soft, lingering kiss and when we pull away, I rest my forehead against hers. "I'm head over heels for you, Jules. I know it hasn't been long, but it's been long enough for me to know that you mean something to me. I want to try with you to make this work."

She sighs, taking my face in her hands. "I want that too."

"Beck..." she says, her voice feathery, and I kiss her with words left unsaid on her lips.

I groan. "You can't whisper my name like that in a room full of people. My suit pants will hide nothing."

"Control yourself, Mr. Wonder."

"Not easy when I'm around you," I say, loving the way

her cheeks have pinkened. "Where are you sleeping tonight?"

Her hands grip my lapels, and she goes up on her tiptoes, her face millimeters from mine.

"Wherever you want me to," she says against my lips.

"With me."

Then I kiss her again.

# Chapter Twenty-Six

Jules

I wake up and my house feels empty. It's quiet. So quiet, I swear you could hear a pin drop.

I get out of bed, pad to the kitchen and turn on the coffee maker. Even the grinding of the coffee beans isn't enough noise to make this feeling go away. The quiet should feel peaceful but instead it just feels… empty.

I woke up to Beckett's side of the bed—yes, he has a side already—cold and empty. He left before I woke up this morning to meet the guys for a bike ride.

I'm used to waking up to one of Beck's arms draped over my body, to his kiss on my shoulder or my cheek. I know I shouldn't get used to having him around so much, it's going to make him leaving so much harder. Easier said than done.

Once the coffee brews, I pour myself a cup while something deep inside me feels like it's unraveling, like a small windstorm is gathering speed. Getting my first taste of waking up without Beckett feels horrible, but I guess I better get used to it.

I take my cup of coffee to the patio, peering into Bella's room along the way. Her bedroom door is open a few inches and I can see that she didn't come home last night.

Folding my legs underneath me, I sink into the small wicker couch on my patio and take my first sip of liquid heaven. I look out towards White Haven beach, taking another slow sip. The blue of the ocean, the oranges, reds, yellows as the morning sun rises higher.

I think about last night and the conversation on the dance floor Beck and I never did finish because we couldn't keep our hands off of one another when we got to my place. His jacket came off on the walk to my front door, followed by my dress in the hallway, then five seconds after the door shut his pants were on the floor in my bedroom.

And after we both finished, we laid next to one another, exhausted and sated. Beck fell asleep minutes later, but I stayed awake for an hour just staring at the ceiling. Thinking of Beck's voice whispering into my ear under the twinkling lights of the dance floor.

Now, with my mind clear, I replay the words he said to me.

*Come with me to London.*

I swallow hard, both nervous and excited, still half-convinced that I dreamed the whole thing up.

*Come with me to London.*

No, he definitely said it.

A shiver rolls down my spine.

Could I move away with him? Is it insane to even consider it? I take another sip of coffee mulling it all over in my mind.

We've only known each other for weeks.

Every excuse I gave him last night is true. Reed Point is my home. It's where my family is, and I can't imagine myself living anywhere else. I have good friends here. I love living near the beach, being five minutes from the marina, sailing whenever I feel like it. There's a lot I love about living here, and I can't see myself ever leaving.

I get up, take a shower, and rinse the sex we had last night off of me. I'm drying my hair when Liam texts me an invite for ice-cream and a walk along the beach this morning with him and Hudson. Ellie, Parker and Olivia are coming too.

My heart dips in my chest at the last sentence my brother writes in the text. *Beckett is welcome too.*

He can't make it, of course, but the fact that Liam thought to invite Beckett makes me happy. I reply that I'll be there, then drag myself to my bedroom to get changed. No use sitting around here feeling sorry for myself all day.

Later, I'm strolling White Harbor beach, watching Hudson make a mess of his ice-cream while tripping through the sand. Ellie takes the cone from him, licks all around the edges where the strawberry has dripped. Liam cleans Hudson's sticky hands with a napkin. He's got it all down his T-shirt too, but it only seems to make him look even more adorable.

It feels good to be with my family. I wasn't going to meet them today when they asked me to join them at the beach, but now that I'm here I'm happy I came. It's just Liam and Ellie, Parker and Olivia, and of course Hudson too. Miles and Rylee are busy filming an interview for a celebrity news show at my parents' beach house, where the two of them are staying for the weekend.

"Beckett couldn't make it?" Olivia asks.

My eyes drift over to the ocean. "He's mountain biking with some friends. A Sunday ritual. But you'll see him tonight at Mom and Dad's place for dinner."

"Good, I'm glad. He's great, Jules," she says, reaching

over to give my hand a squeeze. "Your brothers like him, which is a miracle in and of itself."

I smile as we walk further down the crowded beach, weaving through striped umbrellas and kids building sand-castles. The salty smell of the ocean drifts on the warm seaside air. Tourist season is in full swing. My mind wanders to Beckett and last night at the charity gala. To him meeting my parents. To us agreeing to try to make things work. *How?* I wish I knew.

What I *do* know is that these past weeks with Beck have been bliss. We send text messages back and forth all day, he picks me up from work and we go out to dinner or stay in and cook. We hold hands, he gives me foot rubs at night, and I have a toothbrush and a pair of pajamas in one of his drawers.

"—still having nightmares over that, Ells," Liam calls from ahead of us. I realize I haven't been paying any atten-tion to the conversation, too caught up in my own thoughts.

Beside me, Ellie stops in the sand. Hands on her hips, she stares at Liam and shakes her head. This ought to be good.

"My mom is a free spirit, Liam. You should know how she is by now. I don't understand why you're still so hung up on this."

Ellie's parents are hippies. They live in a motor home full-time, traveling the country, giving their money away to people they meet along the way who they feel could use a little help. Her dad wears layers upon layers of crystals around his neck and her mom always has a DIY crown of flowers in her hair.

"Like, what is the big deal?" Ellie says, looking to me for moral support. "My mom answers *one* Facetime call topless and your brother acts like it's the end of the world."

My hand flies to my mouth, but not in time to stop the laugh that escapes me.

"Woah. Back that train up," Parker says from behind us, where he and Olivia are walking hand-in-hand. "She wasn't wearing a shirt? A bra? Nothing…?"

"She was at a nudist beach and she forgot that her boobs were out when she answered," Ellie explains. "She and my dad think nudism helps to accept the skin you're given, or something like that. What the hell do I know?" she says, throwing up her hands.

"What the hell, Ells? Are you serious?" Parker asks.

"Yeah, their thought process goes something like—the more you see the human body, the more comfortable you become with it. Suddenly your penis isn't that small, your boobs really aren't that uneven, your birthmark doesn't look so strange, you're not overweight," Ellie tries to explain. No one's buying it.

I start laughing and I can't stop. Olivia is laughing too and soon there's a tear running down my face and then another.

"I feel like I've just entered the twilight zone," Parker says straight-faced. "So, what, you saw your mother-in-law naked?" he asks Liam.

"Not everything… fuck," Liam says, covering both of his eyes with his hands. "But I saw more than I will ever be able to forget."

"Language, babe," Ellie says, hands on both hips. "I thought Liam was going to have a coronary. Red face, eyes about ready to pop off his face."

"I'm heartbroken I missed that," I deadpan, licking the side of my cone.

"I told him he ought to give it a try," Ellie jokes. "What do you think, babe? Quick weekend away at a nudist colony before the new baby gets here?"

"Shoot me," Liam replies.

We walk a little further down the beach, finishing our cones. Hudson gets tired of waking, so Parker hoists him up on his shoulders for a while, until he decides he does want to walk after all.

The five of us stop to watch Hudson jump the tiny waves in the ocean. I get lost in his little feet, his giggles. I wonder what it will be like when two more nieces or nephews join the family. It makes me sad to know Beckett won't be here to enjoy it with me.

"Something on your mind, Jules?" Olivia asks. "You seem a little lost in space."

"Beckett is moving to London," I tell her. I look down at my feet, sinking deeper into the wet sand with every wave. I'm not sure I meant to say it loud enough for everyone to hear, but it's too late now. My family is watching me like they're not quite sure what to say.

"Shit, are you serious?" Ellie asks, a concerned look on her face.

"Dead. He interviewed for a promotion before we met and found out he got the job after we started seeing each other." I fill them in, my voice sounding like it's on autopilot, like it's something I've been programmed to say.

My mouth is dry. I get the words out and I don't think it sounds like I'm not dying inside when in reality, I'm sick to my stomach over it.

"Are you okay?" Olivia asks, her eyes searching mine.

I'm quiet for the longest time, because I'm afraid if I answer the question I will break down in tears. My head hurts from trying to contain the emotions that have been swirling around inside of me.

"I will be," I finally answer her. "It might just take some time."

"I'm going to fucking kill him," Parker says. "I knew he was a bad idea. What the hell did I tell you? I knew it—"

"Parker. Enough. Did you not hear a thing she just said?" Olivia says, staring hard at her husband. "He didn't find out until *after* they started dating."

"He still knew there was a chance. Fuck him."

"Parker," I say, perfectly calm. "I knew from the second we started talking that he was being considered for a promotion. He didn't hide anything."

I start from the beginning and bit by bit, I tell them everything. Well not *everything*, but I start with Miami and end with today.

"You could ask him to stay? Or have you thought about moving with him?" Ellie asks.

"I can't ask him to stay. How can I ask him to walk away from a great opportunity? It's a big deal and a position he's been working his way up the Liberty ladder for. What if I ask him to stay, he does, then later realizes he made the biggest mistake of his life and regrets it?"

"Biggest mistake of his life? Come on Jules. There's more to life than a promotion at work," Parker says, eyes squinting in the sun.

"Your brother is sometimes right," Olivia teases. "And in this case, I think he is. Prime example: Parker and I figured it out. We both made sacrifices to be together. You just need to have an open, completely honest conversation with one another."

"Long distance relationships can work too, you know," Ellie adds.

"On what planet?" Liam grumbles. "They never do. You suffer through months of not seeing each other. You're both miserable and mopey and then in the end, you break it off because… well, it was a stupid idea in the first place."

"When did you become the expert on this? Did you

have some sort of secret long-distance affair none of us knew about?" Parker says.

Liam flips him off. "I know a lot of things."

Ellie just looks at him.

"He likes you a lot, Jules. I'm sure you two can figure this out," Ellie says, catching Hudson, giving him a tickle under his chin.

"You've seen us together once," I remind her. "I'm not sure you can tell how much he likes me after a few hours."

"Well, I saw that he never took his eyes off of you all night. I saw how he kissed you on the dance floor," Ellie says, a grin on her face.

"Oh, we *all* saw the way he kissed you," Olivia chimes in. "It was a five-star kiss."

"Okay, moving on," Parker says, while Liam shakes his head in disgust.

"As I was saying," Ellie continues. "He looks at you like you're the sun and he's a field of flowers. And you get all woozy around him—"

"I do *not* get all woozy," I say. It's a lie.

"You actually do. It's cute," Olivia says. "So, have you thought about moving with him to London?"

"What the fuck are you talking about, Livy?" Parker says. "She can't move to London. Her life is here. She can't just leave the Seaside, friends, her family."

"He's right," I say. "I can't—"

"No, he isn't right. Not this time. Everything is here *except* Beckett," Olivia says, wrapping her hand around her husband's arm. "You need to eat all of the words you just said, babe. Did you forget you moved back to Reed Point for me and I moved to Cape May for you? When two people are in love, they make sacrifices. That's just the way love works."

"Right, but Cape May is a hell of a lot closer than London," Parker points out.

I inhale a deep breath and look out at the ocean, the sun casting slanted rays over the turquoise blue of the water. The color reminds me of Beckett's eyes.

"I know it feels complicated, but it doesn't need to be," Ellie says gently. "The way I see it is you are either able to walk away from a relationship with him or you're not, and when you figure out the answer to that question, you take the next steps."

"My fiancée… smart and hot as—"

Ellie lifts a finger at Liam with a watch-your-mouth-around-the-baby look.

"What? I was going to say jalapenos," Liam says matter-of-factly.

I explore my options in my mind—ask Beckett to stay, go with him to London, try long-distance—and for the first time I realize I have options. None of them are easy, but they are options nonetheless.

Liam picks up Hudson, tossing him in the air as the 2-year-old squeals.

"This kid is a mess, Ells. Who thought it was a good idea to buy a toddler his own cone?"

Ellie shrugs. "He likes his food."

"Wonder where he gets that from?" Olivia deadpans.

"Big bullies you are. All of you," Ellie says with a laugh.

We spend another half hour walking back to our cars, chasing Hudson around the sand and jumping in the waves with him. He's sleepy in Liam's arms by the time we say our goodbyes.

I check my phone for the time, missing Beckett, wondering how I expect myself to be able to go without him for months when five hours feels like a lifetime.

I wish I was the type of person who always knows exactly what they want, who makes quick decisions and feels confident about them. I'm more of a fly-by-the-seat-of-your- pants person. I improvise, I figure it out along the way.

Sighing, I slip into the seat of my car, done with thinking because it feels like I've reached my limit for the day. I can't keep going back and forth with this. At some point, I'm going to have to make a decision and live with it. Zero regrets.

I roll my window down, turn up the music and drive.

# Chapter Twenty-Seven

Jules

I open the large door to my parents' house and step inside, Beckett following closely behind me. I watch him as he looks around the 10,000-square-foot house, one of the largest in Reed Point. It's a lot to take in, and I can't help but wonder what he thinks. My parents had the home built when I was around two years old. It sits on three acres of land, and has eight bedrooms, ten bathrooms, a six-car garage, a pool, outdoor kitchen and manicured gardens.

The house became the center of our little world. My parents often hosted parties, charity events, family dinners and an annual Christmas party for the neighborhood, where my uncle would dress up as Santa and give out gifts to all of the kids. My parents spared no expense. The doors were always open to friends of mine, and of my brothers, when we were growing up. It's still the place where we all gather to be together.

My parents' money was inherited from my dad's parents, who owned a hotel chain they eventually left to my dad. My mom's side of the family was working class—she was raised just outside of Queens, her parents were both teachers. My parents met in college—a love-at-first-sight type of story—and were married months later. They moved to Reed Point soon after.

Beckett's holding a bottle of wine in one hand and a bouquet of flowers in the other when my mom greets us in the kitchen wearing an apron and holding a glass of wine.

She hugs me first, then turns toward Beck with a smile on her face. "It's good to have you here, Beckett. I'm glad you could make it," she says pulling him in for a hug. "Welcome, sweetheart. I want you to make yourself at home."

"Thank you, I'm happy to be here. These are for you."

He hands her the bouquet. She dips her head into the pink-and-white blooms to sniff them. "These are beautiful. Thank you. We didn't get a chance to really get to know you last night, so this will be nice," my mom says. "The others are in the kitchen waiting for the chance to get to know you better too. I've made them promise to go easy on you."

We follow her into the kitchen, and I silently pray that my brothers have taken her advice.

My dad rounds the corner of the island when we walk into the room, greeting me with a hug and then extending his hand to Beckett. "Thank you for joining us. It's good to see you again. What can I get you to drink?" He rattles off an entire list of drink options before Beckett settles on a glass of wine.

Miles stands from his bar stool, clapping Beckett's shoulder, pulling him in for a bro hug. They seem casual, relaxed even, and I admit I am a little surprised. Olivia hugs us both next, followed by Rylee and then Parker.

"Have a seat," Parker says, patting the stool beside him.

Beckett sits down while I pour myself a glass of sangria from the pitcher my mom has set out on the counter. I take the seat next to Beck, taking a quick moment to appreciate the view. He's got on dark jeans and a black crew neck sweater, the sleeves rolled up his forearms, the scruff on his face trimmed close to his skin. The shirt fits him well. His jeans fit him incredibly. I have to remind myself to stop staring.

Liam and Ellie arrive last with Hudson, who beelines it into the house and straight for my mom. Ellie follows him, a diaper bag slung over her shoulder, calling after Hudson to slow down. Liam joins us a minute later, and I notice how his eyes find Ellie first. Wherever she goes, Liam's eyes seem to follow and whenever he looks at her his usual gruff, serious expression disappears. His eyes are full of warmth as he watches her make the rounds, hugging Olivia first, then Parker, Miles, Rylee, Beckett and then me. He adores her.

And it makes me realize how much I want that.

My mom wipes her hand on a tea towel and brings her glass of wine to where we're all sitting. She plucks an olive from the cheese board, then picks up Hudson and gives him a kiss on his cheek.

"Is there something I can help you with?" Beck asks my mom. I smile. Beckett is so charming and I'm happy that my family is seeing it in action.

"I've got it all under control, but thank you for asking," my mom says, looking genuinely touched by the offer. "How sweet of you."

She sets a squirmy Hudson on the floor and before his feet hit the ground, he's already off and running.

"How in the world does a wedding cake cost that much?" Liam is asking, engrossed in a conversation about the cost of wedding planning. "It should be illegal. It's like they hear the word wedding and jack up the prices 300 percent."

"—Hudson," Ellie calls out in a don't-even-think-about-it voice, watching her son extend a chubby hand towards the cheese board.

"It's highway robbery," Miles agrees, while Ellie shakes a finger at her son.

"Hudson, one's enough," Liam admonishes, taking several cubed pieces of cheese from his hand.

And then everyone is talking at once, over each other, while my nephew starts to pout. His bottom lip pulls forward like he's about to cry, and then he does, and it's loud. Then it gets louder.

The house is always like this. I'm used to it—the volume, the chaos—but I look over at Beckett, wondering what he's thinking. He's leaning forward against the counter on his elbows, grinning at me, looking right at home. I'm quickly distracted by his forearms, muscular and tan. Beckett has nice arms. He catches me looking, places his hand on my thigh under the counter, squeezes the area above my knee, and a tingle shoots up my spine.

Once Hudson calms down, he's distracted by Beckett, who asks to see the race car he's holding in his hand. Soon, Hudson is up on his toes at Beckett's feet, asking to be picked up. Beckett lifts him up and sets him on his knee.

All of my brothers, Ellie, Rylee and Olivia too, look at Beckett with Hudson on his lap, then at me. The two of them are making car noises, racing the toy Ferrari around a napkin, a fork and a plate. Hudson giggles, Beck laughs too. It's like they've always known each other, which is incredible to see. Hudson is a friendly kid, but he can take a little while to warm up to strangers.

My ovaries almost burst watching the two of them together. My gorgeous, buff boyfriend with my sweet 2-

year-old nephew in his arms is enough to make me want babies right this minute.

"Who's hungry?" my mom asks, turning off the oven, taking a sip of her wine. "Dinner is ready. Everyone, take your seats."

We sit around the dinner table and dig into a feast of roast chicken, asparagus, rosemary potatoes and a green salad.

Beckett carefully passes me the chicken while Miles tells us about the series he's filming, the actress opposite him who's married to an NFL quarterback, and the talk show he recently made an appearance on where all they wanted to talk about was Rylee. He jokes that fans are now more interested in what Rylee is doing or wearing or what she has to say than anything he has going on. She's definitely become America's sweetheart.

I slice into the chicken on my plate and take my first bite, watching Rylee blush and shake her head.

"I think I see Rylee's face on magazine covers more than I see yours these days" my mom points out.

"Thank God," Liam adds.

"Who even buys magazines anymore?" Rylee says with a wave of her hand. "Don't they know it's free on the internet? Besides, it's all garbage anyways."

"Except for that one time they printed the story about Miles and his secret affair with that 60-something-year-old actress that filmed the Polydent commercials. They finally got it right with that one," Liam jokes. "That reminds me, I really need to have a copy of that cover framed for my desk."

"Miles is into the baby boomers, Mom," I add.

"Eat your dinner," she says, shaking her head.

Miles looks at me like I'm gum on the bottom of his shoe. The rest of the room laughs. I take the opportunity to find Beck's thigh under the table and give it a squeeze. He glances at me, smiles and places his warm palm over my hand. The night is going better than I expected… until Miles slides right into telling stories about me as a kid.

Of course, he tells Beckett all about the time I left the faucet on in my bathroom upstairs and flooded the entire main floor. Then Liam talks about the time I was grounded for three weeks after throwing a house party in 10th grade when my parents went away for the weekend. They came home early to find their house full of people, a keg in the back yard and music so loud the neighbors two blocks over called the cops.

"You should have seen how miserable she was for those three weeks," Parker says to the table. "She moped around the house like her life was ruined."

"Didn't they make you write an essay on the dangers of alcohol poisoning?" Liam asks.

Beckett leans in, our shoulders touching, listening to every word. He glances at me with that smirky-smile on his face, the one where one side of his mouth rises a little higher.

"Yes," I grumble. "It took me hours to write that stupid thing. I had a permanent cramp in my hand."

"Well, you learned your lesson," my mom says, passing the potatoes to Ellie. "That was the last party you ever threw."

"That you found out about," Parker says, eyebrows raised.

My mom and I look at each other. I paste an innocent expression on my face. She sees right through me.

"She kept you on your toes," Beckett says to my mom, laughing, though he doesn't know the half of it.

"She's been a firecracker since day one. It's really amazing she's made it to nearly 25 years old without any major scandals. And now she's all yours," she replies, looking at Beck. I flinch.

*His for a few more weeks.*

I push my potatoes around my plate and try to push all thoughts of Beck's move from my mind. He must notice because he sneaks a few glances at me, squeezes my thigh.

When dinner is over, Beckett helps my mom in the kitchen with the dishes before she shoos him away to the patio with my dad and brothers. I watch them through the window talking, drinking after-dinner drinks. Beckett looks like he fits right in.

"We all really like him, Jules," my mom says next to me at the sink. "Have you thought about inviting him to Liam's wedding?"

"I haven't. It's early, Mom," I lie. I have definitely thought about Beck and I drinking Mai Tais on the beach, taking a surf lesson together, watching sunsets from our lanai. But I know it's a dream and nothing more. He'll be living in London by then, busy with a new job, working hard to make a good impression.

"I think you should, Jules, but no pressure on our end. We will always make room for him," Ellie says, drying a platter with a polka-dot tea towel, placing it on the counter.

"Thanks, Ellie," I say, meaning it. Whatever happens with Beckett and I, their support means so much to me.

Later, after we've had dessert and said our goodbyes, Beckett and I are in his car, still parked in my parent's driveway.

"Thanks for including me tonight," he says, thumb stroking my cheek. "I had a great time. Your family is awesome."

"Thank you for coming," I tell him. "You made an impression."

"That so?"

"It is," I say as his hand moves to the nape of my neck. Lust rushes through me, slow but sure.

He leans in to kiss me. Then he kisses me again, soft and slow like I'm the finest wine he's ever tasted and he's a sommelier. The kiss turns deeper, it's heart-meltingly perfect, and all I want to do is drown in Beck and never come up for air. But I force myself to pull back.

"No funny business, Wonder," I tease. "My brothers like you now, but they might not like you for long if they catch you making out with me in the driveway."

"Can I make out with you when we get back to my house?"

"I'm expecting you to, unless the stories my brothers told you about me tonight scared you off?"

"Nothing you do could scare me off."

"Give it time."

He laughs, closes his fingers around mine. He looks magnificent in the dark, the lamps on the driveway shining a dim light across his profile.

I'm happy here, in a moment I know isn't going to last.

But for now, I'm going to hold on to every one of these moments for as long as I can.

# Chapter Twenty-Eight

**B**eckett

I stare at my computer screen, a pit in my stomach.

It's eleven-thirty in the morning and I'm in my office, a file opened on my computer, the official offer for the new job in London staring back at me.

The salary is almost twice as much as I'm making now. The job is larger in scope, a C-suite position in a huge city. It's always been the dream, but I can't bring myself to be excited about it. For starters, I won't know a single soul. Sure, I can meet people and make new friends, but that all takes time, and most people are too worn out to put forth the energy into getting to know people these days. Second, I'm sure I'll be living in an apartment the size of a tree-house. Third, they drive on the opposite side of the road, but maybe that doesn't mean shit, because I probably won't want to drive in London's insane traffic anyways. So, that means I'd be taking the Underground, if I can figure the damn thing out.

I stare at the still-blank signature space with my name

typed underneath it. I should have signed the agreement days ago, but every time I open the file to do so, I find something else to do, something that I convince myself needs my immediate attention.

I take a deep breath.

The problem is that I don't know that the job is worth it.

I can't stop thinking about what my mom said: *Can I live without the dream of London? Can I live without Jules?*

Closing out the tab once again, I open a contract that I decide can't wait.

I crack my knuckles and get to work.

Later that day, I'm in my bedroom getting dressed for dinner. I tug on a pair of black jeans and grab a gray Henley from my drawer on the way to my kitchen.

"Ready," I say to Jules, who's leaning against the counter, her eyes on me as I fumble with my shirt, trying to find the hem so I can slip it over my head.

"Hi," she says grinning, eyes smoky, brows raised. "Do you really need to put that on?"

"I might get cold," I say with an innocent expression. She likes me with my shirt off. I flex and watch her eyes widen slightly. I do it again because I know what Jules likes.

"Bet you won't," she says, shamelessly drinking me in. I like her eyes all over me.

"I'm not sure they'll allow me into the restaurant looking like this. Isn't there some kind of health code that forces you to wear shoes and a shirt?" I ask, taking a few steps towards her. I'm playing with fire. "Or is that just a Kenny Chesney song?"

"Maybe we could ask your family to picnic at the park

instead?" she offers. "Then it would be completely appropriate for you to be shirtless in public."

I made plans for us to have dinner with my family, against my better judgement. I know how my mom is going to react once she meets Jules. For years, she's been hoping I would find someone who makes me happy. And now I have. When she meets Jules, she's going to fall in love with her. How could she not? And that is going to make me leaving for London even harder.

But ever since I told her about Jules, she's been asking to meet her. She wants to get to know the girl who puts this damn smile on my face and has me questioning my life's dreams. Those are her words not mine, but they're true.

I suggested a restaurant so my mom could have a night out and not have to worry about cooking. She reluctantly agreed, but it took some persuading. She hates it when I pay for things, and she knows there's no way I would let her pick up the tab.

"Or—and just hear me out on this one—I could just wear a shirt and we could eat like the civilized people?"

"But then how will I gawk at your abs?" Jules teases, pushing off from the counter, taking two steps towards me, reaching for my t-shirt.

"A compromise?" she asks, grabbing the fabric of my T-shirt from my hands, tossing it on a kitchen chair. My pulse beats faster under my skin. I want her to touch me. I love it when her hands are on my skin.

"I'm listening."

"You leave the shirt off until we have to leave," she says, looping her finger through one of my belt loops, tugging me into her. Her fingers skate over my abs then a little lower. I shiver. "And you can put it on when it's time to go."

"That's in 10 minutes," I tell her, grinning.

"I'll take what I can get." The words are barely out of her mouth before I lean down to kiss her, my hand stroking the side of her jaw.

Our eyes lock when the kiss ends and the ground shifts under my feet, the hardwood rolling like a tiny earthquake until it stops and gently rights itself.

*I love her.*

*I fucking love her.*

But I don't know how to tell her.


## Jules


For the third time since we left Beck's apartment, I'm checking my appearance in the tiny mirror in the visor. First I check my lips, reapplying another coat of a peachy-tinted lip-gloss, smacking my lips together. Then I smooth my hair, which is down in waves, one side pinned behind my ear. Then I check once more, just in case I look any different than I did four seconds ago. I don't. I can feel Beck's eyes on me, and I know he's wearing that very Beck-ett-y smirk. When I look in his direction, my suspicions are confirmed.

"You know they're going to love you, right?" he says, all soft and smoky.

"And what if they don't? What if they think I'm weird, or not funny, and wonder what the hell it is that you see in me?" I say, flipping the visor up.

"Are you listening to yourself? They would never think any of those things. Unless you tell them a really terrible joke that crashes and burns or say something strange. Then maybe—"

"Beck!" I say, giving him a glare. "You're not helping."

He laughs. "Relax, beautiful. I promise you don't have to worry."

I exhale a breath, feeling his eyes roaming over me and the romper that I'm wearing. It's a floral pattern, long sleeves, a plunging neckline with a tie around the waist. His eyes stop on mine, and the look in them tells me he likes what he sees. Mine say be-a-good-boy-until-after-dinner.

"You look beautiful," he tells me, his voice low and smooth, my body softening as we walk closer to the restaurant, our hands laced together.

We're meeting his parents and sister at Cocina Caliente, a trendy Mexican spot a little removed from First Street and tourists. Beck quickly spots them already seated at a table when we walk into the restaurant. I suck in a sharp breath, gathering my courage. Beckett squeezes my hand.

"Beck, my boy," his dad says, getting up from his seat and slapping his back.

"Hi Dad," Beckett says, grinning back at him. His mom stands next and then his sister. "This is Jules, everyone."

His mom is shorter, with dark, straight hair to her shoulders and a ready smile. His sister Bean is the spitting image of her mom, but a little taller and slimmer. They both move in for a hug at the same time.

"—it's so good to meet you."

"—hi, Jules."

"—gosh, you're so pretty."

"—please call me Cindy."

His mom and sister talk over each other as they take turns giving me a hug, smiling like I'm Oprah Winfrey and I've just given them each a car.

We take our seats, Beck's warm hand on my back. "See?" he whispers in my ear. "They love you already."

My body hums. I want them to like me. I want tonight to go well.

"Alright, now that introductions are out of the way, how was everyone's day?" Beck says as we all take our seats.

I sit next to Bean, who quickly starts telling me about her job at a boutique clothing store on First Street, then about the courses she's taking in the fall. She has a bubbly way about her, and an infectious smile and I find myself liking her already.

Beck's mom sips on a lime margarita and talks about Beckett like he's won a Nobel Peace Prize. Soon she's telling me about the year he won MVP at a little league championship, the candy he used to hide underneath his bed, and the time he broke his arm riding a skateboard. When I can get a word in, I ask her what keeps her busy in her spare time. She enjoys knitting, she says, but she's a terrible baker. And she's a bit of a homebody, she admits. In fact, she's never been anywhere outside of the U.S.

Becks shoots me an *are-you-doing-okay* look from beside me. I grin and for what feels like the hundredth time I notice the color of his eyes: ocean blue with flecks of green. It's tough not to get lost in them. I find his foot under the table with mine.

We have dinner, then churros, then a second round of churros because they're just that good. And I forget that I was ever nervous to meet them. Beck's mom reminds me so much of him. She's strong and confident, sweet and charming. His dad Pete is quiet, laid back, a listener rather than a talker. And Bean is sweet, she's someone I could easily be friends with. I feel relaxed around them, like I can just be myself.

Cindy sets her fork down on her plate. "Beckett tells us you have a birthday coming up."

"He did, did he?" I focus on my boyfriend, who's reclined in his chair, an elbow resting on the arm rest, the side of his face in his hand. He smiles. I quirk an eyebrow.

"What? I talk to my mom about you," he says. "That can't surprise you."

"It does a little," I say, then turn my focus to his mom before this starts to get weird. Beck has a way of tugging at my heart, making me forget everyone else around us. "My birthday is on Friday. My 25th."

"A quarter century. That's an exciting one. Do you have plans?" Cindy asks, before taking a sip of her coffee.

"For now, just dinner with my family on Sunday, but Beck has asked me to keep the weekend free."

Cindy glances at her son.

"My lips are sealed. It's a surprise," Beck says.

"But he's been given strict orders not to make a big deal over it," I add, looking pointedly at him.

"You're not big on celebrating your birthday?" Bean asks, sucking a spoon of whipped cream into her mouth from the top of her vanilla bean latte.

"My mom has been throwing elaborate parties for me since, well, forever. And I love them. But with Beckett leaving... I just want..." I pause to remove my foot from my mouth.

"To spend some time with him," Cindy says finishing my sentence. "That's understandable."

I glance at the table next to us and then back to Cindy. "Exactly," I nod, feeling like a heel. This has been such a nice evening and then I have to go and bring up a really sucky topic that I'm sure is just as painful for his family as it is for me.

Beck reaches for my hand in my lap, sensing something's wrong, and I can't help but notice the way Cindy goes quiet, fiddling with her necklace and looking a little heartbroken.

*I'm such a dummy.*

Our waitress breaks the tension when she arrives at our table and asks if there's anything else she can get us. "Just the bill, thanks," Beck replies, and then steers the conversation to safer ground, asking Pete about a game that's coming up. Soon we're all chatting happily again, each of us pretending that Beckett isn't leaving in just a few short weeks.

After saying our goodbyes, Beckett and I walk to his car. "Did you have a good night?" he asks when we're inside, reaching for my hand, kissing my knuckles instead of starting the engine.

"Wasn't it obvious?"

"I'm a man, Jules. Nothing is obvious."

"I did," I say after a moment, shifting in my seat to face him. "I like your parents a lot and Bean is fantastic. They're all really nice."

"My mom didn't scare you off?" he asks, watching me over our joined hands, my knuckles still against his lips. "I thought maybe the comment about looking forward to grandchildren might have terrified you." He rolls his eyes.

"It was sweet. And you leave your mom alone," I say, leaning over the console, looking for a kiss. He drops my hand and meets me half-way, kissing me, his hand in my hair. I'm not sure how many minutes pass before he lets me go and cranks the engine to life.

"Your place or mine?" he asks, pulling out of the parking spot, reaching again for my hand.

"Yours. It's closer."

He takes us back to his place where I quickly remove his shirt and he's exactly the way I like him.

## Chapter Twenty-Nine

Jules

We didn't get much sleep last night, and I'm paying for that today. I survived my 10 a.m. client, barely, having to hide a yawn more than once. After that, I had a meeting with Dad, Parker and Liam. Thankfully, they were discussing a contract with Liam for most of the time and didn't notice my head nod forward a couple of times.

I let out a heavy exhale. Beckett is leaving soon and I'm going to spend every minute I can with him until he gets on that plane. I don't care if it breaks me. Speaking of Beck, I've lost track of time and he's probably been waiting in the parking lot for the past 10 minutes wondering where I am. I'll finish this email, then shoot him a text that I'll be right out.

I'm still typing when I hear footsteps outside of my door. When I raise my eyes my heart rate kicks up five notches.

"You're still here," Beck says from my doorway. My stomach does a flip, happiness filling every inch of my body at his mere presence. He smiles that damn smile that hits me every time. Suddenly, the exhaustion that's hounded me all day is gone.

Beckett looks relaxed, almost cocky, and hotter than hell in his suit. Stubble covers his jaw. He's taken off his jacket, giving me a mouth-watering view of his button-down clinging to his athletic frame.

And now I'm thinking inappropriate thoughts while at work in the office next door to my dad's.

I want him to touch me.

I want him to kiss me.

I want him to do so much more.

"Just responding to an email emergency," I say with a sigh. "But I'm done now. Sorry I'm late."

Beckett just smiles, walking further into my office, leaving the door open, which is probably a good thing. I sense that this could be a recipe for disaster. I need to sit on my hands, avert my eyes and pray he stays on the other side of my mahogany desk.

Too late, because in a just a few strides, he's beside me, swivelling my chair to face him. He tips my chin in his hands, then leans down and kisses me.

His fingers linger on my face long after we break the kiss, and that little bit of contact makes my skin erupt in fireworks.

"Are you sure you're ready to go?" he asks, pure sex in his voice. "Because I like looking at you sitting there in that skirt and your heels. Do you think you could find another email that needs your attention?"

God, I want him to take me right here on my desk. I want to take off his shirt and run my hands over his rippling muscles, inhale his scent while my tongue travels from his neck down to his abs. Instead, I tear my eyes away from Beck and to my still-open office door, knowing that someone could walk by at any moment. But I'm having too much fun and the thrill of possibly getting caught is winning the battle inside of me.

"I'm sure I could find someone to email," I say in a teasing tone.

His hip is on my desk, his legs touching mine. He's so close to me I can smell his aftershave. I look again to the open door. I have no idea who is still around at this hour. Most would have filtered out by now, but not knowing who might wander by sends a thrill up my spine.

"I hope I'm not distracting you," Beck says in a low voice. His smile is smooth, arrogant. "Unless maybe you want me to, then I'm happy to give you something else to focus on."

My breath catches somewhere deep in my throat when he leans forward and kisses my neck, and I have to cross my legs to ease the ache between my thighs. Taking notice, he smirks a smug grin that months ago would have infuriated me. Now it turns me on like a million stars glowing in a jet-black sky.

"Beck… the door," I say just above a whisper. My pulse is frantic. "Anyone could walk by. This is a dangerous game you're playing."

He kisses me again fervently, this time on the lips, in zero rush, taking his time with his tongue, his lips, his hand in my hair.

It feels so good.

The kiss is demanding and merciless. He's taking what he wants. It's enough to make me forget my name, forget where I am. His strong hand grips the back of my neck and I straighten my back to gain better access to his mouth. I kiss him back with everything in me. And I keep kissing him until my hands are pushed up against his hard chest, wishing he would lift me onto my desk and push my skirt up past my waist.

This might be the worst idea I've ever gone along with, but I can't seem to care.

The moment the kiss ends, he groans against my mouth. "I want you to turn off your computer and get rid of every damn thing on your desk," he says, pulling me to my feet. His hands find my ass, pulling me flat against him. Our bodies press together like we belong like this.

He's hard behind his zipper, the long ridge of him pressed firmly against my stomach. I want to take him out, run my fingers over his length then feel him erupt in my hand, but I remember where I am.

"Have you forgotten about the door to my office that is wide open for anyone who happens to pass by?"

He squeezes my ass and I gasp quietly, pressing myself up against him.

"I haven't forgotten. I just don't give a damn," he says. My heart beats so strong in my chest I wonder if he can feel it. "I've waited all day to kiss you. I need to kiss you now."

*Dammit. This is dangerous. You're at work. You need to stop this.*

But I don't. How can I when his fingers brush over my nipple through my blouse, his thumb plucking the sensitive area until my jaw falls open. I squeeze my eyes shut as a shiver skates over my skin. He doesn't stop, softly tormenting me until a fire blazes straight through my bones.

I suck my bottom lip under my teeth to stop from moaning. My breathing is hard. His is too when I tug gently on the imprint of him behind his slacks. His mouth finds mine, his tongue licking into my mouth. We don't stop.

It's only when I hear voices coming from the hall that I jump back, my desk chair breaking my fall. My hands fumble through my hair while Beckett walks to the bookshelf behind me, casually adjusting himself in his pants.

"What are you still doing here?" William from the sales department has suddenly appeared in my doorway. "Oh, I'm sorry to interrupt. I didn't realize you're in a meeting."

William's eyes look to Beckett then back to me. If he has any idea of what just went on in my office, he doesn't show it.

"Not a meeting. This is Beckett Taylor," I say. "My—"

"Jules' boyfriend." He finishes my sentence, moving towards William, shaking his hand. "Pleasure to meet you. We were just about to head out of here."

"I'm on my way out too," William says, with a nod. "Have a good night. It was nice to meet you."

He walks away and Beckett turns to face me with a smirk on his face, then laughs. I cover my face with my hand, shaking my head.

"That could very easily have been my *dad*, Beck. What the hell were we thinking?"

He walks back to me, taking my face in his hands. "We weren't and it was fun as hell. I don't regret a thing," he says before dropping a kiss to my lips.

"Come on, beautiful. Let me take you home."

"And then what?" I ask against his lips. He swallows, like he's trying to control himself.

"Then we finish what we started here," he says, and it feels like the most delicious form of foreplay.

"Promise?"

"Is that even a question?" he whispers, inches from my face. "I promise you, beautiful, that I will fuck you just the way you like it. It'll be hard and filthy, just the way you want, and you won't be able to stop thinking about it for the next two weeks."

Twenty minutes later, I'm in my bedroom, slipping out of my work clothes while he grabs us each a glass of water from the kitchen. I'm down to my lace bra and matching underwear when I hear my bedroom door shut behind me and the sound of the lock click in place.

I turn towards Beckett. His dress shirt is unbuttoned and untucked, his chest making me salivate. He strides towards me, shoulders back, melting me with an I'm-in-control look in his eyes. He has my full attention.

Then his lips are on mine. His hand is in my hair, his other on my neck, his body pressed firmly against mine.

He kisses me softly, with care, as if I'm delicate and he's afraid I might break. His hands gently skim over my skin instead of how he usually grips me, as if to mark me. I melt under his touch, feeling cared for, feeling wanted like I've never felt before.

When he pulls back from the kiss, his thumb traces tiny circles along my jaw, his blue eyes soaking me in.

Silence fills the room, and we stand here, my hands clutching his waist. He gazes at me intently.

"I love you, Jules," he murmurs. "I love our mornings together, drinking coffee in bed until your crankiness has worn off." He quietly laughs and I do too, my heart in his hands. "I love trying new restaurants with you and rating the food. I could never have a Nutella milkshake without you because they remind me of you and our first sort-of date when I was starting to fall for you. I was, Jules. Even back then, I was. But it's so much more than that." He swallows. "I love that you're smart and so damn good at your job. I love how much you love your family, and the way you make me laugh. You're real and vulnerable and I don't deserve you, but somehow life has brought us together and I feel so damn lucky. You blow me away every day."

I blink back the tears that are welling up at his words. My vision is blurry until I wipe at my eyes with the back of my hands.

My eyes dart to his mouth and I can feel my cheeks warming. "Kiss me."

His head lowers and then his lips are on mine. I sink into the kiss, into this moment that feels like it's everything I've waited my whole life for. Sparks ignite, my pulse beats rapidly, and I will it to slow down so I can breathe again. I pull back to look at him.

"I'm not always easy, Beck. I'm a handful."

"You're *my* handful." He brushes his fingers over my cheek. "My heart wants you, and all I know is that I've fallen so hard for you."

My heart trembles, emotion tugs at me. I've fallen for him too.

"I love you too. I love you so much," I whisper.

Astonishment washes over his face. His lips part. "Jules… my beautiful." He kisses me long and slow, his lips soft and tender. The kiss is perfect and sensual and the kind of kiss that makes your heart skip two beats.

Then he lifts me off of the ground, his arms wrapped securely around me, and I squeal laughing into his neck.

When he sets me down on the bed, a smile curls his lips. "You're mine."

I nod, then I nod once more. "And you're mine."

I'm never going to let him go.

"What time is it?" he asks me.

"Why? You have somewhere to be?" I sass back, because it's what we do.

He laughs. "What time is Bella home from work? I'm wondering if we need to be quiet."

"She has tennis lessons today. She won't be home for hours."

"Bella is the best roommate ever."

I laugh, "You haven't even met her yet."

"No, but I really love the fact that she's taking tennis lessons."

I roll my eyes. "You are too much."

He squeezes me and when my head falls back, he kisses my throat. "But you love my too much."

"Stop arguing and kiss me," I say.

And he does. And we don't stop until I'm moaning into his mouth.

He moves my hand to his dick. It's hard and ready for me, and I can't stop myself from squeezing him through his pants.

He groans. "I can't wait to be inside you. We aren't going to fuck, Jules. I'm going to make love to you."

My heart squeezes. I'm ready for this crazy ride with him. It's not going to be easy and I know it might hurt like hell, but we'll figure it out together. For now, I refuse to think about it.

I slide my hand up the ridge in his pants to his button, unzip him and pull him out. He's hot in my hand, thick and veiny. His pants are on the floor at his ankles, my hand shoved into his boxer briefs.

He groans again when I pump him in my hand. "Fuck, Jules."

"We'll get to that, baby." I tease. "We have all night."

He responds by removing my bra, then my panties, his hand slipping between my legs as he teases me. One finger, then two, his other hand gripping my ass while he kisses me until I'm panting against his mouth. My hand is still wrapped around his shaft, but it's not moving because I can't when he touches me like this. My brain has short-circuited.

I'm so close, on the verge, his fingers relentless as they stroke inside of me.

"I promised you in your office I would finish what I started. Didn't I, Jules? I always make good on my promises," he growls. "Do you remember what else I promised you?"

"Yes…." My eyes are squeezed shut. I'm so close, I'm aching. I grip him tighter, his hips thrust towards me and I remember what I was doing before his fingers began stroking me.

"What did I promise you? I want to hear you say it," he demands.

"You… said… you…" I'm panting, gasping, trying to put a sentence together. My hand strokes up and down his length, his fingers moving faster.

"What, Jules? What did I say?"

"You said you would fuck me hard and filthy."

He removes his hand from inside me. My eyes startle open. I was hovering on the edge, tingles pooling every-where, and he just stops. Just fucking stops.

"I was so close," I say with a sulk.

"When you come, I'll be fucking you."

I watch him rip his briefs down his legs, stroke himself in one long even stroke while I'm left aching for his hand back inside me. He flashes that cocky smile of his that says I-know-how-to-make-you-crazy. And he's right, he does. So fucking crazy.

"Get up and face the mirror, beautiful." *Fuck.* He's so bossy.

"What are you going to do to me?" I ask, every inch of me vibrating.

"Exactly what I promised you."

He follows me to my dresser where I lay my hands flat against the wood's surface. I face the mirror like he asked me to, watching him through the reflection. His hands reach for the dresser on either side of me, caging me in, and I watch his mouth trail open-mouth kisses from my shoulder to my neck to my ear. He sucks the fleshy part of my lobe into his mouth, not taking his eyes off of me for a second while rolling his erection into my lower back. Arching my back, I push back against him. He growls again, but this time louder against my ear. It's a sound I've never heard from him before. It's the single most erotic moment of my life.

Then he grips my hips, digging his fingers into my skin. I watch him, mesmerized, waiting for what he's going to do to me next. His eyes stay glued to mine, never leaving.

"Look at you, baby. You're beautiful," he whispers.

"Yours," I say, and he groans.

"Mine." He kisses my neck, drags his tongue over my skin.

"And you promised me things you haven't delivered on," I say.

"So impatient. Have I teased you enough?"

I want him now. I want him more than I've ever wanted anything. I want to be ruined by him, enraptured. I want there to be no doubt that I am his. I want him to remember me, to never be able forget how good we are together.

"Can we get to the part where you're making me scream?" I say.

"I'm getting there. You're so bossy."

"Only when I need to be," I say, looking at him over my shoulder. Then he kisses me like he's a man lost in the desert and I'm the rain.

"We're arguing again," he says, breaking the kiss.

"We wouldn't be if you would hurry up and fuck me."

"You ready, baby?" I can feel him teasing my entrance with the head of his erection.

"Yes, Beck. Please… I want you."

Relief crosses his face, his thumb caressing my hip, then he blinks. "I don't have a condom," he says against my ear. "But I'm clean."

I want him that way. "I'm on protection."

He stares at me in the reflection, looking as if I've taken his breath away.

"Tell me you want it that way, so I know that you mean it."

"I want you bare, Beckett," I murmur. "I want nothing between us."

Then he's pushing inside of me in one long thrust, his lips still on my neck, his eyes still locked on mine. His fingers dig into my hips. It's perfect, the most beautiful thing I've ever felt.

When he's buried all the way in, he stills, exhaling a long breath. He's settled deep inside of me, his arms anchored to the desk on either side of my hips, the rough shadow on his jaw scraping across my shoulder.

"Fuck, you feel so good like this. I didn't think it could get better with you, but it has," he murmurs. "You're mine, Jules. Tell me you're mine."

I don't answer, I just nod, pushing my ass into him, needing him to start moving again. I've never done it this way before, without a barrier, and I have to bite my bottom lip to stop myself from coming.

"Tell me you're mine," he says. His splayed hand moves to my stomach, holding me as close to him as he can, the other one palming my breast.

"I'm yours," I answer, reaching for his face, but my hand slides down the slope of his neck instead.

Then he starts moving again. He pulls out slowly, then slides in slowly. He does it again and again, each time a little faster, a little deeper, a little harder, until he's pumping into me, pinning me against the edge of the dresser.

I bite my lip at the intense pleasure that roars like thunder in my veins, rocking back into him, balancing on my tiptoes. The dresser shakes against the wall, a picture frame falls over.

I moan and my eyes roll back in my head, holding on as he pumps into me at a furious pace.

Beckett's hand pulls me upright, my back into his chest. His face is next to mine, his mouth against my ear, our eyes locked on each other in the mirror.

"We're perfect together. See us, Jules. We fit perfectly."

We do, he's right. It's like we were tailor-made for each other, the missing pieces to one another's puzzles. He knows my body and exactly what it wants and soon, I'm coming so hard my vision blurs.

He follows me over the edge a second later, my name on his lips. He holds me tight as aftershocks tremor through him.

He spins me around in his arms and without letting me go walks backwards to my bed, falling onto the edge and taking me with him. I straddle his thighs, my arms wound around his neck.

I'm going to miss him, desperately, but I can't think about that right now, so I kiss him hard like tonight is all we have.

Beckett is mine. For now, he's mine and that is going to have to be enough.

"I've never done that before, Jules. I always use condoms, every single time," he confesses, his heart split wide open for me to see.

"Tell me you love me again," he asks, the tip of my nose against his.

I'm lost in his ocean-blue eyes. "I love you, Wonder."

"I love you too, beautiful."

My heart jumps at his words. He kisses me, then holds me close and I stare at the headboard wondering how I could let this happen. How could I let myself fall this hard? How could I ever think I could let him go?

And it terrifies me. I'm afraid of making a terrible decision, one that I will regret down the line. I'll have my job, and my family, but without Beck will I really be happy? Or just… alone?

# Chapter Thirty

Beckett

We never talk about London. We go out for dinner, just the two of us, and we rate every meal. We're together every night in my bed or hers, we stay up late talking about almost everything. We walk the beach, we eat ice cream, we even double date with Bella and her boyfriend, Jack. We slow dance in her living room when her favorite song comes on over the Sonos speaker. But what we don't do is talk about me leaving.

Two nights after that incredible evening at her place when I told Jules I love her, I take her to a movie. We sit near the back, sharing a bucket of popcorn. Halfway through the film, my hand is on her thigh, her shoulder is up against mine. Then we're kissing and making out like horny teenagers, and we have to leave before I pull her onto my lap and fuck her right there on the folding seat. We run to my car, just barely making it home.

Every day seems to be better than the last. Unbelievably, I even have coffee with my dad. He didn't wait for me to text him after that day in the produce section. I got a message from him shortly after, apologizing for being too eager but wanting me to know how serious he is about seeing me.

My dad is trying. Over coffee at Dream Bean, he even pulled out a crumpled, worn photo of me as a baby that he's kept in his wallet since the year I was born.

Gobsmacked is how I felt when he handed it to me. I rubbed the image between my fingers, my throat clenched and stinging. He hadn't totally forgotten about me. He'd kept a small part of me close to him and I was surprised at how much that tiny gesture affected me.

He told me about my baseball games that he watched from his car instead of in the stands, knowing it would upset my mom and me and about all of the times he drove by our house to try and get a glimpse of me playing in the yard. I was floored.

When we finished our coffees, he handed me an envelope with two tickets to the Yankees. Told me to take Jules with me, not pushing me for more of myself than I was comfortable giving.

Tickets to the game wouldn't fix the 26 years of not seeing my dad, but it felt like a step in the right direction.

The part where I'm having the most trouble is spending time with his wife and my stepsister. He mentioned she'd like to have Jules and I over for dinner sometime, but I politely declined. My dad seemed to understand and didn't push. We aren't going to build a relationship overnight. It's going to take time and a ton of work, but we're making progress, and that's good enough for now.

I throw a few things in my duffle, hiding the small velvet box at the bottom. Jules is all mine for a little while longer and tonight we're celebrating her birthday. I'm taking her away for the night, having booked us a room at a bed and breakfast in the next town over.

When I pull up outside of Jules' place, she's standing at her front door with her bag at her feet, sunglasses hiding her eyes. I jump out and pull her into my arms.

"Happy birthday, beautiful."

"Thank you," she says, taking my jaw in her hand, kissing me chastely. "For the fifth time today, but I'm not complaining."

"Your birthday is a big deal."

"If you say so, my handsome man."

We hop in my SUV and drive out of the city, windows down, Jules' hair a wild mess blowing everywhere. She turns up the radio. "More Than My Hometown" by Morgan Wallen plays, and she belts out the lyrics. I just watch her and smile. She's fearless, joyful, a wild beauty. I tap my palm to the beat of the song on my thigh, listening to her sing. My wild girl.

Two hours later, we've checked into the bed and breakfast, a white 18th century, Cape Cod-style home with a wrap-around veranda and a panoramic view of the town. An older couple in their 60s show us to our room and suggest the nearby Dockside Bistro if we're hungry.

Jules flops onto the bed when they leave, starfish style, and looks up at the ceiling.

"If these old walls could talk," she says. "I bet they've seen things."

I lay down next to her on my side, lift her hand off of the white duvet and place it in mine. "Yeah, like what?"

"Like artists and poets wandering through town on their way to the next city or maybe politicians bringing their mistresses for a sexy fling. Or way back when fishermen who needed to take cover from the storms in the winter, like that old wooden sailing ship they have bronzed in the park that we drove by."

"And us? What would these walls say about us, one day ages from now, if they could talk?"

She shifts so she's on her side facing me. Her answer is effortless, "They would say that they were a couple so madly in love that they couldn't stop kissing and touching; that they needed each other like the sun needs the moon. Mad in love. So mad in love."

I trace the curve of her nose with the tip of my finger, the peak of her lip, run the pad over her pink bottom lip. "They'd say he couldn't get enough of her. He wanted to be with her every second he could. She was all he ever wanted."

"And she was lost in him. She was under his spell. She loved him more than Nutella milkshakes."

I smile and turn over onto my stomach, hitch my leg over hers, slip my hand to her cheek. "Jules baby, I'm so gone for you. Like so, so mad in love."

Then I kiss her.

---

Jules is wearing a skirt with a fitted yellow off-the-shoulder top and a pair of wedge shoes that make her legs look 10 inches longer. We walk down the main street in town, past a community garden, a bookstore, a coffee shop. At the end of the street there's a huge fountain with a tall, stone sculpture of a man holding a little girl's hand. We find the restaurant I made a reservation at, where we sit by the window sipping white wine and eating Dungeness crab with melted butter and warm, freshly baked sourdough bread.

After dinner, we walk back toward the bed and breakfast, her hand in mine, the sun setting in gold and pinks. I tighten her hand in mine, pulling her to the fountain we passed earlier, and she giggles.

"Are we making wishes?" she asks,

"Only if you want to."

I pull some loose change from my pocket, handing her three coins. I keep a penny and a dime for myself. Jules turns her back to the monument, squeezes her eyes shut for a second then tosses the first coin over her shoulder.

I'm watching her, smiling at the twinkle in her eyes, the gleam in her smile. "Do you have a better chance of your wish coming true by doing it this way?" I tease her, rubbing the coins between my fingers.

"I know this way works if you're in Rome and you're tossing coins into the Trevi fountain." She shrugs, squeezes her eyes shut, tossing the second coin into the water over her shoulder. "The myth says the first coin will guarantee your return to Rome. The second coin means you will fall in love with an attractive Italian—"

"Where does that leave me?" I tease. "Last time I checked I have zero Italian in me."

"It's just a myth, Beck. Don't be so sensitive. I only want you." She rolls her eyes and it's fucking cute.

"What's the third coin for?" I ask, curious.

"That one means you'll marry the one you love." *Splash.* There goes the third coin.

"Come here." I sit on the edge of the fountain and pull her down beside me. "It isn't a ring, but I have your birthday present in my pocket."

I pull the little blue box from my pocket and hand it to her. She looks back at me, warmth filling her face.

She unties the ribbon and opens the velvet box, and gasps.

"Beck, this is beautiful." She holds up the gold locket,

the initial J in tiny diamonds sparkle under the string of Edison lights hanging over the fountain.

"Open it."

She looks down to the locket in her hands. She flips it open using her thumb nail and sees a photo of me on one side and one of her on the other. Her tear-filled eyes find mine.

"I love it. I love you. Will you put it on me?" She lifts up her hair, and I fasten the necklace around her neck. She fingers the locket against her chest. "I'll wear it every day."

"You'll think of us."

"I'll think of you and how you're the best man I know."

"The one who loves you."

"Mine," she murmurs as I lean in for a kiss.

After I kiss her, I tell her my thoughts for the rest of her birthday. "I thought we could go dancing."

She scrunches her nose.

"What would you like to do then?" I ask her, pulling her up from the stone fountain, bringing her into my chest.

Her hazel eyes gaze up at me, a small smile on her lips. "I want to go eat junk food and popcorn and watch a movie with you in bed."

I laugh. "Jules, it's your birthday."

"And that's what I want to do."

"All right, then, let's go to Target."

Twenty minutes later, we're cruising the candy aisle. I'm pushing a red buggy. She's standing on the front as I wheel her through aisles while she reaches for junk food. The cart is half full by the time we hit the checkout.

When we get back to the hotel room an hour later, Jules dumps her enormous candy haul out on the bed: chocolate bars, bags of Skittles and Sour Patch Kids, rainbow Twizzlers. Two pairs of fuzzy socks somehow made it in the bag too.

I shake my head. She makes every day better. Within months, Jules has become my world, the person I want to spend all of my time with, the one I want to tell all of my secrets to.

"You know how to crush a Target," I tell her, laughing.

"Thank you," she says. "I consider that the ultimate compliment."

She grabs a mini-Crunch bar from the pile in front of her and tosses it at me. I catch it, unwrap the bar and pop it into my mouth. I don't even like Crunch bars but if she wants me to eat the thing, I will. It's the spell she has over me, I'm helpless to resist her. "I'm going to eat everything on this bed if you don't stop me," she says, tearing open the bag of Skittles.

"Savage."

"You love me."

"Yeah, I do."

"Come here," I say, hopping on the bed, sending candy flying everywhere. She follows me, giggling.

A few minutes later, we've changed into our pajamas—a pair of black boxers for me and a light yellow, silk camisole and a pair of matching underwear for her. Killing me slowly.

We're settled into bed, both eating from the same bag of popcorn and we both have on the fuzzy socks she slipped into the cart on our candy run.

I flick on *When Harry Met Sally* because Jules asks me to and it's her birthday so what she wants, she gets. She says it reminds her of the night she started to fall for me. I'll watch anything with her, it could be those stupid Real Housewives, and I'd sit with her without saying a word.

Besides, what more could a guy ask for? I'm lying in

bed with a 10, who's also smart, hilarious and somehow digs me.

Fifteen minutes into the movie, she catches my eye. "If I look really happy, it's because I am. Thanks for the best birthday."

I kiss the tip of her nose. "Better than the over-the-top parties your mom threw you when you were a kid?"

"They don't hold a candle," she whispers. "Not even close."

I pull her to me so she's between my spread legs. She nuzzles in close and we watch the rest of the movie with candy bars spread out all over the bed. And I realize she's right… it feels a little like Miami, but 10 times better with her in my arms this time, her summer, orange blossom scent all over my skin.

Later, after the movie and a pillow fight and a bubble bath in the claw foot tub, it's two in the morning and Jules is lying naked between the V of my legs. Her head on my chest, fast asleep. My arms tighten around her middle. I kiss the top of her head and pull the duvet up over the two of us. I reach over and flick off the lamp on the bedside table.

I exhale. This room, this night, her between my legs—I wish we could stay like this forever.

One last thought flits through my mind before my eyes fall closed….

Does Jules Bennett mean more to me than my career?

## Chapter Thirty-One

Jules

My birthday spills over to the next day, when I come home to a birthday banner and balloons in my living room from Bella and a giant bouquet of flowers on my kitchen table from Sierra. Bella insists on taking me out to lunch, so we sit together on the patio at Catch 21, basking in the sunshine while we eat fish tacos and sip on Diet Cokes. I tell her all about my night away with Beckett and she squeals. She swears Beckett can't really be real.

Back at our apartment, Bella packs a few things into an overnight bag and tells me she's going to spend the night at Jack's place so that I can birthday bone my boyfriend all weekend. I tell her that's the worst example of an alliteration I've ever heard, but it's a damn good idea.

After she's gone, I jump in the shower, then slip into a matching lace bra and underwear set that I haven't had the chance to wear for Beckett yet. I blow dry my hair into long waves down my back and apply some mascara and lip gloss. Beckett and I are going to my parents' house for my birthday dinner tonight, and he plans on coming over here straight from his bike ride to shower and change before we go. I'm slathering a mango-scented body cream over my body when I hear the door open and Beck's voice coming from the foyer.

I quickly adjust my boobs so I have the perfect amount of cleavage—as much as my B-cups will allow—and walk into the hallway, trying to look as sultry as I can.

And then I freeze.

Beckett is sweaty in a tight, short-sleeved athletic shirt that's stretched across his broad frame. His wide, heated blue eyes rake over me. My skin feels like it's melting under his heady gaze.

And then I realize that he's not alone.

Grayson walks through the door behind Beck, eyes wide, "Holy—"

"Shit! Turn the fuck around, Grayson, and pretend you never saw a thing. You got me?"

My hands shoot across my body like a shield and I make a beeline for my bedroom, where I lock the door behind me and then bury my face in my pillows, mortified.

"Your girl is hot," I hear Grayson say.

"Shut the fuck up, asshole," Beck rasps. "You never saw a thing."

"But—"

"No fucking buts!"

I throw a T-shirt and jeans over my lingerie and slump onto my bed, wishing I could erase the last 10 minutes of my life, when a soft knock on the door startles me.

"Let me in, beautiful," Beck says from the other side of the door. I weigh my options and decide that staying in this room for the rest of time sounds better than opening that door and facing him.

"Please," he says softly.

I relent.

When I open the door, he walks through and pulls me into his arms by my hips. "I love what you were wearing," he says into my hair.

"I can't even talk about it. I'm going to donate it or set it on fire," I say into his damp workout shirt.

"Or you could wear it for me tonight?" he says, running a finger down the arch of my back.

"Is Grayson still outside?"

"I'm not sure, but I'll ask him to leave."

"No, it's fine. I can deal," I say, stepping out of the embrace and sitting on the edge of my bed. "It's not like he hasn't seen me in a swimsuit, I guess."

"No other man will ever see you in a swimsuit that looks like what I just saw, yeah?" he says, stepping in between my parted thighs. He tilts my head up with his finger to meet his eyes. "Mine, baby. Only for my eyes."

"Caveman," I tease.

"Possessive," he admits.

A few minutes later, I follow Beck into the kitchen. Grayson is sitting at the table with his phone in his hand, drinking a glass of water. He looks up with an expression on his face that is half-sheepish, half-smirk.

"Not a word," I hear Beck mumble under his breath. Grayson raises a brow and looks at me, an awkward grin on his face.

"Long time no see," he says, while Beck growls at him from across the kitchen.

"I mean, Miami, obviously," Grayson stammers. "Miami was fun, right? It's just been a while since I saw you. At the hotel, I mean. Not here. Fuck, I'm sorry, I'm doing a shit job of pretending I didn't just see you in your bra and—"

"Dammit, Gray," Beck says, closing the refrigerator

door with more force than is necessary. "All you had to do was say nothing. How hard is that?"

"It's okay, Beck," I say, sitting across from Grayson. "It could have been worse."

Beck looks at me, eyebrows raised. I mean, it would have been worse if I was bare-ass naked. I guess I wasn't far off.

"Now that we got me flashing your friend out of the way, what's new with you, Grayson?" I grin like I know something he doesn't know I know, because I kind of do. I'm not going to tell him that Sierra told me about their hook-up, but I can have a little fun with him.

His cheeks turn red. "The usual. Kicking ass and taking names at the office." Beck rolls his eyes. "And chasing away women before they fall for me."

"Uh huh." My eyes narrow. "So, no one woman in particular then?"

He scoffs. "Jules, a gentleman never kisses and tells."

"Atta boy," Beckett calls out.

Grayson throws two thumbs up at Beck, then pushes up from the table and looks at me. "I gotta jet, Jules. It was good *seeing* you." He smirks, drawing out the word "see."

I throw a hair scrunchie at him because it's the closest thing to me. Beckett glares at him, pointing to the door.

"You, out!" Beck grabs him by the shoulder and ushers him to the door.

Grayson laughs. "I'm sorry, I'm sorry. I couldn't resist."

"Goodbye, Gray," Beck says, shutting the door behind him. He shakes his head, his hand over his face, then looks at me with a thoughtful smile.

"You okay?" Beck asks, tugging his sweaty shirt over his head.

*I am now.*

"Jules?" he says, and I snap my gaze from his abs. "You seem a little distracted."

*I am very distracted.* "I'm fine."

"Do we still have time for the surprise I fucked up?" he asks, dragging his hand over his abdomen and the soft hairs of his happy trail that my fingers love to play with.

*Stay strong. You have a birthday dinner you need to get to.*

"Get in the shower," I say. "We have—" He's in front of me, kissing me, before I can finish the sentence. It takes every ounce of willpower, but I put my hands on his chest and push him away. "Go! And maybe we'll have time after you shower." He kisses my neck and I giggle. "You're sweaty, go!"

His hand cups my jaw gently while his lips suck on my neck one last time. Then he's walking towards the bathroom, opening the door and tugging his shorts down his thighs before disappearing.

"I could use some help in here," he calls, before I hear him turn on the water.

The man never stops. He's insatiable.

The shower is over in two and a half minutes, and when he walks into the bedroom with just a towel around his waist I know we're going to be late for dinner.

---

The next day, Beck picks me up from work and instead of turning left in the direction of both of our apartments, he turns right. Five minutes later we're parked at the beach, the sun reflecting off the ocean.

He looks at me, so damn handsome in a pair of Ray Bans, his dress shirt unbuttoned at the collar. The air conditioning is on high thanks to the temperature hitting 103 degrees this afternoon.

"We're both a little overdressed for the beach. don't you think?"

"I guess I didn't think this through," he admits, pulling a paper bag with a take-out order from Cocina Caliente from the back seat. "Should we take this back to your place?"

"Let's stay. It's a beautiful night. We can dip our feet in the ocean and cool down."

He smiles and reaches for the handle of the door.

"Wait!" I grab his arm. "My bag is in your trunk. Our swimsuits might still be in there."

Beck hops out of the car, grabs the duffle from the trunk and sits back down in the driver's seat. He searches through the bag. "Voila! Here's yours," he says, handing my pale blue bikini to me before digging around some more and pulling out a pair of trunks. "And mine too."

"See? It pays to go back and forth between two different apartments sometimes."

Beck reclines in his seat and seconds later, he's shimmied his pants and boxers off and slipped into his swim shorts. Meanwhile, I've changed into my bikini bottoms and am struggling to get the top on without flashing the entire beach. He cracks up as he watches me, clearly enjoying himself. Finally, he helps me tie the strings in the back and I slip my white dress over top.

We find a spot in the sand, take off our shoes and eat our take-out tacos. The sun is so warm that soon there's a light sheen of sweat over both of our bodies. "Want to go for a swim?" Beckett asks as he packs the remnants of our dinner back into the paper bag.

I answer him by standing, reaching for his hand and pulling him up. He takes that as a yes, and we both run toward the water, Beck pulling me in alongside him.

"My dress, Beck," I giggle, not really caring that it's going to get wet.

We're both laughing as we run straight into the ocean, crashing into the turquoise water that immediately cools our skin. We stop when the water is up to our shoulders and Beck pulls me into his arms, a shiver rolling over my skin as the water laps at my shoulders. My legs wrap around his waist, my hands grasp the back of his neck. His smooth, wet skin presses up against my chest.

"Sorry about your dress," he says, his big hands cupping each of my ass cheeks, his thickening dick pressed against my core.

I smile. "It's fine. It's nothing special," I say, running my hand through his hair.

"Beckett?" I ask, and his expression changes at the shift in my tone.

"Yeah? What is it?"

"When can you come home for a visit?"

He tenses, and I worry about his answer. "I think Thanksgiving will be the first chance I'll get."

I frown. "But maybe you can visit me in September?" he suggests.

I inhale a deep breath. We've been avoiding this conversation, but it's one I know we need to have. We can't pretend this isn't happening. He's going to be an ocean away, busy learning a new job in a new city. It's going to be me who is going to need to do the travelling to see him for the first little while, until he's established and comfortable in his role. "I can do that," I say, playing with the short strands of his hair at the base of his neck.

"How about this…"

I listen as he tells me what he's thinking and when he finishes we have a plan in place. Even though we've been avoiding the topic, it's clearly been on his mind just as much as it's been on mine. It will be nowhere near enough time together, but it's going to have to be enough for now.

"Are you okay?" he asks, tilting his head slightly, concern in his eyes. I lean in and kiss him, deeply, under the glare of the sun, wrapped in his arms.

"I love you, baby. So much," I tell him, trying to make this as easy on him as I can. "We'll take it day by day." Then I kiss him again.

When our lips part, his eyes are on mine, a soft smile curving his lips.

"You in this dress…wet…is seriously a fantasy. I don't know what I did to deserve you."

My smile is all the evidence he needs to know how ridiculously happy he makes me. This man owns my heart and soul.

"I'm yours, Wonder. And don't you ever doubt that."

---

Later that night, we're at Beck's apartment and all I can think about is the fact that every second that ticks by brings us closer to Beck having to leave for London. It's Monday night and his plane departs early Wednesday morning, so we're spending every second we can together.

We've worked out a plan. I'll try to fly out to see him once every couple of months and he'll come home for Thanksgiving and Christmas. I've thought about all of the things I could say to make Beck change his mind and stay. I could tell him that I want him to stay. I could ask him to go for a year, to experience the position, then promise to come back to me. But I'm not going to say any of those things. This is his dream, and who am I to get in the way of that?

The late-day sun streams through the open patio door

and I inhale the scent of the ocean breeze from my seat on the couch next to Beckett. My phone vibrates with a text and I reach forward to grab it from the coffee table.

> Parker: I'm assuming you're with Beckett.
> Give him the message… safe travels, bud.
> The Seaside isn't going to miss you.

I shake my head, then show the screen to Beck. He grins and then grabs my phone, and his thumbs fly over the screen.

> Beckett: It's Beckett. Thanks for the well
> wishes. Your numbers should skyrocket
> with me gone. You're welcome.

> Parker: Can't wait! Go get 'em in London.
> Show them how it's done.

> Beckett: Thanks, man. Appreciate it.

After a quick reply to my brother to let him know I'll be late to the office tomorrow, I set the phone down. Tomorrow is Beckett's last day and we're going to have breakfast together before he heads into the office.

"A friendly text from Parker is not something I ever thought I'd receive," Beck admits, with a happy expression on his face.

"My family loves you, babe. They're all going to miss you."

"I'm going to miss them too," he says, pulling me onto his lap. It has finally hit me that he's really leaving, and that tomorrow is our last day together. With shaking hands, my fingers cling to him.

*Tell him not to go. Ask him to stay. He'll listen to you, and he'll change his mind and then everything will be okay.*

But I can't, so I push down the thoughts and kiss him with urgency, my mouth colliding with his, words I can't say dying on my tongue.

Then his lips are on mine, his fingers in my hair, and I forget about Wednesday, and about London, and I'm just here in the moment with Beck.

"Jules, baby, I'm going to miss you…so much."

Tears sting my eyes, threatening to fall, and my throat burns. Finally, a single tear rolls down my cheek.

"Baby, don't cry."

"Don't ever stop loving me. Ever, Beck," I say against his lips. "You have to promise me. I can't be without you. I need you even if there's distance. I will never not want you."

It feels hard to breathe, the air thick all around us, heavy and tangled. I feel desperate, heartbroken. But I need to remember that this is what Beck has worked so long and so hard for. I need to be happy for him.

"We can do this, Jules. We can make it work. I'll come home for Thanksgiving and two weeks at Christmas, just like we planned. We can Facetime, you can fly out to visit, baby." His eyes are glued to mine. His words shred through me like a knife. It feels like I'm bleeding slowly, losing the life he's given me in two short months.

He rubs the tear from my cheek with his thumb. "You're mine, Jules. No matter where we live, you're mine." My eyes shut, and I inhale a deep breath. "You always will be. Us…baby, we're perfect. What we have is perfect. I love you so damn much."

I squeeze my eyes shut, fighting to get control over my emotions. I need to be strong for Beckett. I can fall apart into a million tiny pieces after he's gone. But for now, I want him to be happy.

I dig deep, steel myself and ignore the ache in my chest. "I'm so proud of you," I tell him, meaning every word. "And we're going to be okay. We'll just take it one day at a time. Don't worry about me for a second. This is such an amazing opportunity for you. You deserve it, Beck."

I stop talking, because it's all I can take. Soon I'll be weeping at his feet, begging him to stay.

He pulls me into his chest, kisses my temple, strokes his hand through the strands of my hair. I cling to him, wrapping my hands around his back, inhaling his fresh scent.

*Please don't go.*

He stares down at me, his baby-blues glassy, agony and heartache etched into his face. He leans in to kiss me, soft and slow, and the kiss feels like an apology and a goodbye.

"I had no idea a love like this existed until I met you," he murmurs into my hair, my hands clutching his shirt. "There's no one in this world for me but you, Jules."

"I love you, Beckett Taylor," I say, lifting my chin to see his face. "I will see you soon. I promise. I'll visit the first chance I get."

I hold him close against me, feeling my heart beat slowly in my chest.

*My heart is his. He's taking it with him. Please come back to me.*

## Chapter Thirty-Two

Beckett

The contract I've been ignoring for days is heavy in my hands and time has run out. Marco, my boss, sits across from me in his office. He's talking about work visas and the documents I still need to fill out, the relocation package that I haven't yet picked up.

I only absorb some of what he's saying, most of it sounds muffled, like we're underwater. My throbbing head isn't helping either.

I scrub my hand over my face, unease settling into me as I try to loosen the knots in my shoulder. I try again to focus, but all I can think about is Jules. Am I crazy to think I could ask for a future with her already? Make us permanent? We fell so hard, so fast. I see now that I never stood a chance. I'm in love with her, she's all I want. But things end. People leave. Hell, I know that better than anyone. How do I know she won't leave one day too?

*Because it's fucking Jules, you idiot. She's not the leaving kind.*

Then why the fuck am *I* leaving?

On paper, this is an incredible opportunity for me. The

title, the salary, the city. But everything feels wrong. The tension in my shoulders is like a vice. Memories of these past months with Jules run through my head. And then I see moments that haven't happened yet—her brothers' weddings, the births of her nieces or nephews—and I'm not there to share them with her.

Marco sits in his chair, his eyes fixed on me. "Is something the matter, Beckett? If you have a question about the move, the job, now's the time to ask. That's what I'm here for."

I exhale, clench and unclench my hands in my lap. I feel on the verge of a full-blown panic attack.

This time four days from now I will be in London, alone, while Jules is at Sunday dinner with her family. I think about her in that yellow dress she wore to the gala, the way the strands of gold in her hair shimmer under the sun. I think about how grumpy she is when she wakes up in the morning, but how happy she is after I bring her a cup of coffee.

I look again at the contract, trying to steady myself, hoping to find clarity. All I see are a blur of black lines across the page. I scrub the back of my neck.

"Beck, are you feeling okay?"

If I take this job, I'll see her what…three times a year, until she gets tired of long distance, until maintaining a real relationship becomes impossible, until she meets someone else? It isn't fair to ask her to wait around for years while I build my career in another country. I can't even give her a timeline as to when we might be together again. I'm a fucking idiot to believe I could ever move halfway across the world and think we could make things work.

"I'm feeling fine… sort of."

"Look, Beckett. I've been making excuses for you for

two weeks and I can't do it anymore. You need to sign the contract. The guys in London are breathing down my neck. What is the issue here?"

"I'm sorry, Marco. I can't take the job," I blurt out.

I can't have Jules *and* London. I see that now. And I want Jules. I want her more than a job. I want her more than anything else. I'm choosing her.

Marco puts his hands flat on his desk and gives me an uneasy look, his jaw clenched. "Jesus Beckett, what's going on with you? You've been off for weeks."

"I'm sorry," I exhale. "I should have figured this out sooner, I shouldn't have let this drag on the way I did. Long story short, I met a girl, and I'm in love with her and she's more important than a job promotion. She's the one, Marco. She's the one for me, and I'm so damn sorry to do this to you, but I have to go with my heart."

He stares back at me, disappointment and confusion seared in his eyes. He shakes his head in disbelief. "You've wanted this position since the day you took the job here. I hope you know what you're doing, Beckett."

"I'm sure. I'm sorry, Marco. I need you to know that I am grateful for every opportunity you've given me, and for the chance to work with you and to learn from you. I'm sorry for this, truly. But I know it's what I need to do. It's been a real pleasure working with you." I reach out my hand, anxious to get out of here and *home* to Jules.

I jog out of Marco's office, relief washing over me. For the first time in weeks, a weight has been lifted off of me. The questions that have been haunting me are gone. I can't wait to see Jules and tell her the news.

I don't give a fuck about the job. I couldn't care less about the money. I want Jules, and I want her all the fucking time, not three times a year.

I'm coming for you, baby.

## Chapter Thirty-Three

Beckett

I knock on her door for the fourth time and still no answer. She's not at work and she's not picking up my calls either. Where the fuck is she? I rake my hands through my hair, then pace the parking lot until it dawns on me where she is, and I jump into my car.

I drive the 10 minutes, find the first available parking spot and jog to the gate. I have to wait five minutes or so for someone to let me in. Thankfully he believes me when I explain that my girlfriend has the keys with her. It's a little white lie for a good cause.

A warm breeze tangles my hair as I race to where I know she'll be. The place she goes to forget everything, to clear her mind.

My breath catches when I see her, her golden hair lit up in the sun. She is so fucking beautiful.

Jules steps out onto the stern of her dad's boat and it feels as though the earth shifts.

I walk to the dock where the sleek white boat is moored, "Hi," I say, both hands shoved in my pockets.

She looks over her shoulder at me, stares for a moment, confusion in her eyes. "Beck, what are you doing here?"

I take a deep breath, settle my nerves. "I need to talk to you."

She frowns. Her hand moves to her wrist, massaging the anchor tattoo. "You're supposed to be——"

"This is more important."

I'm standing now on the swim grid of the boat. Jules is wearing an old pair of athletic shorts and a worn-out T-shirt. She has no makeup on, and her hair is tied up with a yellow tie. There's a couple playing cards four boats down, a man scrubbing the hull of his catamaran in the slip across from us.

None of it matters. I'm here with Jules.

"I don't know how to not be with you," I say, feeling the sun on my neck. "I'll have no one to watch movies with or cook spaghetti dinners for. Now my favorite damn color is yellow and I'm going to miss seeing you in it."

"Beck, we can eat spaghetti together over Facetime," she says. "I promise you… we're going to be okay."

I smile at her attempts to calm my nerves. She has no fucking clue why I'm here.

"It's not enough," I say simply. "Not even close. I love you too much to eat pasta together over a computer screen."

She watches me, waiting. A crease between her eyebrows slowly forms.

"Okay?" she says carefully, waiting for me to say more.

"I love you too much not to bring you coffee in the morning. I love you too much to wonder when I'll see you next. I love you, Jules, way more than I love London and way more than I love the idea of being president of a hotel company."

Her hazel eyes are hesitant, but they sparkle when she asks quietly, "What are you saying, Beck?"

I swallow hard. "I'm saying… be with me."

She tucks a loose strand of her hair behind her ear, exhales a deep breath. Steadies herself. "How, Beck? How are we going to do that?"

I keep my hands planted firmly in my pockets because if I don't, they will be in her hair, and then I'll be kissing her, and I won't be able to stop. And she needs to hear this.

"We'll do it here, beautiful. Right here in Reed Point."

She looks back at me like she can't quite believe what she just heard. Finally, a small smile crosses her face and in this moment, this simple few seconds with the girl I've fallen deeply and madly in love with, I realize what happiness means to me. The thing that makes my heart burst at the seams is not what I ever expected. Not too long ago if someone would have asked me what would make me happy I would have said a job promotion, a new Porsche 911, a trip around the world.

But it turns out that's not what it's about. Not even close.

It's Jules and I on her boat, sailing to Twin Islands. It's eating tacos while watching the sunset. It's going to bed with someone after a long, stressful day and feeling finally at peace.

"I've made my decision, beautiful. I'm not taking the job. I'm staying right here in Reed Point with you."

Jules' face softens and she tilts her head slightly, like everything I'm saying is making sense.

"That job was my dream for a long time, but that was before I met you. Everything is different now, Jules. *I'm* different now. I want you more than some job in a city that, if I'm being honest with myself, has nothing on Reed Point. I love you more than I love my work or any *thing* that

I could ever own. *You* make me happy, Jules. I'm sorry it took me this long to realize it."

I can think of 50 more things I want to say to her, and I want her to hear them all. Luckily, I have the next month to tell her, and the one after that. I'm silently hoping that I have forever.

There's a long pause where nothing seems to move. The breeze stops blowing, birds stop chirping. The world around us feels frozen in time.

"I love you too. I can't believe it…" she finally says.

"Jules, it's done. I told my boss today that I'm not taking the job."

"You did?"

"I did."

"How did he take it?"

"Not great," I say, removing one hand from my pocket, scratching the back of my neck. "Honestly, I have no idea if I have a job to go back to, but it doesn't matter. There are other jobs. I'm telling you none of it matters without you. I need you, and I want you and I'll be yours until the day I die."

Jules steps forward, touches my cheek with her fingertips, a half-smile on her lips. Her cheeks are pink, her eyes slightly glassy as if tears could spill out at any minute. I wait.

"I don't deserve you, Beck," she says softly and my eyes close and I swallow the lump down in my throat. "But I love you. You will always be it for me."

Now tears run down both of her cheeks and she's smiling that Jules smile that takes my breath away.

I kiss her. My hands are on either side of her face, carefully, gently, like she'll disappear from my grasp if I hold her too tightly.

Then I kiss her again because I don't want to stop.

"I knew I'd never be able to get on that plane the night we went to the movies," I say softly after breaking the kiss.

"The night we made out in the back of the theater like two crazy horn-dogs?"

"That's the one," I say, pulling her closer.

"You're so romantic."

I'm smiling. She is too.

"I thought to myself… how am I going to survive not seeing this woman for weeks on end if I can't even wait until the movie ends to get my tongue in her mouth?"

"Eww," she says, laughing.

"What? I thought you like it when I talk dirty to you?"

"I do," she says, wrapping her arms around my neck, pulling me down so her lips are millimeters from mine. "Now tell me what you plan on doing to me when we go inside the cabin."

My entire body shivers. She excites me. She's bold and daring and not afraid to be stripped down to her soul. And she's never coy about how she likes to be fucked.

"Are we alone?" I ask.

"Yup," she says, popping the "p" sound at the end of the word.

My hand slips under her shirt and her eyes turn a hazy green.

"I want you naked underneath me while I taste every inch of your skin, until you're helpless and needy and can't remember your own name. I want my hands fisted in your hair, my scent all over you. I want to be inside of you until you don't know where I begin and you end, and then I'm going to make you come and do it again and again," I tell her, watching as her cheeks pinken. "Is that dirty enough for you?"

She nods with fire in her eyes, then takes my hand and leads me down the three steps into the cabin.

Five hours later, we're in my kitchen. I'm wearing jeans, button undone, no shirt, bare feet and Jules is in nothing but my T-shirt. She made us sandwiches after we got dressed, once I was finished fucking her in every position I could think of. We ate lunch on the bow of the boat then went for a walk along the beach. We held hands and I chased her into the water, but only up to her knees this time, and we talked about tomorrow, and the day after that and the day after that, because we're pretty sure that what we have is a forever type of thing. We talk about dogs versus cats and agree on a dog. We talk about kids—she wants four, I want less, but she's pretty positive she can convince me. I know she can too. I don't think I could say no to anything when it comes to her. Jules has turned on the lights for me. She's given my life a brand new meaning. She has my whole heart in her small hands.

We talk about moving in together when the time is right, but for now, we both agree we're happy as it is. This insane connection, the passion and intimacy we have together, is more than enough.

"You're sure, Beck? I mean… about London. I don't—"

"Come here," I say, holding my hand out to her. She steps into my arms and my hand slides around her neck, drawing her into me. I kiss her hair.

"I'm sure. Never been more."

"What's going to happen?"

"With work?" I ask.

"Yes," she says, softly into my chest.

"I have no idea what's going to happen," I say honestly. "But I'm not worried."

I hold her a little tighter. She smells like fresh rain, her hair like strawberries, and I marvel again at the fact that's she's mine. I don't plan on ever letting her go.

"You're really not worried?"

"Not at all," I say, pulling back just an inch, and her head tips back to look me in the eyes. "I got the girl and that's all I really wanted. The rest I'll figure out, and I'll figure it out with you next to me."

Her hands tighten around my back, my shirt in her fists, a smile on her face. Her eyes sparkle, full of happiness, love and want, and I lean down and kiss her. Her body melts into me, soft and warm, and I thank God that I found her.

When the kiss ends, she rests her forehead against mine. Her eyes are closed, her lips parted.

"Come to bed," I say to her, slipping my hand up her shirt and over her nipple, pinching gently, feeling it stiffen between my fingers.

"It's five o'clock in the afternoon," she points out. "We haven't even had dinner."

"I'm only hungry for you," I say, pinching her nipple a little harder, my other hand gripping her ass.

"That was cheesy, Beck," she says through a moan, running her teeth over her bottom lip, squeezing her eyes shut.

"It was cheesy, but that's what you do to me, Jules. I can't think when you've got me this hard."

She finds my hard-on behind the zipper of my jeans and squeezes. I stifle a groan watching her, knowing she wants me just as bad as I want her.

I walk her backwards into her room. The blinds are open, and the bedroom is bright, lit by the sun. It lets me see every inch of her as I slip her shirt over her head, her shorts and her panties down her legs, toss her bra to the floor.

She's beautiful. So fucking beautiful. Mine.

And when I fuck her, she's on top. We go slow, then speed up because control is nonexistent when we're together. She rides me, my hands roam her chest, her ass and her hips. The image of her on my dick will be seared into my brain forever.

She's sated and sleepy when we're done, so I pull her into my chest. We're quiet. We don't say a word.

Jules falls asleep in my arms, and I drift off to sleep soon after, right where I want to be.

# Chapter Thirty-Four

6 WEEKS LATER

Jules

I stir the pasta in the boiling water, then take a sip of my wine, watching Beckett slice a handful of cherry tomatoes for the salad. It's a regular dinner routine that all couples do, mundane, but I've never been happier. I've been happy ever since Beckett showed up at the marina six weeks ago and changed my life forever.

After dinner, I'm standing at the sink, hands covered in soap suds when he cages me against the counter from behind. He sucks on my neck, then nips at my earlobe and unties the apron at the back of my waist.

"What are you doing?" I giggle as he attempts to slip the apron over my head. "I'm not finished. I still have the pot to wash over there on the stove. Pass it to me, would you?"

Ignoring me, Beckett turns me in his arms and removes the apron over my head. "The pot can wait. Put on your shoes, beautiful. I have somewhere I want to take you."

"Now? Where are we going?" I ask as he takes my hand and leads me to the front door.

"I'm not telling," he says, swinging open the door. When it closes his hands find my ass, squeezing, his lips on mine.

Minutes later, he's tucking me into his car and when he slips into the driver's seat, he takes my hand in his. It reminds me of our first real date when he drove me home from the bonfire, and of every date since then.

He pulls his car out of my parking lot, and 10 minutes later we're parked right where we had our first date… the beach with the bonfire.

*He's going to propose.*

He shifts the gear into park then turns off the engine, then looks at me and palms the nape of my neck, pulling me in for a kiss. Our lips linger; the kiss is sweet and hot all at once. My body feels like a soda bottle that's been shaken and is ready to explode.

"Come on," he says when he breaks the kiss.

"It's a Saturday night, Beck. You know there won't be a fire pit free at this hour. A little planning goes a long way," I tell him, because I love to wind him up.

"Would you just trust me?" he asks in a can-you-just-go-along-with-it tone.

We get out of the car and walk the path to the beach. I follow him to the fire pit where we had our first date. It's the only one on the beach that's free, and there's a fire already going.

"Did you call ahead, and have it reserved?" I tease.

He shrugs. "I know people. I've been coming to this beach since I was a kid."

Then he takes both of my hands in his and drops to one knee. My heart takes flight.

He's my whole world. It's him. Down on one knee.

He looks up at me, his face illuminated by the flames. He's not wearing his Beckett-smirk; instead, his expression is thoughtful, mixed with hope and love and a promise for the future. He's so damn beautiful it leaves me breathless.

"I love you, Jules. From the moment that you kissed me I hoped that you'd love me one day," he says and my heart throbs. "You've opened my eyes to what I never knew I needed, but it was you all along. Baby, I was missing you. It's *you* I want. It's *you* I was looking for, and I want a million good mornings with you, and a million sunsets with you in my arms."

He pulls a diamond ring from his pocket, holds it between his thumb and his fingers and I gasp. The rectangular diamond is big and beautiful, and a slim row of diamonds sparkle around the band. It's the most gorgeous piece of jewelry I've ever seen.

I gasp.

This is happening. It's really happening.

With steady hands, he slips it on my ring finger, looking up at me with want in his eyes. "I want to love you for forever, Jules. If you'll let me. Will you marry me?"

Without waiting for my answer, he stands, takes my face in his hands, his lips brush over mine. How did I ever think I could watch him go? I wouldn't have lasted a week without him.

"Yes, Beck. Yes. I will marry you," I choke out, my voice broken, my eyes wet. "Beck, you are the one. It's you and me, together forever with a house and babies and sunrises that lead to sunsets. I want to spend my eternity with you."

My hands tighten around him and he bends forward and kisses me under a blanket of stars, his hands around my waist, my hands gripping his neck.

And it's perfect.

He's perfect.

And we have forever waiting for us.

**Eight weeks later.**

The sun streams through the window as I sip from my Nutella milkshake.

It's a perfect summer day to sit in Sweet Spots and share my favorite mason jar dessert with my fiancé. After I swallow the little brownie bite I scooped up with my spoon, I set down the cute little plastic utensil and gaze at Beckett sitting across from me.

"It really is the best thing I've ever had," I say to Beck, a huge smile on my face. I feel like I've been smiling for weeks. I want to pinch myself… life is so good.

Marco called Beckett two days after he refused the job and told him he wanted to see him in his office. It didn't seem to matter to Beck if he'd lost his job. He said he was prepared for it, that there were plenty of other opportunities for him and he'd find something else. Turns out, Beckett didn't need to worry. Marco offered him his old job back and told him that even though he'd given him a couple more gray hairs with how it all went down, in the end he admired Beck for listening to his gut. Since then, Beck has been working his ass off. The Liberty's occupancy rate has never been higher, and they landed at number two in most profitable hotels on the east coast—behind The Seaside, of course. I'm so freaking proud of him. He may have turned down the job in London, but he's going places, and he deserves it all.

But today, we're not thinking about work. Today, my favorite person on the planet and I are in Miami, where our love story first started. We flew down for the weekend to get away and have some time to ourselves. It was his idea to get some rest and relaxation, and who am I to argue over a weekend away in a fancy hotel with my man?

I rub my foot up his thigh a few times until he grabs my shoe under the table, sets my foot in his lap and removes my sneaker. I sigh, closing my eyes. It feels so good. "Three of your favorite things. You deserve every one of them," Beck tells me.

"Three?" I ask.

He rubs the arch of my foot in soft circles, and says, "A Nutella milkshake, a foot rub and me."

I lean in closer, grab his free hand and flip it over so my finger can trace the lines of his palm. "But not in that order. You, my Wonder, are my most favorite. Forever."

And there will be a forever. We set a date. We're getting married next summer.

I take him in—the granite jaw, the peace in his sea-blue eyes.

"So, what are you rating it?" I ask, eying his milkshake.

"A 10, definitely," he says with enthusiasm. "You've made me a fan."

"What can I say? I have good taste," I tell him, a gleam in my eye. Pulling my foot from his hand, I lean over the table for a kiss and he soon deepens it, kissing me harder. We're so caught up in one another that we barely notice the sounds of spoons clinking in glasses, the low tones of others sitting at tables around us. But I haven't forgotten how lucky we are to be here together, remembering the days not so long ago when our time together had an end date and a relationship felt out of reach. Now, we live every single day together to the fullest.

"I think they're looking at us," I say when I pull back from the kiss.

"Which is why this is fun," he replies, my hand still tightly wrapped in his. "I just wish we were at the hotel,

Jules, and that you were on your knees giving me what I want."

"Beck…" I say, a little breathless.

"If you keep saying my name like that, I'm going to pull you into the washroom and fuck you in there."

And soon, we're walking out of Sweet Spots, just Beck and me, way too wrapped up in each other to be out in public. When we step outside, I pull him in closer, in the city where our love story began. "Mine forever."

"Forever," he murmurs.

## Epilogue

NEW YEARS EVE

**J**ules

Hudson stares up at me in his suit and bowtie, a cheeky grin showing off all six of his teeth.

"My turn," he says, but it sounds more like *ma tun*. Thankfully, I've mastered the art of toddler talk.

"Not yet, bud," I tell him. "Auntie Rylee goes first and then it's your turn."

He scowls, scrunching up his little face while I balance his 5-month-old sister Lyla on my hip. My big bear of a brother is now a girl dad, and Lyla has Liam wrapped tightly around her tiny finger.

Around us, people are primping Ellie, adjusting the straps of her white Vera Wang dress, applying one last coat of lip gloss. A light breeze cools our skin under the warm Hawaiian sun.

It's a beautiful day for a wedding and today, Liam is finally getting his wish. He's marrying Ellie on the beach in front of the Grand Wailea Hotel in Maui. Two years and two kids later.

I look down at my bouquet of white and soft pink

orchids, catch the pale gold satin of my dress flutter in the wind around my feet. My feet are warm, bare, sinking into the sand below them. Palm trees sway all around us.

Liam is standing with Parker and Miles in front of a giant arch made of white orchids, the ocean providing the perfect backdrop. Rows of white folded chairs line either side of a makeshift aisle in the sand that's lined with flowers and candles in cylinder vases.

Guests are seated— only around 30 of them because both Ellie and Liam wanted something small. The music starts, and all heads turn to watch Rylee walk down the aisle first.

Hudson watches her go then looks up at me with a coy smile, making him look just like his dad. His eyes are wide, and his light brown hair is perfectly gelled in place. The golden hair is all Ellie, and his personality all Liam.

"My turn," he says again, and I nod.

As soon as I let go of his hand, he's off like a rocket, running to the end of the aisle where my brother, Liam, is waiting with a giant smile on his face. I'm not sure I've ever seen him happier.

I take a step forward, remember to breathe, adjust Lyla on my hip and find Beck's eyes in the second row, just behind my parents. He mouths the words *I love you* and they're all I need to take the first step towards the altar. His eyes don't leave mine the entire time I walk down the sand, until I hand Lyla to my mom. My dad is seated next to Mom, with Parker and Olivia's daughter Marigold on his lap.

Our family has grown. Two weeks before Ellie gave birth to Lyla, Olivia delivered Marigold, who instantly became the apple of my brother Parker's eye. He is head over heels for his baby girl and will talk anyone's ear off about how she's already starting to sit up on her own, how she loves carrots and being pushed around the neighborhood in her stroller. Sunday dinners are even more fun with Hudson, Lyla and Marigold around.

I take my place next to Rylee at the altar and wait for the rest of the bridal party. Olivia, the maid of honor, makes her way down the aisle and then the music changes and Ellie appears on her dad's arm. She walks down the aisle barefoot, her dress simple and flowy, white and almost backless with a plunging V neckline.

My gaze shifts to Liam, who's looking at his bride with tears in his eyes. When Ellie reaches him, he takes her hand in his and brings it to his lips and kisses her knuckles.

Hudson grins from where he's sitting and Lyla squeals, then she reaches for her brother because she's obsessed with him. The sound catches Liam and Ellie's attention, and they look over at their babies, beaming.

Vows are read. Liam's hands are in Ellie's as the minister talks about commitment and love and growing old together. Ellie cries while Liam says his vows. They slip rings onto each other's fingers and the minister pronounces them man and wife.

Everyone cheers as the newlyweds kiss and half an hour later we're mingling on the lanai of the hotel, drinking Mai Tais.

"Smile!" Rylee calls, stepping towards us with her camera. Beckett pulls me into his side, kissing my cheek, making me giggle.

*Click, click, click.* Her camera snaps away until she's happy with what she sees in the tiny window at the back of her camera. She mostly does family photography back in L.A., her waitlist months long. Even though Liam and Ellie told her they wanted her to enjoy herself rather than take photos tonight, she can't help herself.

Beckett turns around to face the ocean, leaning against

the railing, drink in hand. It's golden hour and the horizon is a mix of oranges and reds, the air warm like a blanket wrapped around us.

I turn and lean on the railing next to him. "Having fun, beautiful?" he asks, his eyes finding mine.

"I'm having one of the best weeks of my life," I tell him. We landed in Maui six days ago and we've been to a luau, went whale watching and have been hopping back and forth between the ocean and the pool all week. Bliss.

"Me too," he says, leaning towards me, finding my lips with his. He kisses me. It's not the kiss that I want from him, the one I've been dying for since I left him this morning to get ready, but it will have to do.

When he pulls back, he's smiling that cocky, confident grin that I love.

He's taken off his suit jacket, his sleeves are rolled up his arms, his skin tan from six days by the pool. He looks fucking gorgeous, for the record.

"They're going to serve dinner soon," I say, wiping my lip gloss from his lips with my thumb.

"Good, I'm hungry," he says, and slips his hand down to my lower back.

Then it travels lower to my ass. He lightly grabs, clutches, caresses.

"My dad is standing right over there," I point out.

"He's busy talking to Liam," Beckett says, moving his hand higher, up to my hip, to my exposed collarbone, then to my neck. His thumb gently brushes over my jaw.

And just like that, I forget all about my dad watching my fiancé feel me up.

"I want all of this too, Jules," he says with determination in his eyes. "The wedding, the cake, dancing, all of it. I want this with you."

"Beckett, I want all of that too," I tell him.

I go up on my toes, cup his face in my hands. "Only with you," I whisper against his lips.

We kiss and it feels like fireworks on the 4th of July.

"I'm crazy over you, Jules Taylor."

"Taylor?" I ask, eyebrows raised. "You're getting ahead of yourself now."

"I'm trying it on. I like the way it sounds."

*I do too.*

He kisses me again, lingering and slow and full of promises.

Then we hear a giggle and look down to see Hudson at Beckett's feet, a cookie in his chubby hand, a sly grin on his adorable face.

"Up Uncle Beck!" he says, arms reaching up for Beckett. The two of them have become best buds. He scoops Hudson up into his arms and pretends to take a bite of his cookie.

"How did you get a cookie before dinner, you monkey?" I ask as he holds it as far away as he can from Beckett's mouth.

"I bet you took it when no one was looking," Beck says, looking at me with a laugh.

"I want one of these too," Beck says to me, looking at my nephew adoringly. "Maybe two, a boy and a girl."

"How about four?" I ask him, because Beck is sexy holding a baby.

"Didn't we talk about this?" he asks. "How about we try one before we sign up for an entire baseball team of kids?"

I smirk, because I know Beckett can never say no to me. He knows it too.

I smile and kiss him chastely, then kiss my nephew on the nose. Then the three of us walk inside for dinner.

Later that night we're in our hotel room. I'm standing in front of the bathroom mirror in a silk chemise slip dress, taking my hair down.

Beck steps through the door in nothing but briefs, his hair tousled, eyes sleepy, with a glass of water in his hand. My eyes can't help but take a slow path down his body.

"For you, my beautiful girl," he says watching me in the mirror, setting the glass on the bathroom counter as I pluck out another bobby pin. I thank him for the water, take several long gulps, then keep searching my hair for more pins.

"I thought you might be thirsty after all of the dancing. I just drank an entire bottle."

"I might be here awhile," I say. "Possibly until Christmas. The hairdresser wouldn't stop with the pins."

"They did their job. You were the most beautiful girl in the room tonight. Isn't there some sort of rule about not showing up a bride on her wedding day?" he says, stepping behind me, looking at me over my shoulder in the mirror.

He slips one strap of the silk dress down my shoulder and kisses me there, then slides the strap back in place.

"You are biased and it's sweet, but I know there are a handful of men telling their girlfriends the same thing right now."

"Maybe so, but I actually mean it," he says, gently running his fingers over my hair, finding a pin and softly pulling it out. "Do you think Liam and Ellie are happy with how the day turned out?"

I smile. "How could they not be? It was beautiful. My gorgeous boy, Hudson, stole the show. He is going to be wiped tomorrow."

"We should probably take him and Lyla off of your parents' hands in the morning," Beckett suggests. My parents offered to keep the kids with them so Liam and Ellie could enjoy their wedding night. "We can take them to the pool."

My heart beats double time. He loves my family just as much as I do.

He finds another pin, his fingers massaging my scalp looking for more, I sigh. His hands feel so good.

"We should," I answer him, my eyes closed. "That sounds fun. But first we're going to have to have room service here with an endless amount of coffee in order for that plan to work."

He laughs. "You think I don't already know that?"

I lean back into him and one of his hands slides around my waist. I open my eyes, find his blue ones glued to mine in the reflection. Then we go back to my hair.

I pull out a pin. Beck's fingers search for another.

"You know, I'm going to miss having your family around for the next little while," he says, quietly.

"Yeah? You've gotten used to the chaos?"

Miles and Rylee are flying to Tennessee from Hawaii to spend some time with her family before Miles starts a new movie. Liam and Ellie are honeymooning here for the next two weeks, and Parker and Olivia are going to their beach house for a few days.

"I kinda prefer the chaos now," he says, loosening my hair from its bun, lightly combing his fingers through the curls.

It feels so good. My eyes close for a second again, tingles scattering over my neck.

"You can keep doing that for as long as you want," I tell him, leaning into him.

"And if I do, do I get you in bed on all fours?"

I can't open my eyes to smirk at him, it feels too good. "It feels so good, I would say yes to anything you ask."

I move my head slowly from left to right while Beckett runs his fingers through my hair.

"I think we got them all," I say, looking at my hair, still stiff from all of the hairspray. "I've looked better, but this feels so good. You don't know how easy you have it being a man."

He pushes my hair to one shoulder, kisses my neck, then slides the silk slip off of one shoulder again.

"Mmm," he says, his lips sucking on the base of my neck, his eyes brimming with lust.

This time he slides the slip dress from both shoulders, and it falls to the floor. He begins to kiss a path over one shoulder until I turn in his arms and he's pushing me against the bathroom counter like he's going to fuck me right here.

His hands are on either side of me, flat on the marble counter, my hands around his neck. He pushes his erection even harder into me and I roll my hips against him because I know by now what he likes. Beckett is a book I know every word of.

"Ever have sex in a hotel bathroom?" he asks, sucking on my neck, rolling the hard ridge of his dick into my center. I moan.

"Nope," I pant, reaching for the waistband of his briefs, hooking my fingers under the elastic, easing the fabric over his hard dick. Mr. Wonder.

"You're about to."

"I can't wait. And Beck?"

"What is it, baby?"

"You are the best thing to ever happen to me."

## Another Epilogue



**J**ules

Beck jumps feet first into the water, splashing anyone within five feet of the pool. I shriek, turning my face to the side and covering myself on instinct with my arm. "Beck, you are the biggest kid in that pool," I call out when his head breaks the surface of the water. He shakes his wet hair from side-to-side like a dog. I swoon like a fool.

"Who thinks I should go grab Mom and dunk her in here with us?" he asks the pool full of kids, ours included, some swimming on their own, others in puddle jumpers. Parker and Liam are in there too.

"Do it, Daddy!" I hear my 4-year-old holler, then Hudson and Lyla at the same time screaming, "Do it!" and "Throw her in!"

These kids are little stinkers.

"Do it and you will be sleeping on the couch tonight," I yell back, pretending to be annoyed. The truth is I could never be, not with him.

Beckett swims over to Hudson and throws him in the

air. Parker tips the floatie that Marigold is riding, and she crashes into the water with a scream. I laugh at the antics while smiling like a loon, revelling in the deep love my family shares for one another. I've never been this happy in all my life. A deep contentment pours through me as I watch my entire family in my parents' back yard. My mom and dad sit on a lounger underneath an umbrella, sipping their iced tea at a safe distance from the madness going on in the pool. Ellie, Olivia and Rylee lie beside me on pool chairs as all of the cousins squeal and splash one another. It's a perfect August afternoon, and we're here to celebrate my mom's birthday.

I think back to the last five years. Beck kept his job at The Liberty, then eventually was promoted to president when his boss Marco decided on an early retirement. It's funny how things sometimes fall into place. With the promotion at work and a signing bonus, we bought a house together on the same street as Liam and Ellie. A 5,000 square-foot home with a pool and an indoor basketball court and plenty of room for four or five kids. We got married in my parent's backyard, and of course my mom was in heaven, doing what she loves, planning the most perfect day. It was a summer wedding with 200 guests. Hudson was our ring bearer and Ellie, Olivia, Rylee, Bella and Beckett's sister, Bean, were my bridesmaids. Beckett had my three brothers as his groomsmen, as well as his buddies, Grayson and Carter. I remember walking down the aisle just trying to convince myself it wasn't all a dream.

And what I couldn't have imagined was Beckett's dad, wife and stepsister attending our wedding, never mind sitting right there in the front row beside his mom, Pete and Bean. Beck's relationship with his dad has grown stronger every day and he's become an amazing grandpa to our three kids. He tells them silly jokes, takes them to the park. It means the world to Beck.

It was just six months after our wedding when I found out I was pregnant.

These days, I mostly work from home, too busy with the kids to manage the commute to and from the office. We have Maya, who is four and a spitting image of her dad, and Chase, who is two and has my personality and Beck's blue eyes, and Poppy who is brand new, an angel, and so far, the easiest of our three. Our house is busy. It's loud and chaotic most days and there's almost always a baby who needs my attention, but I wouldn't want it any other way. Life is pretty perfect.

I watch Beck lift Maya out of the pool, and then she's at my side, shaking her little body like a wet golden retriever. "Maya, you monkey," I giggle, drops of water flying from her, getting me wet, giving me goosebumps. "Did your dad put you up to this?"

"Maybe," she giggles. She has dark brown curls and light blue eyes like her dad, with dimples that make me melt. I tickle her tummy, then she walks back to the edge of the pool and yells "Catch me, Dad!" to Beck. He holds out his hands just in time.

"I will get even with you later," I say to my husband, who's got Maya in one arm and Chase in his other.

"You better," he says with a wink and a smile.

Miles looks thoroughly grossed out. "Get a room, you two," he says beside me, a sleeping Clementine in his arms. She's three and is Miles' and Rylee's oldest. Their 1-year-old son Blake is napping in the family room with my youngest, Poppy. "I don't know why we constantly have to witness all the nauseating PDA from you two."

"Leave the lovebirds alone, Miles. It's sweet," my mom says from where she's sitting next to my dad.

I look around at my family, the one I've always dreamed of, and see Beckett at the center of it all. His smile so full, his relationship with my family so strong. I sometimes wonder how we got so lucky. And then I remember that this is just the beginning of a long and happy life together, making memories like today with the family that I love.

My wandering thoughts are interrupted by the soft cries of Poppy coming from the baby monitor and after a few seconds I push up from my chair and walk inside to check on her.

She's stirring, her pacifier on the mattress next to her, a mess of dark curls on her head. I gently hold her pacifier in place against her cherub lips while my other hand rubs her tummy in tiny circles, attempting to coax her back to sleep. I'm still there a few minutes later when Beck walks into the family room with a towel wrapped around his waist, his hair wet and messy. He leans over my shoulder and kisses my cheek, wrapping his arms around me.

Smiling, I put a hand over his and lean my head back against his hard chest. "She looks so much like you," I sigh, looking down at Poppy. "It always amazes me."

He kisses the top of my head. "I don't see it. I only see you. She's beautiful just like her momma."

"You're sweet, Beck."

"It's true. We sure make beautiful babies," he says, burying his face in my neck.

"Yeah, we do."

"It looks like my princess is done with her nap," he says, watching Poppy stir in the bassinet.

"Seems like it," I nod, lifting her into my arms. She settles right away as I nuzzle her against my chest.

Beck caresses the top of her head, then he takes Poppy

from me. He whispers sweet words to her. *I love you my beautiful girl. You'll always be my baby.*

I look at Beck and think again that our kids are the luckiest in the world to have him for a daddy.

"My Poppy girl is up?" my mom asks, walking into the living room.

"She is," I say, clipping her pacifier to the sleeper she's wearing.

"Oh, let me take her," Grace offers, her hands held out towards Poppy. "You two need a break."

That I do. I don't think I've had a good night's sleep in four years. If I'm not up feeding Poppy every couple of hours, I have Chase's arm in my face, sleeping between me and his daddy. He's been crawling into our bed in the middle of the night for as long as I can remember.

"Come to Mimi, my sunshine," Grace says, scooping a sleepy Poppy into her arms. "Time for some Mimi cuddles in the shade," she says, smiling over her shoulder on her way out to the patio. She disappears outside, leaving Beck and I all alone.

When she closes the patio door behind her, I waste no time pulling the towel from around my husband's waist so I can appreciate his naked torso. His body is still damp from the pool, droplets of water dripping down his muscled abs. The air around us is thick, heat simmering. Over five years with this man and I still find it hard to keep my hands off him.

He pulls me into him, kissing me chastely, rubbing his hands up and down my back. I run my hands through his wet hair.

"I love you, Jules," he says, kissing me softly.

I kiss him back. "I love you too."

And I'll never stop. Our life together is better than I could have ever expected. It's everything I dreamed of when I was a young girl and so much more. Beck is the kind of husband who looks at me adoringly, who tells me I'm the only woman he'll ever love, who says the sweetest things to our children. I'm not sure I'll ever understand how I got so lucky to be loved by this man, but I choose not to question it and just be grateful that he's mine.

That he's ours.

The five of us.

And I'll thank my lucky stars for my lifetime.

The End.

(I mean it this time :))

Thank you for reading! I hope you enjoyed your time in Reed Point as much as I loved writing this pretty coastal town.

Not quite ready to leave? Let me welcome you to Haven Harbor! A secluded little street tucked in Reed Point, where four irresistible hot best friends each get their HEA and set the pages on fire. The series is A LOT spicier… so get ready!

Start with Grayson and Sierra in One Good Move. A brother's best friend, forbidden and secret relationship, neighbours to lovers romance.

# Acknowledgments

To my readers, thank you from the bottom of my heart for supporting me and taking a chance on my books. I love being able to write happily-ever-afters for you. You continue to inspire me with your excitement and passion for my stories. I hope you know how much you all mean to me, I feel like the luckiest author in the world.

To my Beta readers, Brandee, Erin and Carmen and my girls, Natalie, Leah, Mary and Janelle, for making this story so much better. Thank you for listening to me ramble on about Jules and Beckett for months, being with me every step of the way and for the pages of notes you take for me that make me smile. If it wasn't for you all, I wouldn't be sane.

To my editor and good friend, Carolyn, for helping me tell stories and turning them into so much more. How did we get here from house parties and late-night dancing at Kits Pub? I'm so lucky you continue to sprinkle magic over my books. You're stuck with me forever.

To Emily Silver, for the daily writing sprints, the encouraging dm's and for being the best writing partner a girl could ask for. I love that we're on this journey together. You are the best friend a girl could ask for.

To my cover designer Jayde Ubels, for always creating the covers of my dreams. I don't know how you do it every time, but each cover keeps getting better. I owe you for bringing my ideas to life. I feel so lucky to work with you.

To Katie and Brey PA, for introducing Crazy Over You to the world with your book tours and book hype.

To my ARC readers and the many Bookstagrammers that have become my friends, I will never be able to thank you enough for everything you do for me. Thank you for every edit, post, TikTok, review and author group you support me through. A special shout-out to my girl gang, Indie Author Love on Insta. You mean more to me than you'll ever know. I'm surrounded by the best and I'll never take you all for granted. I love you beyond the moon.

To my family, thank you for allowing me to lock myself away from the world for hours on end and write. You give me the space to do what I love, and I could never do all of this without your support. I love you more than a lifetime.

Lily xo

# Afterword

**Thank you for reading!** If you loved the story, I'd be so grateful if you left an honest review—it helps more than you know. Your time and thoughts mean the world.

**Want to stay connected?** Join Lily's newsletter to get the latest updates, special sales, audiobook news, and first looks at new releases.

Lily Miller Newsletter

# About the Author

Lily Miller lives in Vancouver, BC with her husband—her real-life book boyfriend—and their two daughters. When she's not writing love stories full of heat, heart, and happily-ever-afters, you can usually find her in the kitchen cooking, sailing the Pacific Ocean, or with country music playing in the background.

A lifelong romantic, Lily has been hooked on happy endings since she was a kid, and now she channels that passion into writing small-town, contemporary spicy romance that celebrates love in all its messy, swoony, unforgettable forms.

9 781738 289943